VERONICA AIMED THE LIGHT AND SAW THE GHOST.

Although the ghost's attacker was not visible, it was clear she was being strangled. Her bare belly was indented as though a weight was pressed upon it, and Veronica could see her neck constricting like a sponge. The girl made an attempt to remove the unseen murderous hands, but lost hope quickly and tried some faint punches.

The girl, her eyes like Ping-Pong balls as she managed to lift her arm, was pointing. Right at Veronica.

Veronica tried to hold the light steady while she screamed for Kirk.

1

I walk through walls. I whisper at the window when I watch her leave our home. I flicker at the edges of my own memory.

She sleeps now, her breath ruffling the edge of her pillowcase. I don't know if it is my presence at the foot of her bed that causes her to roll over. Her arm, suddenly free of her comforter cocoon, stretches back over her head, and her pretty face, framed by long auburn hair, turns toward the ceiling.

She looks so much like Mary, I feel the familiar ache that is like death but deeper. I reach toward her, intending only to stroke her cheek, but she whimpers and I wonder what walks through her dreams.

Her alarm sounds, playing a song recorded many years after my death, a song I like. I fall through the floor as her eyes begin to flutter.

Her mother is already in the kitchen, rattling pans, brewing coffee, pouring orange juice. She pauses every three heartbeats to look back at the kitchen table, where the rest of her family will soon sit, her face wrung and lined with worry, as though she feels there is never enough time. And she is right, of course. There never is. She doesn't see me standing in the archway, as it takes effort by me to be seen. For all I know, it may take effort

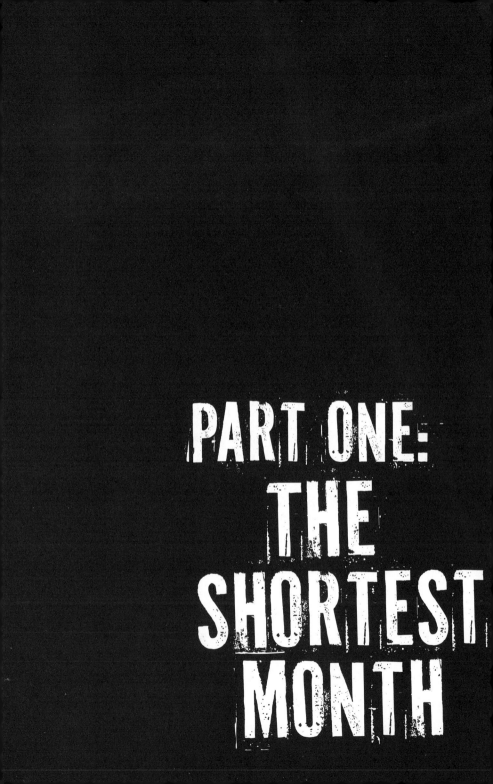

PART ONE: THE SHORTEST MONTH

For Kayleigh, and for Cormac

Copyright © 2012 by Daniel Waters

All rights reserved. Published by Hyperion, an imprint of Disney Book Group. No part of this book may be reproduced or transmitted in any form or by any means, electronic or mechanical, including photocopying, recording, or by any information storage and retrieval system, without written permission from the publisher. For information address Hyperion, 125 West End Avenue, New York, New York 10023-6387.

Printed in the United States of America

First Hyperion paperback edition, 2013

10 9 8 7 6 5 4 3 2 1

V475-2873-0-13213

Text is set in 12-point Adobe Garamond

Library of Congress Control Number for Hardcover: 2012009395
ISBN 978-1-4231-2228-9 (pbk.)

Visit www.un-requiredreading.com

SUSTAINABLE FORESTRY INITIATIVE
Certified Chain of Custody
Promoting Sustainable Forestry
www.sfiprogram.org
SFI-01054
The SFI label applies to the text stock

BREAK MY HEART 1,000 TIMES

DANIEL WATERS

HYPERION
NEW YORK

to see also. She lifts her eyes toward the ceiling through which I just fell, hearing the padding of her daughter's feet as she rises to shut off the alarm. I wait until I hear the screech and groan of plumbing above as she runs hot water for her shower.

I pass through the kitchen wall. Inside the cavity there is an ancient bottle cap and the skeleton of a mouse, its tiny spirit long fled. There are wires, and when I pass through them I tingle and hum and the light in the kitchen dims and then flares.

I enter the living room, so different now than when I was alive. Two recliners, a long sun-blanched sofa, and a huge television with a dusty screen. I peer into the dark mirror of the television, but I'm not reflected at all, not until I lean forward and brush my "hand" across the dull surface, where lingering static renders it visible briefly as a white blur that waves and recedes. I look down and see that I have disrupted the clock on the DVR again; a quartet of zeroes blinks on and off at me.

Her energy guides me upstairs to her like a beacon, and I can see puffs of steam curling out from under the bathroom door. I pass through the unlocked door; I'm pulled to the place of my death as though drawn by a magnet. I pass through steam and shower curtain, and she is there, and I would blush if I still had the ability to do so.

Averting my eyes, I look in the tub, where water swirls down the drain. As I watch, the water turns to blood, and then the swirling blood overwhelms the drain and rises to her ankles and continues to fill and oh no I remember I remember. . . .

I remember. What a strange thing for one such as me to think. Strange because I am no more than a memory myself. A memory that no one other than myself holds any longer.

There are others like me but not like me. Others who appear and fade, but for them consciousness has not returned, they exist as memory alone. Or do they? The wall between the worlds of life and afterlife was always permeable, even before the holes began to appear in its foundation.

The blood recedes and turns to water yet again. She's noticed none of this. She has her eyes closed against the possibility of trickling shampoo, and I watch her flesh stipple as I stand there, my invisible spirit bisected by the plastic curtain. My presence brings a subtle chill. I can still have an effect on the tangible universe.

I step back from the shower and wait by the sink. I prepare. What is easiest is to find a moment in time gone by and hold on to that moment. With effort and energy, the memory of a memory may become visible again. Time is not entirely linear. She shuts the water off, and the towel slung over the curtain rod slips.

I make the effort. The curtain draws back, and she sees me.

ll

Veronica didn't fear the ghosts every waking moment, the way some people did. Ghosts were an established fact of her life since the Event; there was just no avoiding them. But the one place she did not want them at all was in the bathroom. The bathroom, in her mind, should be a permanent ghost-free zone. So when she got out of the shower at 6:49 that Tuesday morning before school and saw a ghost standing in front of the mirror that would not reflect his image, she shrieked. She clutched her towel and rushed past him to her bedroom.

She sat on the edge of her bed and steadied her breathing. She dried her body and wondered if the ghost had left yet. Sometimes they stayed around for as long as fifteen minutes, but usually they were there and gone in the time it took to snap a photograph. She hoped it was the latter. She'd left her clothes in the bathroom, and it was too much effort to pick out another outfit. Now dry, she wrapped herself in her towel, deciding she'd give the bathroom another try.

He was already gone. Why did it have to be a boy? she thought. He looked like he was about her age. He'd been shaving or combing his hair, she thought, and then she decided he must have been combing his hair, because he'd been wearing a shirt, and who shaves with his shirt on?

There were pockets of warm moist air in the cramped bathroom, but the mirror above the sink was clear. She stepped in front of the mirror and got goose bumps. There was a definite chill where the ghost had been standing. She shuddered. How many people had stood in front of this sink over the past seventy years?

Too many, she thought, plugging in her hair dryer. She wouldn't have been surprised if there were an endless parade of ghosts traipsing through the house and the acre of grass and gardens outside. Ghosts walking up the carpeted stairs in twos and threes, ghosts staring out a window that is no longer there, ghosts wedged in the breakfast nook, sitting in front of invisible tea sets. Sometimes they left an aroma; even now she thought she could smell a hint of cologne, a subtle, faded smell; woodsy, not at all like the body sprays jocks in her class applied by the gallon.

It was a nice smell, she decided. She wished she hadn't been so startled and that she'd actually taken the time to look at the boy; but all she'd had time to notice was his blond hair, which had just begun to curl over his collar. Maybe he's cute, she thought.

"How morbid," she said to her reflection, which she then shot with a blast of hot air from the dryer. There were more than enough cute boys in her class at Montcrief High to choose from, all of them with heartbeats and pulses and modern wardrobes. James, for example. He'd asked her to go out with him this weekend, and she hadn't answered him yet. James,

James. She would let him wonder about it through homeroom and then let him know she was free on Friday, in the English class they shared. So many boys, so many choices, but she felt as though she didn't really know what made one more attractive than another. Sure, looks—that was the obvious category—but what beyond that made her want to say yes or no?

She switched off the hair dryer and heard her mother's voice drifting up the stairs.

"Veronica. It's almost time. I have breakfast for you."

"Thanks, Ma," she called back, and dressed.

Veronica normally wore very little makeup, just some foundation to smooth her freckles out, but she did like perfume. Today she stepped out into the hallway to spray her wrists and dab her neck, not wanting to cover the scent that the ghost had brought with him, even though it had dissipated considerably.

She walked into the kitchen and hugged her mother, who was washing the frying pan. Her mom leaned in to her but kept scrubbing. Scrub, scrub, scrub, with vigor, the eggs having been scorched in the pan. Veronica looked at her father, who sat in his usual place at their small kitchen table, reading the newspaper. She turned to the clock, which read 7:13.

"Are you okay, Mom?" Veronica said.

"I'm fine, honey," she said, and sniffed. "Just a cold."

It was more than just a cold, Veronica knew. Her father didn't look up from his newspaper.

"Are you sure?"

"I'm sure," her mother said, her voice as brittle as the icicles that hung from the dormer above the kitchen window. "Did you hurt yourself upstairs? I thought I heard you cry out."

Veronica licked her lips. She noticed the worry lines around her mother's eyes and the gray streaks in hair that she'd stopped bothering to color.

"There's a ghost in the upstairs bathroom."

She could feel a new tension in her mother's shoulders, where a moment ago there was only resignation.

"Oh, Veronica," her mother said, and dropped the soapy pan into the sink. Thin strips of fried egg clung to the curves. She turned and looked at her husband, silently thumbing through the newspaper. Always the business section first, then the local news. The sports section would go unread, always.

Veronica watched him as well, hoping for a show of sympathy. He did not look up. "I'm sorry, Mom," she said.

"The ghosts, the ghosts," her mother said. Water and soap were dripping from her fingers onto her dark slacks and the old linoleum floor, which Dad was supposed to have replaced years ago. "Always the ghosts."

"I was startled, that's all," Veronica said, feeling her mother disconnecting. She talked fast before her mom's attention floated away like the bubbles dripping from her cracked and bitten nails. "A teenage boy. He was combing his hair, which was long and feathered—sort of like those pictures of Dad when he was a kid."

There was a brief flicker of movement as her father turned the page. Her mother just stared at him with no real focus in her eyes.

"He must have been pretty vain," Veronica said, hoping for a reaction but getting none. "He wasn't scary or anything."

She wished she hadn't said the last part, because she hadn't stayed around to watch him fade away. Veronica knew of a ghost at the corner of Case Street, a woman who picks herself off the pavement, and when she stands, she's smiling. But then the grin goes lopsided and she starts bleeding from different places on her bare arms, and then red blots appear and widen on her blue dress, and finally blood starts running through her blond hair, from the top of her head. She walks three staggering steps toward the sidewalk and then disappears.

The Case Street ghost was almost willfully creepy. The boy in the bathroom didn't seem to be like that, although it was pretty disturbing that he had been standing right in front of a mirror and had no reflection.

"Mom?" Veronica said. She touched her arm.

"The ghosts are the worst part," her mother whispered, and Veronica wanted to hug her, but part of her was afraid to.

Her father looked up at them, smiled, like he always did at this time in the morning, and vanished.

The ghosts are the worst part.

Veronica thought about that as the cold February air kissed her cheek. It wasn't the first time her mother had said it, and Veronica had heard similar sentiments expressed by people her mother's age and older. Veronica found it incomprehensible that the worst part of the Event—which had taken the lives of anywhere between one and four million people, depending on whose statistics you read—could be a few ghosts. The ghosts, much like the sickness and lingering death, environmental damage, and general chaos that followed, were merely the unfortunate by-products of the horror of the Event itself.

The Event had expunged human beings with the nonchalant disdain of a hand wiping away spilled grains of salt, and the ghosts were the worst part? Even the creepiest of ghosts did not seem capable of malevolence. In Veronica's eyes, the ghosts were, at worst, an irritant, nothing more.

Veronica actually liked seeing her father most mornings. She had been terrified at first, and she'd cried, but in time she decided that the ghostly image of her father at the breakfast table was better than nothing at all. She knew that it wasn't really "him," that "he" was like a hologram or a digital recording. He was a pleasant memory rendered visible in the material world by whatever strange alchemy the Event had caused. The memory couldn't communicate beyond showing up.

But he smiled. Every day that he appeared, he smiled. She and her mother always made certain they were standing just so in front of the sink, because if they stood there, his eyes met theirs and they had the illusion of contact, a brief feeling that he was staring at them from beyond the realm of death. For a moment, he was there. Really there.

But then the moment would pass, and she'd find herself again wishing that she could see him do something, anything, other than sit and read the paper.

"Veronica!" she heard Janine call. "Veronica, wait up."

She saw Janine hurrying toward her, her slight shoulders stooped and her eyes downcast. Janine was afraid of ghosts— deathly afraid of them. She was one of a tragic, but surprisingly small, group of people who had difficulty coping with the pro- liferation of ghosts in the post-Event world. Veronica knew it was an effort for Janine to even leave her house, especially when their short walk to school together took them past at least one specter every day.

Janine was wearing a scarf, heavy coat, and a knit Peruvian hat with long tassels, as though the extra insulation could keep out spirits as well as the cold.

"Careful, Janine," Veronica said, not stopping but slowing her pace a little. "There are some icy spots on the sidewalk."

Janine's cheeks were flushed and pink. "Aren't you cold, Veronica?" she said, her voice as rapid and clipped as her footsteps. "It's so cold."

"It isn't so bad," Veronica said, but before the words were fully out of her mouth, Janine shivered. Veronica wanted to hug her, knowing there was a part of Janine that could never be warmed by extra layers; but she also knew that a hug wasn't going to make the ghosts go away. Everyone needed to find a way to cope with their reality, Janine included.

"Is she there yet?" Janine asked. Veronica noticed that Janine was wearing her knit gloves where the fingers were each a different color; they twitched and clenched into nervous rainbow fists. A red pom-pom drooped on the side of her matching hat. Janine had been Veronica's first friend when she'd moved to town about seven years ago, but she wasn't the same feisty kid that Veronica had been drawn to. This was a girl who had, soon after they'd met, faced down two older boys who'd thrown rocks at them while they were walking in the woods; but that was before the ghosts leeched all the bravery out of her. Again, Veronica fought the urge to hug her; she was worried that Janine would remain a little girl forever if she didn't find a way to face her fears.

"I don't see her," Veronica replied. "Are you doing anything this weekend?"

"Oh, no," Janine said, too quickly. "Do you want to come over?"

"I'm working," Veronica said. She'd tried to get Janine a job at the theater with her, but there was no chance—ghosts were drawn to the Cineplex like moths to a flame, for some reason. Veronica had thought she could attract Janine by telling her that there were always plenty of living people around, too, but instead of being relieved, Janine had been even more horrified. "How can you tell them apart?" she'd said.

Janine made a disappointed noise so soft it was nearly drowned out by the sound of their boots in the snow. There were alternate streets to take to school, but none as direct as the one that took them by Mary Greer. Veronica didn't want to go the long way, and Janine was more afraid of encountering a new ghost alone than she was passing a familiar one with Veronica. She often tried to get Veronica to leave earlier or later, but Veronica refused. And to her credit, Janine forced herself out the door each morning. It made Veronica hopeful that her lingering spark of bravery might one day be nurtured into a flame.

"I have a date, too," Veronica said, smiling.

"You always have a date," Janine said, and nudged Veronica as though to convey that she was only kidding about the "always" part, but Veronica knew that one of Janine's nervous tics was making frequent, slight physical contact with the few people she was close to, as though to reassure herself that they were really there.

"You're only saying that because it's true," Veronica said, nudging her back. Maybe a hug was too much, but contact couldn't be a bad thing.

"Who with this time?"

"Janine! You make me sound like an incorrigible flirt!"

"You *are* an incorrigible flirt."

Veronica heard the change of tone and knew that Janine was icing over in anticipation of passing the ghost.

"I'm going out with James, if you must know," she said, hoping to distract her. "Why don't you come, too? I'm sure James has a friend who would love to go out with you."

"Oh, no, no," Janine said. "I couldn't. I really couldn't."

Across the street, Veronica saw Mary Greer ascend the stairs to Mr. Bittner's house. She seemed to be walking on air, and her thin bare arms and slender legs were unseasonably tanned.

Janine's breath quickened, and she stumbled into Veronica again, the multicolored fingers fluttering against her sleeve. Veronica knew she needed to say something to distract her.

"I get a birthday this year," she blurted.

Mary Greer's knocks were not making any sound on the heavy door of Mr. Bittner's house. Janine made an inarticulate noise, her fingers pinching and releasing, and then spoke up with a quavering voice.

"Oh, that's right," she said. "You get a birthday this year!" Stronger now, happier. Veronica was pleased she'd thought of the right thing to say.

"How old will you be now? Four?"

"Yep, four," Veronica said. "The joys of being a leap day baby."

"You should have a p . . . p . . . party," Janine said, her confidence wavering. They had pulled even with the ghost on Mr. Bittner's porch.

Be strong, Janine, Veronica thought. We're almost past.

"If I did, would you come?" she said.

"P . . . probably not," Janine said, and then the ghost was behind them.

"Why not?" Veronica asked her, still allowing herself to be plucked at and pinched.

"Your house is huh-haunted," Janine said.

The whole world is haunted now, Janine, Veronica thought, but she kept silent and led Janine up the hill toward school.

III

August Bittner watched Veronica and her timid friend through the gap in his drapes, tucking his favorite red scarf into his topcoat. They'd barely broken stride to look at his house and the girl floating onto his porch. They didn't stop, but they looked.

Every school day he saw them watching his home as they made their way toward Jewell City's Dr. Charles E. Montcrief High School, where he'd been teaching for the past thirty years. Them watching the ghost, him watching them, her watching the door. She didn't appear every day, and sometimes the children were too late to see her, but on the days that they and Mary were at their appointed spots, a nervous warmth would radiate up from the center of his gut and spread until his extremities tingled. On some days, like this one, he would feel his neck dampen with sweat. And yet he was at his spot just inside the shadow of the heavy curtains on time every day. Despite the guilty feelings it produced, he found that he looked forward to the brief moment of terrible synchronicity.

"She's our daughter, you know."

Bittner turned back toward his wife, who was sitting in the shadows at the bottom of the staircase.

"Who?" he said.

"Her. The bold one, walking."

He removed his leather gloves from the pockets of his coat and pulled them to his wrists until the smooth leather creaked. A pretty girl, Veronica Calder. She was in his history class and she paid attention, unlike most of her classmates. Veronica's coat looked more stylish than warm, and he wondered why girls her age seemed to be more immune to the elements than the girls he'd known when he was a younger man.

This made him think of the girl on his porch, of her soft ribbed cotton top, the straps of which were no thicker than a pencil. Last February, when the streets were empty because of the thick, gray snow that had washed over their town, changing the terrain to a spectral moonscape, August Bittner had taken a risk and stood outside to look at her. He'd gotten close enough to see the fine hairs on her perfect chestnut-colored skin. They were shiny and golden, as though reflecting the sun, which, on this winter day, was blotted out by a gray and swirling sky. He'd stood and leaned close, intending to kiss her ghostly cheek, but in that moment a shearing blast of crystalline snow had blown through her body, stinging his face and blinding him so that he staggered back into the deep drifts that had gathered on his porch. When he'd cleared his eyes he could see the snow whirling within her body. She'd raised her hand to knock on their door, and he'd lost his nerve, not daring to walk back into his warm house until she disappeared.

"Our daughter," Madeline whispered.

"That's what you said about Mary," he said. "And the others." These last words were just a whisper, but Madeline always heard him. She could hear things that he never voiced, even. She could hear his thoughts before he thought them.

"And I was right then, too," she said, her words echoing in the stairwell. He could imagine her voice filling the rooms upstairs, their bedroom, the study. Eva's room. "You know I was. You felt it. You feel it every day she comes back."

"Yes," he agreed.

He'd killed Mary in February, eight years ago. It didn't seem right that as a ghost she appeared dressed as she had been when she visited him for lessons in the summer. Not right, but he was so happy to see her he didn't care, not even when her appearance led to whispered rumors that he'd killed her. And in school, it wasn't just whispering—Mary had been one of the first ghosts in town to make regular appearances, her initial visit coming just a few days after the Event. She had been dead nearly two years by then, but the local paper had run a picture of August, looking appropriately grave and standing on the porch, where she appeared. (The pictures of Mary did not develop well, reducing her to a digitized blur of pale amber light that would not look impressive in the newspaper.) Her reappearance had been an unwelcome reminder of an incident that the town, by now fatigued by the death and horror of the Event, was all too eager to forget.

The teens at Montcrief had longer memories and had lost no time in naming August as Mary's killer, even though the police eliminated him as a suspect very early on in the investigation. Someone had dropped a typed sheet on his desk just two days after the photo ran, with a poem:

GUS HAS MARY
HANGING FROM A TREE
K-I-L-L-I-N-G
FIRST COMES BLOOD
THEN COMES MARRIAGE
THEN COMES BITTNER IN A BABY CARRIAGE

Not exactly Robert Frost, but the memory of the poem—which at the time had shocked August, and left him awake at nights fearing the discovery of his many crimes—made him smile today.

"It will be her anniversary soon," Madeline said.

"I know," he whispered.

"And you must deliver her. Again."

He rubbed his forehead with his gloved hand. "Must I?"

"You must, August. Her birthday is the only day it is possible for her to be reborn. How can our little girl be reborn if you do not deliver her?"

He could feel a tear gathering at the corner of his eye.

"Old fool," his wife said, her voice echoing. "Go hug our daughter. Let her in."

August wet his lips. He opened the door, but Mary never set foot in their home.

Despite the rumors and rhymes, few bothered to question him about the girl, perhaps because by the time of her appearance in the newspaper, there were dozens of ghosts all over town, each with a story as mysterious as his own ghost's.

He frowned as he retrieved his briefcase from the floor. That ten-cent philosopher Stephen Pescatelli was one of the few who were suspicious; he had insinuated something in the teachers' lounge many years ago.

"Mary was a student of yours, wasn't she, Gus?" he'd said, his eyes dark and rimmed with red in his round face. He had a face like that of a black squirrel's, its furry cheeks stuffed with nuts. "Why do you think she's on your doorstep for all eternity?"

This was when Pescatelli was still drinking, before Principal Evans, bless her heart, had staged an intervention in the form of a stern warning: *Stop coming into work hungover, or you are done.* In the days when he was drinking, Pescatelli was liable to say just about anything to anyone at anytime, and seemed to take special delight in irritating his colleagues, especially August Bittner.

"She used to visit me," August had said, so surprised by Pescatelli's aggression he'd revealed more than he'd wanted to regarding his relationship with Mary Greer.

"Really?" Pescatelli had said, leaning forward so that August could smell the beer in his sweat and the cinnamon gum that didn't quite mask the odor of his breath. "What for?"

"I . . . tutored her," he'd said, and lifted his hand to his mouth, feeling wrinkles that hadn't been there when Mary was alive. "She was not a strong student."

The despair he'd felt at that moment was not feigned, although he thought that Pescatelli probably expected it was. But it was real. In taking Mary from this life into the next, he'd lost something. She was his forever, but that did not mean he was free from loss.

Each girl had taken a little piece of his soul with him when he'd taken their lives.

"What are you waiting for?" his wife said, and he blinked, as though waking from a nap. "Stop your foolish daydreaming."

When August turned back to look at his wife, she was gone. The girl remained, staring right through him as though waiting for him to answer the door.

"You are not the one I want," he whispered. "You aren't Eva." The girl's happy-go-lucky expression did not change.

He got his hat from the hook inside the coat closet and took his long black umbrella from the bucket next to the door. The girl raised her head as though noticing him for the first time, the smile that he loved so much just starting on her lips. Instantly his spirits rose. Today was going to be a good day; he'd timed it perfectly.

He opened his arms and stepped through her just as she vanished, and warmth spread throughout his body. The feeling was similar to the guilty little thrill he got when Veronica would look at his house. He loved when Mary vanished inside him. It made him feel as though she were a part of him. More, it made him feel that she was his, and would be forever.

He loved her though she was a poor substitute for his daughter. He loved her and he loved his wife, even when her voice grew sharp—her nagging was better than the long silences between. He loved them and he would do anything to have them back with him.

The day was coming. In just a few weeks, it would be here.

The Calder girl and her friend were far up the hill now. Bittner was whistling by the time he reached the sidewalk.

||||

"Life is short," Mr. Pescatelli said, and his sophomore English class braced themselves.

Veronica bit her lower lip. She hated when she had his class in the morning; the day seemed to progress much more smoothly when she had English later in the day. The Fish—so-called because of a loose translation of his last name, and because his thick glasses gave his face a fish-eyed appearance—was about to go down one of his winding, twisty roads to ghost land. When a student asked Mrs. Trask to discuss bee pollen, she discussed bee pollen. When Mr. Bittner was queried about Prohibition, he would discuss Prohibition. When Mr. Pescatelli was asked a question on anything at all, the answer would be lengthy, open-ended, and about ghosts.

"Life is short," he repeated, his voice growing in volume but not in strength. "And death is forever."

Veronica glanced over at Janine, who looked like she was about to be sick. Veronica stuck out her tongue, making her smile.

"But we don't really know that, do we?" Mr. Pescatelli said. He was leaning back in his chair with his feet up on his desk, stroking the chin he'd forgotten to shave that morning. "Seeing all of our phantom friends sort of puts that thought into question, doesn't it?"

The class was like a single body, a still, small animal holding its breath in the hope that its predator would pass it by. Sometimes Mr. Pescatelli intended these questions to be rhetorical; other times he expected answers and was furious when he didn't get them.

He wasn't really looking at the students; he was looking through them as though they were "phantom friends." He picked up a tented copy of *Hiroshima* from his desk, looked at a random page, and then dropped the book flat.

"One hundred and forty thousand people," he said, "gone in a blink. And a hundred forty thousand more a few days later in Nagasaki. And many more over the weeks and months that followed."

Two seats in front of Veronica, Kirk Lane closed his notebook with a grunt of disgust. He slumped back against his seat, and although Veronica was not at an angle where she could see it, she could imagine the expression on his face. Beside him, her date for this weekend, James, was smirking.

"Gone," Mr. Pescatelli was saying. "But that was just a fraction of the people lost in the Event. Two *million* people, if you can believe even the lowest number our government offered as an estimate. Higher estimates said four or five. But can you imagine *two* million deaths all at the same instant? Two million people gone in an eye blink." His own eyes were blinking rapidly, and he leaned forward and then back in his chair as though in the grip of some sort of seizure.

Veronica reached over to put a steadying hand on Janine's bony shoulder, feeling her shiver.

"Mr. Pescatelli," she said, knowing that she was taking a big risk, "you are upsetting Janine."

He stopped stroking his stubble for a moment and swung his legs back under his desk, and when he answered, his voice was inappropriately loud, but he was smiling.

"I'm upsetting her?" he said. "Good! She should be upset! We should all be upset! The problem is that the world did not get upset enough after Hiroshima and Nagasaki. We forgot. The whole world forgot!

"How many of you realize that the sixth anniversary of the Event is in just a few days?" he asked, a strange, almost triumphant look on his face. Only a few hands went up; Veronica's was not one of them.

"You forgot," he said. "And thus, we get—"

"Ghost," Janine whispered, and Mr. Pescatelli must have seen it flickering at the edge of his vision, because he stopped midsentence to stare at it.

She was a young woman, pretty in a pink dress, with reddish hair in tight curls. She was holding a piece of chalk, and pointed at something on the blackboard, waited a moment, and then laughed, her face glowing in soundless mirth.

"My God," Mr. Pescatelli said. "That's Eileen."

The woman turned, the long skirt of her dress billowing, and she walked toward Mr. Pescatelli and then through his desk until the lower half of her spectral body was invisible beneath it. Veronica felt a tingle in her chest as the woman pivoted to look back at the class—at her, it seemed—and smiled with such warmth that Veronica was sorry when she disappeared a moment later.

Mr. Pescatelli was having difficulty regaining his composure. His class was restless; ghosts were commonplace, but a new ghost was always a topic of discussion. Even Kirk had reengaged, and was discussing the apparition with James.

Beside Veronica, Janine was sobbing and had put her head into the crook of her folded arms.

"Mr. Pescatelli?" Veronica called, raising her hand. "Mr. Pescatelli, can I bring Janine to the nurse?"

He turned toward her and moved with less animation than the spirit who'd appeared and disappeared like a memory. She got the feeling that he was looking right through her, as though she and all of her classmates were ghosts already fading from view.

"Mr. Pescatelli?" she said.

"Sure," he said. "Sure. Go."

Kirk watched the girls go, especially Veronica. Green was a good color on her, he thought. But then, so was red. And blue. And eggshell, taupe, vermillion, and colors that hadn't even been invented yet.

At the front of the room, Mr. Pescatelli was still rubbing away at his jaw like he thought he could erase his beard stubble. Kirk thought that maybe he should go over and help him and erase his whole head for him.

He didn't know why he was so irritated. Kirk actually liked the Fish, unlike most of his classmates. Even now James was sneaking a look at Kirk, shaking his head with glee. It wasn't because of the ghost talk, exactly—Kirk found the subject as interesting as the next person—but he thought the Fish was so obsessed with ghosts that he used up all his class time talking about them. Every book they'd read thus far had had some disastrous or apocalyptic theme—*Hiroshima, On the Beach*, and some stupid zombie book. If the book featured hundreds of thousands of deaths and at least a ghost or two, it was required reading for the Fish.

"Read the next three chapters," the Fish said, slumping down into his chair, apparently calling it a day, as far as lecturing went. Kirk watched him take off his glasses and rub at his eye with the heel of a hand.

Kirk opened *Hiroshima*. He'd already read it through and highlighted everything that interested him, and everything that he thought would interest the Fish. There would be an essay test at the end of the following week, and Kirk would get an A. He reread a paragraph where he'd highlighted a single word and then stopped.

Most of the students were reading, except for James, who was trying to carve his initials into his desk with the tip of his pen. The Fish was looking at the spot where his former colleague had stood many years ago in life—and just moments ago in death.

A twinge of guilt irritated Kirk like an unscratchable itch; he was ashamed that he'd forgotten about the impending anniversary. He remembered that the media had latched on to the date with a fervor for the first few months after the Event; there had even been talk about shifting Memorial Day. But soon after, everyone—the media included—seemed to want to put the memory behind them and to forget.

Everyone, that is, except the Fish. Rumor had it that he had lost his wife in the Event. He had been on the outskirts of the city when it happened, and knowing that his wife died in the city left cracks in his brain. Kirk reminded himself to be more charitable.

But it bothered him, all Pescatelli's talk. The Fish, to his knowledge, had never offered to work at ground zero in the aftermath, the way Kirk's parents had. Talking about the Event and the ghosts was one thing; actually trying to do something about them was another.

Then again, Kirk thought, he hadn't done anything about his attraction to Veronica other than sit with her in the cafeteria. For six months he'd been carrying a torch and had done nothing. And now she and James, who was at that very moment working on the curve of his *J*, were on the verge of going on their first date.

That's it, he thought. That's what's really bothering me.

The Fish licked his lips and looked over at his class. Kirk lowered his eyes back to his book.

Everybody's haunted by something, he thought.

####### ||||

The nurse had Janine call her mother to come pick her up. Janine had made a stop at her locker to get her hat and gloves, objects of talismanic protection for her. She sat in a puffy green vinyl chair outside the nurse's office and occasionally leaned to the side to bump her head against Veronica's shoulder.

The strings of Janine's hat drooped low, and she twisted them up in her multicolored fingers. She didn't open her eyes when she thanked Veronica for staying with her.

"There aren't any ghosts at my house," Janine said. "How do you stay with them, Veronica?"

The answer that came first to Veronica was a complicated one, and one that was unlikely to bring Janine any comfort.

"I try to focus on the living," she said. "Then I'm no longer afraid of the dead."

Janine rocked forward, bumping lightly against Veronica, who put a reassuring hand on the back of her head. "Don't go yet," Janine whispered. "Don't go."

Veronica felt terrible for her, but didn't choke up until then. "I won't," she said, and looked away so that Janine wouldn't see her cry.

Janine's mother arrived, her face and tone conveying

impatience and a lack of sympathy. Veronica left the office with Janine's whispered words ringing in her head. *Don't go.* Janine had brought out the thing that disturbed Veronica most about the ghosts. It was that the people she saw were gone, and yet they weren't. To see her father every morning but to know that he was gone, that was the most disturbing thing. She didn't find the ghosts frightening, she found them tragic. *She* should be the one they reduced to a quivering wreck, not Janine.

Lost in thought, she was on her way to her next class when Mr. Bittner stopped her.

"Veronica," he said. He was a tall man, one of the few male teachers in the school and the only one who maintained a sense of formality in his classroom by wearing a jacket and tie, something he did even when the air conditioners weren't working in early September. "Do you have a hall pass?"

Veronica noticed the intense focus of his eyes. He was someone who she thought saw people clearly, and didn't squint at you as though wondering if you were about to disappear.

"No, Mr. Bittner," she said. She explained what had happened in Mr. Pescatelli's class, and how she had escorted Janine away without waiting for him to write them a pass. "He seemed, I don't know, a little shell-shocked."

A wry smile crossed Mr. Bittner's heavily lined face, as though he thought Veronica had chosen the perfect word to describe his colleague.

"I see," he said. "A new ghost, you say? A teacher?"

Veronica nodded. "I think Mr. Pescatelli knew her. He called her Eileen."

"Ah," Mr. Bittner said, and paused a moment. "You have

your books already? Why don't you walk with me to class? We've only got five minutes until history," he said. "But who knows what history could be made in the next five minutes?"

He smiled at her. His grin wasn't quite as winning as the one she'd received from the ghost, set as it was in an aging, craggy face, but she'd take it over Mr. Pescatelli's empty smiles any day.

̶L̶H̶T̶ I

"Eileen Janus," Pescatelli was saying in between slurps on a can of Mountain Dew. August thought it was bad enough that he was drinking a sugary children's beverage, but to slurp it from a can like some uncivilized street urchin, he found almost unbearable. They were in the teachers' lounge, just he and Stephen Pescatelli, Amateur Ghost Hunter.

August found his padded cooler in the back of the refrigerator and got his mug from the rack next to the sink. Someone had drained the last of the coffee and had been too rude to start another pot, but he withdrew the filters and the bag of coffee from the cabinet without complaint.

"I almost shit a brick," Stephen said.

"Are you sure it was Eileen?" August said. The news of her apparition had lightened his mood after the initial shock. Eileen was a lovely young woman who'd taught at the school for eight years before developing some form of cancer. She'd died . . . when? Five years ago? Six?

"Pretty sure," Pescatelli said. "Maybe you ought to come see her, if she is going to start making regular appearances."

"Eileen was a fine teacher," August said.

"Yeah. I was just going to tell the class that more and more ghosts are appearing all the time, and then ping, there she was. It startled me. I have to admit, I still get a little spooked every time I see a ghost. There's this one . . ."

. . . *who rakes leaves, like every day, in my neighbor's yard,* August thought as he scooped the coffee into the filter. *And it still creeps me out every time.*

". . . who rakes leaves, like every day, in my neighbor's yard, and it still freaks me out every time."

Freaks, August thought, I almost had it.

"You really believe that?" August asked.

"What?" Pescatelli said, still slurping although it was obvious the can was empty.

"That more ghosts are appearing every day?"

"Of course. Don't you? I mean, doesn't Eileen prove it?"

"Eileen proves that there is one more ghost." August watched the coffee begin to drip. "Not an epidemic."

"There are tons of new ones all over the place, Gus," Pescatelli replied. "And they appear more often, too. How many times have you seen Mary this week?"

"Three," August lied, trying to keep the edge out of his voice. Mary had appeared at his doorstep at the same time twenty-three consecutive days, the longest stretch since her first appearance. "What do you think it means? More ghosts, more visitations?"

"I haven't figured that one out yet," Pescatelli said. "You'd think that fewer would appear the further we get away from the Event. Ghost activity after the Boxing Day tsunami peaked about three years later, and seems to have crested in Hiroshima and Nagasaki a decade after the bombs were dropped. And then there was Sendai . . . they still appear with some regularity. I'm talking visible ghosts, of course. To this day you can't walk onto a concentration-camp site without feeling haunted." Pescatelli reddened a shade beneath August's gaze. "From what I've read," he added.

August sat at the table with Pescatelli and unwrapped his tuna fish sandwich. Why only human ghosts, he thought. Why am I not haunted by the schools of tuna I have consumed these many years?

He looked across the table at his coworker, who'd removed his glasses and was rubbing his eye with the heel of his hand. I'm haunted by but one Fish, Bittner thought, swallowing a bite of his sandwich.

"What about ghost activity before the events?" he asked.

"What do you mean?" Pescatelli asked.

"Well," he said, "I thought you told me once that quite often ghosts appear prior to a catastrophic event. 'Crisis apparitions,' I think you called them. Didn't you tell me about some 'ghost wave' or some such that thousands of people saw weeks before the actual Boxing Day tsunami?"

Pescatelli swallowed as though his throat was dry, even though he'd just downed a can of unnaturally yellow soda. "Yeah, but—"

"Well," August continued, chewing his sandwich and enjoying the crunch of the chopped-up bits of celery, "maybe we're seeing more of these ghosts because we've got another Event on the horizon."

He smiled, both at the poetry of the thought and at having finally rendered Motormouth Pescatelli speechless. *Event horizon*; he liked that.

"Now there is a cheery thought," Pescatelli said, frowning.

"Yes," August replied, "isn't it."

~~IIII~~ II

Veronica had been hoping for a quiet lunch, but James was talkative, and with regret she realized that all his talk was to impress her. He seemed to have no clue that his efforts were having the opposite effect.

"I think there are more ghosts than ever," James said. He and Holly Blackstone were sitting across from Veronica and Kirk, who instantly bristled at the subject.

"Ghosts, ghosts," he said. "Next subject."

"Well, sure, Kirk," James said, his tone laden with sarcasm, "why don't we talk about what you want to talk about?"

He made eye contact with Veronica, who was wishing she'd never accepted his invitation to go out. He was good-looking, and sat straight and tall in his seat and had clear skin and piercing brown eyes, but he smirked all the time lately. She was having a harder and harder time imagining herself kissing smirking lips.

"I'm just so sick of it," Kirk said, pushing half a meatball around his plate, trying to soak up what little tomato sauce the stingy cafeteria ladies had given him. "Let's talk about something real."

"Uh, that ghost looked pretty real to me, pal," James said,

and Holly Blackstone giggled beside him.

"You know what I mean," Kirk said.

"Not really."

"The ghosts are just . . . *there*, okay?" he said. "They don't do anything other than make people nervous."

"Poor Janine," Holly said, and Veronica caught a mocking look that passed between her and James. It implied she didn't have any sympathy for Janine at all.

"She was really upset," Veronica said, putting enough ice into her voice to warn Holly off the topic. But James's and Holly's covert exchange made her angry. Good, she thought. They can have each other.

"But why?" Kirk said. "The ghosts don't signify anything. They're just like short movie loops played on the wall."

"What do *we* signify?" James said. He was trying to be sarcastic, but Kirk took the question seriously.

"Just by existing, probably nothing," he said. "But we have potential. A ghost doesn't have potential. It is just there."

"For someone who doesn't want to talk about ghosts, you sure are doing a lot of talking," James said.

"Do you guys know any ghosts?" Holly said. "I mean, are any of the ghosts you see people you knew when they were alive? Mrs. Olsen, a neighbor who used to babysit me and my brother, stays out at her mailbox reading a letter every day at 3:47. She looks really sad. I think she lost a son in the Iraq War."

"A guy who used to work with my father appears in his garage," James said. Kirk was shaking his head.

"My father," Veronica said in a voice barely above a whisper.

She'd surprised herself by the admission; her dead father had been a guest at their breakfast table almost daily since the Event, but that wasn't something she shared with just anyone. Prior to today, Janine was the only friend who knew about Veronica's father's ghost; he was the reason that when she and Janine got together it was always at Janine's house. The ghost of the teacher—or Janine's reaction to it—must have disturbed Veronica more than she had realized.

"Your father?" James said. "Holy crow."

James was cute but about as empathetic as a pile of stones baking in the sun. Only Kirk looked like he had any inkling of how Veronica felt. His look told her that she didn't need to say any more if she didn't want to. But she wanted to talk about it.

"He appeared a couple years ago. My mom thought it was because she was planning on selling the house."

"She'll never sell it now," James said.

"Probably not," Veronica said, again surprised and confused by his apparent lack of empathy. Was he saying her mom wouldn't sell it because her father's ghost remained, or that she wouldn't be able to sell it because no potential buyer would want the unevictable ghost of the former owner? "But I'm not so sure that's healthy."

"Is he . . . is he a scary ghost?" Holly asked.

"No," she answered. "He's not scary at all."

But she knew that statement wasn't exactly true. Sometimes his very smile terrified her when she thought about it. She was certain there had been nothing enigmatic about his smile that day. She was able to read the date from the section of the newspaper he held, just above an article entitled "Three Die in Fire in Home for Mentally Ill," but she had no special recollection of that day. Why did he smile? The obvious answer was that he, in that moment—the real moment, when the coffee at his elbow had just been poured and the newspaper he was holding still smelled of newsprint—had looked up at something that either his wife or his daughter had said. But Veronica couldn't actually *remember* it happening, and that was the thing that terrified her. What had she said that had caused her father to look up from the fascinating article on home heating oil to smile at her?

More important, what had caused this forgotten moment to be the one that got played over and over again? What was so special about a cup of coffee, a newspaper, and a father's smile for his daughter?

Just a few weeks later, the Event would come, taking away at least two million lives, including her father's, and bringing thousands of ghosts. Why was this quiet kitchen-sink moment preserved?

"Ronnie?" Kirk said, his voice soft, "are you all right?"

She said she was, and dabbed her eyes with her napkin. Her friends and mother called her Ronnie only occasionally; her father had called her that all the time.

"When did he die?" Holly asked. Like it was another piece of gossip to her and not a tragedy. "How?"

"He died in the Event," Veronica said, looking up at Holly with clear eyes and answering her with a steady voice. Somehow, tying death—anyone's death, not just her father's—to the Event put some distance to the subject. Americans talked of the Event—when they talked of it at all—with a peculiar clinical tone. "He had business in the city. He'd take the train in once every other month or so." She could hear the distance in her own voice, as though she had detached from her true consciousness and taken a train ride far away. "Wrong day, I guess."

"Man," James said, and something in his tone made Veronica consider breaking their date. "That's rough. Why do you suppose—"

"Maybe Ronnie wants to talk about something else," Kirk said.

"Hey, you're the one who brought it up," James shot back. They were friends but Veronica could sense a rivalry intensifying between them. She looked at Kirk, at the tension in his face.

"It's okay," she said, and put her hand on Kirk's arm. "I guess we don't know why any of them come back, do we?" she said, looking at James. "Maybe you can talk it over with Mr. Pescatelli."

"No need to get snotty about it," James said.

"I'm not," she answered. Her hand was still on Kirk's arm. "I'd love to find out why my dad is there every morning. And a new ghost has arrived—there's a teenage boy in my bathroom!"

Holly and James laughed, but Kirk was watching her closely. She realized she was frowning.

"Maybe *I* should talk to Mr. Pescatelli," she said.

Something—she wasn't sure what—passed between her and Kirk. She'd never really noticed him before; not as boyfriend material, anyhow. She wasn't normally attracted to guys who seemed vaguely dissatisfied all the time. But a purposeful look had crept into Kirk's expression that had intrigued her, and his hand was warm when he placed it over hers.

⊥⊢⊢ |||

August left early, as there was no point in staying at work when Simon Schama's book *Landscape and Memory* was lying on the table next to his reading chair at home. He also left early to avoid Mr. Pescatelli, who no doubt had been turning over in his mind everything August had said, mixing and chopping and whirling it all together until it was a fine theoretical paste. August just didn't have time for it. He'd decided what the ghosts were and what they meant years ago, and nothing Pescatelli had to say interested him in the least.

Walking along the curving sidewalk to his car as the last of the day's buses groaned past in a rush of noise and diesel-soaked air, August noticed Veronica far ahead, waiting patiently for the crossing guard to let her pass. She was all alone.

Such a pretty girl. A girl who saw a value in attractive, modest clothing, while most of her classmates seemed to be having a contest to see who could show the most skin. Bared midriff, exposed cleavage, shorts and skirts high up the thigh; this was what passed for fashion these days. August found it ironic that it was the fatherless girl who dressed so modestly, when it was all of the young women with fathers who dressed so cheaply. He could not understand why these fathers, half men all, could stand idly by and watch their daughters march off to school, the mall, and into the cars of quick-handed boys, wearing clothing more appropriate for a strip club than for public view. He wouldn't have stood for it. Although, he admitted to himself, it might be easier to make such a claim knowing that he'd never have the chance again.

He'd wanted a daughter more than anything on earth, and the sixteen years that Eva had been alive were the happiest of his life.

She had been a frail child; both she and her mother had barely survived her birth. She was born with complications—underdeveloped lungs and asthma. Madeline had been hospitalized for a week and would not be able to bear more children. But in his wife's and daughter's weakness, August had grown strong. He had become the rock that he needed to be to guide his family through crisis, something he'd done successfully for sixteen years, right up until the asthma attack that took Eva's life. He hadn't been there, and neither had Madeline. Eva was with her boyfriend and without her inhaler; the panicked call from the cell phone did not summon the ambulance in time. Eva died in a snow-dusted field of grass on a cloudless, sunny day, unable to draw in enough of the clean, sweet, February air to keep her alive.

Surrounded by ghosts, August thought, and I have never seen my daughter again. He was holding the steering wheel tightly enough to rip it right off the column.

Madeline never really recovered from Eva's death. In the long weeks that followed, she was held in the grip of a depression that neither therapy nor medication could break. She became obsessed with the date of Eva's death—February 29. The fact that the 29th occurred once every four years led Madeline to conclude that some cosmic mistake had been made.

"It didn't exist," she would mumble, rocking in the chair where, years before, she'd held her tiny daughter. "It shouldn't exist." August's various attempts to talk with her, to break through the advancing wall of her depression, were met by these muttered phrases, which gradually began to erode the rock he thought he'd become.

August put his car into gear without waiting for the engine to warm up. Veronica wasn't halfway home yet, and he maintained a healthy distance from her. In his younger years he'd enjoy the mile walk to school, but he no longer trusted himself on sidewalks slicked with slush and ice.

He watched her make her careful way down the hill toward his house. She was, he thought, a lot like Eva.

When she walked by his house she did not give it so much as a passing glance as she continued on her way on the opposite side of the street. This made him smile. This was how it was supposed to be. Mary's ghost never appeared in the afternoons, just in the mornings.

If only she hadn't come to his door that day, he thought. He'd locked himself inside his house, trying to ignore Madeline's insistent voice inside his head. He'd known at the time that what he'd done four years prior had been wrong—even if it had worked, it would have been wrong—and was trying to hide until the 29th drifted by for another four years. But he heard Mary knock, and as he held his breath, Madeline whispered in the dark, "It's Eva," and then, as though in a trance, he found himself opening the door.

He'd reached out to her, this girl who had given him such comfort, and he swore to himself that he was reaching out to embrace her, but instead his hands went around her throat, and he squeezed, his fingers pressing into her powder blue scarf. He squeezed. He squeezed until the breath fled her body, and in that moment he looked deep into her eyes, hoping that he could see the soul of his Eva in their flickering, fading light.

After that light was gone, he'd found an essay folded neatly in the pocket of Mary's coat, the A minus written at the top in Mrs. Ellison's no-nonsense hand, evidence of how successful his tutelage of her had been. She'd been flushed with pride and happiness at the hard-earned grade, eager to show her tutor the fruits of their labors. And instead of praise, she'd found . . .

Madeline's nagging voice became more compassionate and supportive after the attempt, even though it was another failure. She spoke more quietly then, but her faith that Eva's soul might be able to enter the body of the girl the moment her spirit fled never wavered. Eva had died on the 29th of February; she could return on the same day, to inhabit the body of a girl whose soul had recently left. Every four years, August tried again, and every four years he looked into the new girl's eyes as she died, hoping for Eva to finally be reborn. The first one—a teenage runaway he'd offered a ride to when visiting the city— had had a light in her eyes that had danced for some moments after her lungs had stopped working.

"Close," Madeline had said. "We were close."

Veronica was nearly at her own home now, the house that

Mary Greer had been walking to the day she shouldn't have stopped by August's home.

Pulling into his driveway, he heard Madeline's voice as clearly as if she were sitting next to him. "She's the one," she said.

This time it would be different. This time he'd hold her and feel her as her last breath escaped, and he would watch her eyes, and he would pray and he would see his daughter walk through the door that he created; he would hear the body draw a new breath—a long, clean, unbroken breath—and then Eva would be back in his arms. Eva, his daughter, returned to him. Veronica would be gone, her spirit severed from the tethers that bound it to her body, and Eva would take her place.

He was sure of it.

He strode up his porch steps to the heavy front door, resisting the urge to knock, the way Mary did, time and time again.

‖‖‖ ‖‖‖

Veronica arrived home and found her mother on the couch, asleep in front of the television, instead of at her job at the Jewell City Town Hall. She'd been watching the Food Network with the sound down low, apparently. There was an advertisement running for Ghost-B-Gone, an aerosol spray that was guaranteed to leave your house specter-free. It came in two pleasing scents, lemon and potpourri. Veronica went upstairs to the linen closet.

She chose a purple-and-blue comforter that her grandmother had made years ago, because it smelled faintly of the cedar blocks her mother stored it with, and because she knew it was her mother's favorite. If only they made cedar-scented Ghost-B-Gone, maybe she'd be able to convince her mom to try it.

Veronica thought she was moving with catlike stealth, but her mother woke up when she started to draw the blanket over her.

"Hi, honey," her mother said, wearing a fragile smile. "How was your day?" she asked, yawning midsentence.

"It was okay," Veronica said. "How was yours? Didn't make it to work?" Her mother worked as a clerk, assisting people in getting their tax records filed.

"No, I was there," she said, drawing the comforter tighter around her shoulders rather than sitting up. "I left after lunch."

"Are you sick?" Veronica was careful to keep her voice neutral when she asked this; her mother called in sick to work frequently, and left early even more frequently. Connecticut, perhaps because of being so close to ground zero, had been one of the first states to recognize Post-Event Stress Disorder as a serious medical condition. As a state employee, Veronica's mother was given all due consideration, but Veronica often worried that her mother might lose her job. She didn't tell her, but Veronica banked almost all of her pay from the movie theater in case that day arrived.

"No," she said. "I came home because a dear sweet little old lady named Mrs. Hergstrom came to the counter. She was wearing a blue coat and a cute rain hat. I said, 'Hello, Mrs. Hergstrom!' but she just smiled at me. Then I remembered that she died two years ago."

"Wow! Is that the first time she—her ghost—appeared?"

Her mother yawned again. "I think so. None of the other women in the office remembered seeing her—not since before she died, anyhow."

She closed her eyes, and Veronica had to resist the urge to smooth out the wrinkles on her mother's forehead. "I don't know why, it just hit me today. I wait for your father every morning, and sometimes when he disappears I'm ready for the day, thankful that I at least got to see him again and he looked happy. Other times I leave and I feel so hollowed out, empty inside. I'm like, 'When we die, this is all that is left? An image that flickers and repeats like an old rerun?'"

Veronica stroked her mother's hair, and her mother groped for her hand and held it against her cheek, as though trying to draw warmth from it.

"I just felt so bad for her. Mrs. Hergstrom. To think that a fragment of her was stuck inside the town hall, waiting at the front counter for service. It sends chills down my spine."

"We don't know if it is really a fragment of her," Veronica said, leaning into her mother, hugging her, partially covering her like another comforter. "Are the videos we shot with the Flip fragments of us?"

"Images, then," her mother said. "Either way, the thought of it makes me sad."

Veronica held her, and could smell her mother's scent mixed with the cedar.

"How about I make dinner tonight?" she said. "Do we have chicken breasts?"

"You don't have to cook, honey," her mom replied, "just because I'm so fainthearted."

"I want to," Veronica told her, rising from the couch. "You can make dinner on one of my nights when I've got too much homework. How about I put on the water for tea?"

"I'd like that," her mother said, but Veronica could hear nothing like enthusiasm in her voice.

Veronica put the water on. She went upstairs and changed into loose sweatpants and an old oversized pink T-shirt with the TaB logo on it. When she returned to the kitchen, the kettle had just begun to whistle, and something about the sound made her look at the table. She stared at the seat where her father's image sat in the mornings. She and her mother had positioned the chair so that when he appeared he looked seated with his elbows propped up on the table at the right angle. It would have been disturbing to see Dad bisected by furniture like the ghost teacher at school, cut in half by Mr. Pescatelli's desk. Of course, her father wasn't there. There was a sugar bowl, a napkin holder with a few thin floral napkins, and salt and pepper shakers in the shape of smiling cows on the table, but no newspaper or coffee cup. Veronica stared until the whistle rose to a shrill, shrieking volume.

Maybe we should have moved, she thought.

She removed the water from the heat, knowing that her mother would never move. Maybe the only thing worse than finding your husband's ghost in the kitchen every morning was not knowing where his ghost was. Mrs. Hergstrom probably had children somewhere, maybe a small tribe of beautiful grandchildren. Which would be worse—to know that your dear sweet nana was haunting the town hall, or to not be sure if she was haunting anything, anywhere?

Veronica selected two of her mother's prettiest, most delicate cups and placed them on a tray along with a small teapot and some spoons, and then she leaned over her father's chair to get the sugar bowl. There was no chill, no subtle scent of newsprint or strong coffee. It wasn't his time.

Her mother was sitting up when she returned with the tray. "You're so sweet to me," she said as Veronica poured hot water over the tea bag in her cup. She was, Veronica saw, on the verge of tears.

"Oops," Veronica said. "I forgot the cream."

She stood up, and as she crossed the room she was struck

by a sudden feeling, an intuition, one that told her she did not want to go into the kitchen. The feeling was so strong, the onset so quick, that for a moment she felt light-headed.

"Veronica?" her mother said. "Are you okay?"

"Stood up too quickly," she answered, forcing herself to take another step forward. From where she was standing she could see into the kitchen; she had a clear view of the stove and the refrigerator, but could not see their little round table.

"Veronica?"

"I'm fine! Really!" she said, and stumbled forward. She needed to be strong for her mother. There was no reason to be scared of ghosts.

She was holding her breath when she walked into the kitchen, but she forced herself to look at the table straightaway.

There was no one there. No one she could see, anyway.

####### ||||| |||||

The effort costs me. And to have spent it so foolishly! I watch her, momentarily afraid in her own home, and I am ashamed.

It has been so long since I could do anything but watch. The idea that I can manifest, and can cause the living to feel emotion, is something new to me. This is something that has been building steadily within me, ever since the cataclysm. I do not know what the cataclysm was, exactly—I have heard the girl and her mother talk of it in only the vaguest of terms as the Event—but I felt it when it happened. Thousands upon thousands of souls migrating into the afterlife, a rushing river of souls. How I wished that river had washed over me and carried me along on its current.

It wasn't the transmigration of millions of souls that left me in this place, though. It was one. Mary's. We were happy, Mary and I, the sort of happy that is so bright it blinds you to the way life really is. At least it blinded me.

We were sixteen, and although the world tells you that sixteen is too young to fall in love, we knew that we were. We were growing up at a time when sixteen wasn't too young to start planning for one's future, in terms of college and career; we were maybe unique in that we were already making those plans together. Mary was going to go into a "helping" field—nursing, social work, elder care—anything that allowed her to console and mitigate human suffering; a role that she was ideally suited for.

She often said that she enjoyed her tutoring sessions with Mr. Bittner because she felt that she was easing some pain, some loneliness that he harbored deep within his heart. She saw him as deserving empathy and pity, a solitary widower who needed occasional contact and conversation with people outside the classroom. She saw him as a poor aging man who had tragically lost his own daughter, and who would benefit from the company of a surrogate.

This is how Mary viewed him, the man who would murder her. With compassion.

The years that followed have been long, but since the Event I have felt an energy building. I am like a sketch that the artist has just begun to apply paint to. Since the cataclysm, the barrier that separates this world from the afterlife has thinned in places. I am not the only pale watercolor beginning to take form.

But Veronica's father and I are different. I'm not even sure that "he" is the correct term, any more than a photograph of the man would be a "he." His appearance at the family breakfast table is certainly a by-product of the Event, but he is not the same as I am. At least I don't think he is.

I think the difference is that I have never passed into the afterlife. I haven't had more than a glimpse of it. Just a brief flash of a brilliant light, light that touched the ethereal me and then was gone. And I've been cold ever since.

Why did I frighten Veronica? Of all the emotions I might have tried to create in her, what made me settle on fear?

Is it just that I know that emotion more than any other?

I reach out and allow spectral fingers to pass over the surface of the Blu-ray player, again disrupting the set time. I consider this disruption a slight ironic joke. Time lengthens and stretches, but endures. Time endures, but there are places where time renders thin the veil between the worlds. Many images are most visible at the hour of their death, or the hour of their birth, or at the time when their emotions burned most incandescent. Soon it will be the rarest of days, the day that only occurs every four years, and that is when the veil is at its thinnest, February 29.

The day when Mary died.

I feel as though I'm coming apart, that whatever it is that allows me a consciousness is beginning to fray and decay. It may take days to gather myself together again. I drift past where Veronica's father appears each morning, and I float upstairs into the bathroom, where I died. The trauma of my death has etched a permanent scar upon that room, a scar that the Event widened. It is part of my curse that the room where I died is now the room where in death I grow strongest. Only there am I able to coalesce into something that appears tangible. Falling into the old pattern—my ghostly loop in front of the bathroom mirror—is easiest to do and requires little effort or energy at all. But moving outside of a memory, doing something that I had not done when alive is a draining experience.

What's left of me drifts to the tub, where I last closed my eyes, where I last drew breath.

I'm so tired.

~~卌~~ ~~卌~~ |

The boy in Veronica's bathroom didn't appear again until Friday. She was ready for him this time, having peered cautiously around the shower curtain each morning when the waterproof clock radio hanging from the showerhead told her it was time for him to arrive. Sometimes ghosts intensified gradually, like a strengthening signal; other times they were simply there, and this ghost was one of the latter. Without any forethought, Veronica decided to name him Brian.

The water was still running hot, sending puffs of steam into the bathroom. She dried her eyes on the soft cotton towel she'd hung over the bar.

Brian's hair was a light blond and feathered back over his collar. He was wearing dark jeans that looked stiff and brand new, and a thick brown leather belt; he'd missed a loop on his right hip. Veronica could only see the side of his face, but she could tell now that he was brushing his teeth. He paused, spit some phantom toothpaste that would never hit the basin, and looked up to smile widely at himself in the mirror.

Veronica smiled as well. It was such a natural thing to do, free from any of the self-consciousness one has in the company of other people. Much less naked teenage girls, although Veronica had curled her fingers around the edge of the shower curtain so that only her face and dripping hair were visible outside the shower.

Brian gave a little flip to his hair, making his shiny, feathered locks bounce into place. He did it again, and Veronica laughed. She'd say that his hair was a length and style that was no longer fashionable, although she could also think of half a dozen boys at school who wore theirs similarly, or longer. But there was something about Brian that made him look out of place in her time.

Then a weird thing happened. Brian lifted his hand to run his fingers through his oh-so beautiful tresses, and when he did, his face became visible in the mirror.

It happened so suddenly that Veronica gasped and closed the curtain, the metal ringlets clinking on the bar.

His eyes were blue. He'd blinked and looked right at her, that's how fast it had happened.

Veronica's heart was beating fast, and her nakedness was something she was now acutely conscious of. Ghosts didn't have reflections. Or did they? And they weren't supposed to change their patterns; they weren't capable of independent thought or action, or so the common belief went. She'd read that the patterns sometimes lengthened, but the actions that the ghosts committed were not supposed to change. But had the pattern just lengthened or had it really changed? Veronica had bolted out of the bathroom on Brian's previous visit and hadn't really caught the whole "show."

She took a deep breath and peeled back the edge of the shower curtain. Brian was still there, comb in hand, but the reflection was gone. And then he was, too.

Veronica turned the water off and began to pat her body dry with a fluffy towel. She wasn't scared, she told herself, just startled. The bathroom was filled with steam, but the mirror wasn't foggy. The ghosts made all sorts of laws of physics go haywire. Veronica went to the sink, and her skin began to tingle the moment she approached the place where Brian had been standing. The cool cone of air surrounding the area was like a frosty caress in the otherwise warm and humid bathroom. She shivered.

Veronica forced herself to look in the mirror. She was seized by a giddy, whimsical feeling, and she drew back her lips to replicate the toothy smile she'd seen Brian give himself. Or give her; that's what it had felt like. The elation she'd felt when he'd smiled was even greater than the quick flash she felt when her father's eyes met hers. She dried her hair and got dressed.

Attraction, she thought. Such a weird, unquantifiable thing. She thought of all the boys in her class and wondered why she'd felt an instant attraction for this ghost boy, and varying levels of attraction for the real boys at school. Back to looks—Brian was handsome, but it wasn't like he was a Greek god or anything, and he had a goofy haircut and had missed a belt loop. He was between James and Kirk in the looks department. What else did they have in common? What else set them apart? She realized that she felt a similar thrill when seeing any of them—and maybe here she'd given the slight edge to Brian because there was something totally magical and unexpected about his morning appearances. James would probably be the best protector, but she didn't really need protecting—and no one could protect you from an Event, anyway. It either happened or it didn't. But to talk to . . . and be understood by . . . she wasn't sure yet, but she'd give that edge to Kirk.

But Brian hovered on the periphery of her thoughts; it was as though the cool air she'd felt in front of the bathroom mirror contained within its atoms deeper memories of him; trace elements of his personality. Veronica thought she could say anything, anything at all to him, and probably be understood perfectly. The only downside, if that's what it was, was that he couldn't talk back.

"I don't know what I want," she said out loud, and the words seemed to hang in the air the way his presence did. Maybe in the end, all she really wanted was someone who was going to be there, really be there for her. "If only you were real."

Downstairs, her mother was sitting across from her father's ghost at the kitchen table, eating a buttered English muffin and having a cup of tea.

"Hi, honey," she said as Veronica entered. "There's hot water if you want some tea, and I left the muffins by the toaster."

Veronica realized that her mother's cheeks were wet with tears. She put her hands on her mother's shoulders.

Veronica watched as her father turned a page. He was turning page four in the business section to page five, to be precise, and he would soon become engrossed in the article about home heating oil. This was how their day began. Yet again.

ⅢⅢ ⅢⅢ ‖

"So what do you got going on tonight?" James said to Kirk as they headed down to Pescatelli's class. "Besides spanking the monkey."

Sometimes, James was a really irritating guy. Most of the time, actually, but Kirk wasn't going to let on. Like rubbing poison ivy, it would only make the irritation worse.

"The monkey is in need of a good spanking, I must admit," he said, "but I'm working tonight."

"You are a damn fine barista, Kirk," James said, clapping him on the back with more force than necessary. "One of the best baristas ever. In fact, to show my appreciation, I will be tipping you a shiny new quarter when I bring Ronnie over for free coffee before the movie. Caffeine is better than alcohol on a date. Gets them . . . excitable, you know what I'm saying?"

Kirk looked at his friend's cocky leer. The fact that he was taking Ronnie out was the proverbial insult to injury.

"I think stopping by for coffee is a great idea, Jimmy," he said. "She'll need it to stay awake. I'll gladly prepare any of our delicious beverages, made from only the finest coffee beans and pure, filtered water, that you would like to purchase."

"Come on," James said, taking the jibe in stride. "Hook a brother up."

"Can't do it, my friend. No free beverages."

"C'mon, those drinks are wicked expensive. And then the movie and the damn snacks . . ."

"Why I make the big bucks."

"Dude . . ."

They reached class as the second bell rang. Kirk returned the clap on the back with enough gusto to make James stumble.

"Dude," Kirk said, "think of it this way. Part of the reason late-night coffee bars were invented was so jerks like you could get away without buying a girl dinner."

Kirk noticed that Veronica was looking over at them as they sat down. Janine's seat beside her was empty. James was a friend, but Kirk couldn't help but hope that his date ended in ruin, hopefully with something really dramatic, like Veronica dumping a caramel macchiato—one that Kirk himself had made—over his head.

Veronica had been on Kirk's radar for a long time. Her confidence, the way she carried herself . . . she was different than most of the girls in their school—who dressed and acted like another Event was on its way.

Funny, he thought. If there was another Event around the corner, he'd rather face it with someone like Veronica. He knew that she was regarded by many as being the class flirt, but that didn't bother him; it just made him think she'd chosen to remain alive. Since the Event, most people lived in a nostalgic past or in the uncertain future. Veronica lived in the present, and if Kirk had to name one quality that made her more vibrant than the crowd of dull girls (and here he thought of poor quivery Janine) at Montcrief, that would be the one.

"How long has she been working at the theater?" James whispered.

"I don't know," Kirk said, but he did know—to the day. The Cineplex was right next door to the Starbucks where he worked, and he often saw Veronica arriving at her own job. He doubted that she ever noticed him. "A couple months, maybe."

"Maybe she could hook us up for a movie, too," James said. "With any luck, I won't have to pay for anything."

"You'll pay," Kirk said. "Oh, how you'll pay."

James, laughing, socked him in the meat of the shoulder, knocking him a little off balance. "We'll see. Maybe I'll get to go in her house, protect her from her ghost."

"Yeah," Kirk said. "I hope instead he protects her from you."

He'd meant it—sort of—as a joke, but it was a joke that brought with it a sudden flash of insight.

He had a great idea on how he could get Veronica to pay attention to him.

Kirk watched his arrogant friend swagger; James's mouth turned up in a self-satisfied little smile.

She doesn't really like you, Kirk thought. So watch out.

"Yeah? Who does she like? You?"

Kirk blinked. Had he really said that out loud?

"Just warning you. All's fair. It isn't like you two are an item or anything; it's just a date."

James looked shocked and a little hurt.

"You ass. You really would try and move in like that?" he said.

"I'm just saying. Let the best man win."

"Yeah, good luck," James said with as much contempt as he could muster. Which was a considerable amount, it turned out.

"That battle has already been decided."

But Kirk had seen the look in Veronica's eyes when she was talking about the ghosts. Her father. The boy in her bathroom. James might have a date with her, but Kirk was beginning to think he had the inside track to her heart.

"Okay," Pescatelli said. "No goofing around today. We're going to get right into it with a quiz. Pick one of the survivors whose tales are told in *Hiroshima* and give me two pages on what you imagine a day in his or her life must have been like between the main narrative and the afterword chapters. You can pick any of the six, the one you think you know the best. Really get into their head. I want you to think like they thought. Creativity is not a crime in this assignment. Questions? Go."

There was a just-audible groan throughout the class, but Kirk was actually relieved. Sometimes it was easier doing work than enduring Pescatelli's endless rambles.

He supposed, though, that he had better get used to those, too, because if what he was planning was going to work, he'd be spending a lot more time with Pescatelli.

Ghosts, he thought. *Ronnie is curious about ghosts.*

"I'll catch up with you later, dude," Kirk said to James as the bell rang.

"Whatever," James replied, looking at him with a strange expression, like he thought it was weird that Kirk was staying after class to talk to the Fish.

Kirk hovered around the edge of Pescatelli's desk, watching as James put his arm around Ronnie's shoulders. Had she recoiled slightly? He could only hope so.

"You want something, Lane?" the Fish said. He sure was a moody guy, Kirk thought. Pescatelli had let loose with a loud, curt laugh when the ghost teacher in the pink dress appeared again, using her as the signal to end the quiz, but right after that his mood and lecture sank down into a depressing swamp of fragmented ideas. Kirk wanted to tell him to give up on *Hiroshima* and *On the Beach* and the so-called "literature of the apocalypse" and switch to something lighter. Something with elves, maybe. Or anthropomorphic animals. Anything.

"Lane?" the Fish repeated. If you could catch Pescatelli at the right angle, his glasses made him look like his eyes were on the sides of his face, like a flounder's.

"Um, I . . . I was wondering," Kirk said, nervous and stuttering without knowing why. "I was wondering if I could do an independent work study. You know. For extra credit."

Pescatelli blinked, and maybe he was aware of how comical his eyes looked refracted by his glasses, because he took them off a second later.

"Are you crazy?" he said, lightly shoving Kirk toward the door. "You've got one of the best grades in the class. Go out. Live a little. You need a tan, not extra credit."

He really is nuts, Kirk thought. No one was getting tanned in February, not in Jewell City.

"I was thinking about studying the ghosts," he said.

Pescatelli leaned forward on his elbows, upsetting the delicate ecosystem of his desk, knocking a couple papers and a pencil to the floor. Kirk watched the pencil roll under a chair in the front row, but made no move to pick it up. When Pescatelli spoke, he sounded even less amused than usual.

"This is a joke, right? What are you trying to do to me here, Lane?"

"Nothing," Kirk said, sounding more defensive than he wanted. "I just thought—"

"Thought what? You'd have a little fun at the Fish's expense?"

Kirk was shocked to hear the nickname—which was rarely used as an endearment—come out of Pescatelli's own mouth. "Really," Kirk said, lifting his notebook and copy of *Hiroshima* shieldlike in front of him. "I just thought it would be interesting, that's all."

"Bullshit," Pescatelli asked. "I mention the ghosts in class and the look of disgust on your face could ward off vampires. What's the game?"

Kirk shrugged, and he knew that the look of disgust was returning to his face. He'd tried to reach out for help—and reach out *to* help, on some level—and got sand in his eye. Screw it.

"I wanted to learn something," he said. "To help a girl I know."

"A girl?"

"Yeah, a girl. They're kind of soft, easier on the eyes, and they smell better than we do."

The sarcasm had a strange effect on Pescatelli. He laughed out loud, and seemed to relax a little when he leaned back in his seat. "You trying to impress this girl, that it?"

"Yeah," Kirk answered. When all else fails, honesty could be a good policy. "And help her with something."

"Veronica Calder?"

"Yeah," Kirk answered, surprised. Pescatelli taught like he didn't even know the class was there, or like he thought they were all ghosts in neat little rows. How he could pick out a minor drama like Kirk's crush on Ronnie was a mystery. "How did you know?"

The Fish snickered. "She's the obvious choice. And the pursuit of a girl's heart is the single best reason to ask for extra credit that I've heard in all my years as a teacher."

"Okay, mockery aside—"

"I'm not mocking you," the Fish said. "My wife used to tell me that one of the things that drew her to me was when she saw me working on one of my projects. That's what she called my books: projects."

"You were married?"

"I was," the Fish said, his eyes lowered. "Do you have a driver's license?"

"Yeah," Kirk replied.

"Okay. We'll do an independent study. With fieldwork. Meet me at the library tonight at five."

"I can't. I'm working."

"Okay. Saturday, then. They open at ten. Can you do that?"

Can do, but don't *want to*, Kirk thought. He was working a full shift on Saturday night, starting at eight o'clock, and had been looking forward to sleeping in and maybe lifting weights, but the image of Ronnie rose up in his mind.

"I'll see you then."

"Right."

Pescatelli turned toward the west windows overlooking the soccer field. The school was high enough on the hill that the black clouds that the Event had kicked miles high into the atmosphere would have been visible from those very windows for weeks.

||||| ||||| |||

Veronica didn't get *really* angry until the second time that James attempted a covert grab of her breast. What made her especially pissed was that they were in public, although in the gloom of a movie theater. He could have at least waited until they'd left and he'd parked the car somewhere. The result would have been the same, but at least he would have been the only person embarrassed by the attempt.

"What?" he said, after she gave him a solid thump with her elbow.

"Just stop it, James." She'd said please the first time, but her patience had run out.

"Don't get mad," he said, rubbing where she'd hit him.

Good, she thought. Let him rub his own chest for awhile.

Veronica was regretting not breaking off their date. All that time ironing her clothes and doing her hair could have been spent in better ways. She could have finished *Hiroshima* or started her history homework. She could have called Janine to see if she was interested in going to a ghost-free mall. She could have vacuumed her room or counted the number of cans of crushed tomatoes in the pantry; at this point, anything would have been preferable. James had picked her up fifteen minutes

63

early and brought her to Starbucks, apparently with the sole intention of humiliating Kirk in front of her. James worked for his father's construction company on the weekends and vacations, and found the idea of his friend working in a coffee chain hilarious.

Veronica didn't. Kirk took the ribbing in stride, even though there seemed to be a nasty undercurrent to it, and Veronica thought that if Kirk showed any interest in her, she'd encourage him. James was a jerk. A handsome, arrogant jerk. She'd seen the signs at school, but they'd simmered just under the surface of his personality, hidden from view. She was distrustful of people who were one person in public and another in private.

She didn't even like coffee, and she much preferred the green tea she made for herself at home.

She'd glanced back at Kirk as they were leaving, and he'd looked more disappointed than angry, even though James had abused him about the taste, the temperature, the various names of the Starbucks sizes, and finally the price of his drink. Veronica smiled at Kirk as she left, but his expression didn't change. She felt bad for him and thought that James had not picked a good way to kick off their date. Totally a tactical error on his part.

The movie was not good. Teens having sex at a lakeside camp until the slasher—a large zombielike creature who had been constructed from the corpses of the most violent criminals executed in the country—shows up. The movie was supposed to be thrilling, Veronica supposed, but she found it to be more than a little icky.

"Do you want to get out of here?" James whispered, giving her a light kiss on the neck.

"No," she said, although she did. Not for whatever reasons James intended, but to leave the terrible movie and go home. But he wanted to leave, so Veronica would make him stay for the whole movie.

When it was over, she slid out of her seat quickly, before he could try to hold her hand, or worse, put his arm around her waist. And then she got her biggest fright of the night: Mr. Bittner had been sitting two rows behind them. "Hello, Veronica," he said, putting on his gray coat and pushing himself out of his seat. "Mr. Trantolo."

"Hello, Mr. Bittner," she said. James grunted in a "we're not in school and don't have to talk to you" sort of way.

"Did you enjoy the movie?" he asked Veronica, not including James. His thin, dry-looking lips were tight, the merest hint of a smile at one of the corners. It was the same expression he wore just before humiliating a student in class for not doing an assigned reading. She was mortified because he must have seen stupid James groping her.

"Um," she said, "not really." Mr. Bittner's eyes were black beneath the brim of his hat.

"You like it?" James asked, putting his arm around Veronica's shoulder. If it had been anyone else they were talking to, she probably would have shrugged it off, and maybe hit James again, but something in Mr. Bittner's expression made her glad James's arm was there, even if the public contact embarrassed her.

Mr. Bittner laughed. "Not my cup of tea, I'm afraid," he said, holding up a broad flat hand. "I don't know why I sat through the whole thing, to be honest with you."

His hand was as wide as her face, Veronica thought. As he

lowered it, her eyes were drawn to the thick, knobby knuckles, each sprouting a tuft of wiry white hair. There was a lot of strength in that hand, she thought. Much more than required for turning the moldering pages of forgotten history books. Mr. Bittner could have been a great guitar player, she thought, or a pipe fitter. The long fingers twitched, and she realized she had been staring.

"Mr. Bittner?" she said, trying to recover.

"Yes?"

"You've lived in the neighborhood a long time, haven't you?"

His expression seemed to darken a shade. "Long enough. Why?"

"There's a . . . there's a ghost in my house. A teenage boy. I wondered if you knew him."

Mr. Bittner almost looked like he was glaring at her. "I'm afraid that I have never been very cognizant of my neighbors," he said. "A great failing, no doubt."

What a weirdo, Veronica thought, shuddering. "Oh, okay."

He stood there, and she had the impression that he was trying to gaze into her eyes, like her mother would sometimes do when she suspected her of lying.

"We've got to be going," she said. "I'll see you on Monday, Mr. Bittner."

He smiled, the wrinkles in his square, pink face deepening. "Take care, Veronica," he said. "Mr. Trantolo."

"Man, what a creepy dude," James said, once they were inside his father's SUV. "He looks like Jack the Ripper with that overcoat and hat."

"He's really pretty nice," Veronica replied, more from the

need to take a contradictory position to whatever James said, although she *had* thought at one time that Mr. Bittner was a nice man. But the truth was, Mr. Bittner *was* creepy.

She realized James was talking.

"What?"

"I said I hate that guy."

"Really? Why?"

"I'll be lucky if I pass."

"That's too bad. I really like Mr. Bittner's class."

"That's because you're a brain. He probably kills all of his dumb students."

Then he asked if she wanted to drive over to the lake.

She didn't know if she should be flattered and admire his persistence, or amazed at his inability to read what she thought were overt signals.

"Not tonight. I couldn't go to the lake after watching a creepy movie like that," she said, letting him off easy. His arm had felt good around her shoulders when they were talking to Mr. Bittner. Protection. Solidity. Those were good things, but then he'd open his mouth.

"Some other time, then?" he said. At least he didn't pull the puppy dog routine. She hated when boys acted all crestfallen and mopey.

There was something to be said for a boy that accepted disappointment with grace. James put the car into gear and drove her home without any nonsense, and they had a pleasant conversation about colleges they were interested in, what they did on the weekends, and what James liked and didn't like about working for his father. There was a point in the conversation when Veronica thought that if their evening had started this way, it might have ended much differently.

They came down the hill past the school, toward her house. Almost there, she looked over at Mr. Bittner's, which was dark except for an amber light that shone down on where the ghost of Mary Greer knocked every morning. His old gray Volvo wasn't in the driveway. Without knowing why, she drew her jacket a little tighter. The creepy feeling was still there a minute later when James pulled the SUV into her short driveway, and because of that feeling, she gave him a quick, friendly kiss before thanking him and stepping out of the car. She stood on the porch and waved as he backed up and drove away, but the kiss had done nothing to dispel her unease.

$$\text{IIII IIII IIII}$$

August had followed them home from the theater at a respectful distance, interested to see whether or not Veronica's cologne-soaked date was going to attempt anything beyond what he'd tried in the theater. He was also curious to see if she would weaken and succumb to her overheated paramour. Most girls her age did, he knew, having so little self-esteem that their token resistance broke quickly under the boy's constant, insistent pressure. He'd seen microcosmic versions of their weakness play out time and again in his classes and in the halls, where young girls allowed themselves to be fondled, squeezed, kissed, and about everything else by dull, sweaty boys.

"You need to be ready," his wife said. "You can bring Eva back, August."

August didn't want to answer, but he knew that his silences only encouraged her.

"It has to be on the day, doesn't it?" he said. "I thought it had to be on the day or it had no chance of working."

"Yes, it has to be on the day, you old fool!" she said. "But you need to prepare! For Eva's sake."

August's jaw tightened as he choked back his reply. He was surprised to find himself on his own street so soon. He'd been certain that the Trantolo boy would have driven Veronica straight to the lake for a backseat rendezvous, like the young fools in that wretched movie they'd just watched.

August wasn't sure what he would have done if they'd driven to Lake Mouse, or to one of the many wooded inlets where hundreds of young couples from Jewell City had gone over the years. He'd had a vague idea of parking the Volvo on the side of the road somewhere and following them into the woods on foot, but the thought of skulking around through the brambles in his overcoat was absurd, not to mention leaving his car on the road to be easily seen and identified by anyone driving by.

Once he was home, he left the porch lamp lit but did not turn on any lights inside. He was thinking how different life would be if his daughter had lived.

"You are sure this time?" he said, his voice soft. "It hasn't worked before, has it? Are we making a mistake to—"

"Mistake?" Madeline said, her voice echoing like a freight train plowing through the cavern of his head. "A mistake? Don't you love our daughter, August? Don't you love Eva?"

August closed his eyes, and he could see her.

"Yes," he whispered.

"And don't you want to see her again? Don't you want to rescue her from this ocean of ghosts and actually see her again?"

"You know that I do."

"If that were true, if you really loved her, you wouldn't fret about a few so-called 'mistakes.' You saw her, didn't you? When the others took their last breaths you saw her in their eyes, looking out at you. Didn't you?"

"Yes," he said. "I think so." He'd seen something in their

eyes, some different type of consciousness or wisdom that hadn't been their moments before.

"'I think so,' he says. You think so. She was there. She almost made it through, and if you couldn't see that, you are a fool, August Bittner. A damned fool. I think you don't love our daughter at all. I think you don't love *me* at all."

"Madeline—"

"Because if you did love her . . . if you loved me, you would do anything you could to bring her back. Anything."

His eyes still closed, August summoned up an image of Veronica in his mind. A sweet, pure, fatherless girl—she could be the one who would help him.

"I would do anything, Madeline," he said. "You know that I would."

"She is the one, August. I'm sure of it. She is the one who will let you bring Eva back."

He had a very clear image of Veronica then, walking down the sidewalk across from his house, the light filtering through her dark auburn hair, and her head tilted at a slight angle toward his house. He would count off her steps until she disappeared from view. He smiled, and he could picture himself smiling in anticipation of seeing her walking by, each and every morning, rain or shine, sixteen forever, her spectral gaze focused on Mary, her spiritual sister, as she beat her silent tattoo against his peeling door. He would turn, and there would be Eva, but Eva solid and real and smiling, and together they would watch the ghosts of the other girls drifting away.

The image was so vivid, it was like she was with him already.

|||| |||| ||||

On Saturday, Kirk found the Fish in a corner of the library behind a rampart of stacked books. The Fish looked up at him and blinked once.

"I didn't think you would come," he said.

"I said I would," Kirk said, sitting across from his English teacher in what must have been the creakiest chair ever constructed. He looked around, embarrassed, but the library wasn't exactly a hot spot early on a Saturday.

"I thought that maybe your ardor for Miss Calder had—"

Kirk lifted his hand. "Okay, I told you why I wanted to do this project," he said, "but I don't want to discuss that again, okay? Let's stick to the ghosts and leave Ronnie out of the conversation. Can we do that?"

The Fish gave a slight nod. "Either way. There are worse places to be stood up than a library."

"Am I going to have to read all of these?" Kirk said, pointing to the stack of books that the Fish had collected. *Ghosts: The Illustrated History*, *Haunted Heartland*, *Ghosts and Poltergeists*. Most of the books looked decades old, their plastic wrappings cracked and torn.

"Yeah, like that would be a difficult thing for you," the Fish said. "My guess is that you read more than anyone in your class. I'm talking your graduating class, not just English. It shows in the essays you write, sarcastic and snotty as they are. You said you wanted extra credit; don't think I'm just going to give it away."

Kirk could feel himself redden, wondering who the Fish was to call anyone sarcastic.

"Okay," he said, dragging the pile of books closer to him. "So I've got to read these. What else?"

The Fish pushed a thick black three-ring binder toward Kirk.

"You've got to read my notes. And then there's the fieldwork. I'm writing a book on modern-day ghosts—and by the way, if you tell anyone that, you can kiss your extra credit good-bye— and you're going to help me compile some research."

"For a generous cut of the royalties?" Kirk said, opening the binder. Inside were over two hundred pages of a typewritten manuscript. He wondered if he should tell the Fish that everyone sort of assumed he was working on a book, and that it wasn't the secret he seemed to think it was.

The Fish frowned. "Get real. If you do a decent job I'll give you credit in the book. There won't be much commercial interest. People don't want to read about anything having to do with the Event."

"So this is about the Event?"

"It has to be," he answered. "Everything is about the Event. My central theory is that images—or the larger percentage of them, anyhow—occur because of a relative proximity to the Event. You don't hear much about ghost activity on the West Coast."

"Why do you call the ghosts 'images'?"

"I want to get people off the idea of thinking they are 'ghosts,' with spookiness and metaphysics implied. They're like photographs, nothing more. We just don't understand the media they're recorded on."

"Really? But what about—"

The Fish lifted his hand, cutting Kirk off. "I know what you are going to say. You're going to bring up a bunch of examples where you think ghosts exhibit consciousness, or 'haunt,' or something. Don't bother. Read the books first, then tell me what you think."

"So you think people will actually want to buy your book?" Kirk said. The Fish's theory didn't sound very interesting.

"Kid," he said, "I'm not giving you any of the proceeds from the book. Maybe you'll get real lucky and I'll leave you something in my will."

Kirk cleared his throat. "You mentioned fieldwork?"

"Yeah. I want you to go around town and visually document as many of the ghosts as you can, and I want you to take good notes on when and where they appear. I also want you to try to figure out why they are appearing."

"Why?" Kirk said. "I thought you said they appear because of the Event. Not an original theory, by the way."

The Fish shook his head. "I'm not talking about the circumstance that caused them to appear," he said. "I'm talking about the circumstance that makes them appear the *way* they appear."

"I'm not following you."

"Just trust the process," the Fish said.

Kirk sighed. "So, basically, you want me to go around videotaping ghosts?"

The Fish nodded and passed Kirk a small leather bag.

"Yep. Here's a video camera for you."

Kirk turned the clunky device over in his hands. "Kind of old-school, isn't it?"

"Just like the library itself. I've got ten tapes in there—the images don't show up as well on digital media, for some reason."

Kirk opened the bag and withdrew the camera, which had a hand strap that held it snugly in his palm. He panned it around the library.

"Cool."

"You can keep the camera when we're done," the Fish said. "Along with the A plus-plus you are already getting in my class."

Kirk trained the camera on him and thumbed the recorder on.

"You can write me a glowing recommendation letter for college, too."

"Done," the Fish said.

"You better," Kirk said. "I've got you on tape."

The Fish smiled, leaning back in his chair. An older woman in a frilly blouse walked by with a stack of books under one arm. She looked at them and lifted a finger to her severe but smiling lips as though to shush them. Then she disappeared.

"You should have gotten *her* on tape," the Fish said.

The Fish had a theory that after hospitals, factories, and schools, libraries were the most haunted places in America. He told Kirk there was also an image—a little girl—downstairs among the picture books if he wanted to check it out.

"You've got seventeen minutes until she arrives," he'd said, glancing at his watch. "Please make careful note of the starting and ending times, and write a brief description in the notes." Then he said good-bye and that he'd talk to Kirk on Monday.

Kirk went down the carpeted stairs, which had been worn smooth by the shuffling of a thousand sneakers. The children's librarian gave him a funny look, and he realized he was still holding the camera and lugging the rest of his gear in a backpack that felt like it weighed three hundred and fifty pounds.

"I'm going to videotape the . . . ghost," he told her. She wasn't someone he recognized, a younger woman with black hair, but there was a time when he'd known all of the librarians in the children's area. His mother used to bring him here every week, letting him take out three or four Thornton Burgess books at a clip. One day he'd stumbled across some Alfred Hitchcock anthologies, older books with slick hard covers in gloomy grays and greens, and then some Ray Bradbury novels a few shelves over. Those were the gateway books that brought him upstairs. Good-bye, Reddy Fox and Blacky the Crow.

"Oh," the woman said, and if she'd told Kirk that that was irregular, highly irregular, he wouldn't have been surprised at all. "Molly. She'll be over by the series books."

"Molly? That's her name?"

The librarian shrugged her round shoulders. "She looks like a Molly," she said. "You've got a few minutes. She's usually here around quarter to eleven."

Kirk nodded and thanked her. The Fish said 10:47.

He turned the camera on and sat at one of the low children's tables so that he could get a clear view of the whole section. Fortunately—or sadly, when he thought about it—the children's section at the moment was not being haunted by any actual children. He looked through the lens, and the display told him it was 10:42. He blinked, and Molly was there, a precious little thing with bouncy red curls and freckles. She was wearing a shirt with a rainbow that sprouted from a cloud, and the rainbow sparkled with glitter. She was reaching for one of the Thornton Burgess books on the top shelf, going up on tiptoe, her shirt hiking up and her baggy jeans drooping an inch or two. She turned away from the shelf and looked up, smiling and nodding as though someone had asked her a question—"Would you like me to help you?" perhaps. Kirk had to fight the urge to rush over to her and grab a book off the shelf. The girl reached up to accept the phantom book, and then she disappeared.

Kirk felt like crying. The little girl had looked so happy. He realized that no one was ever going to be that happy again. That sort of happiness just didn't exist after the Event. Molly hadn't grown up with ghosts, and she hadn't had the larger specter of the Event looming over her at all times, like everyone did today. Kirk hadn't lost a single family member in the Event, something he'd never paused to be thankful for, but the Event and the ghosts that followed had killed part of him and everyone he knew.

But Kirk wasn't just sad for himself; he was sad for Molly, or whatever her real name was. The real Molly was dead. Something had plucked her—bouncy curls, freckles, and all—as easily as plucking a book from the shelf.

He was rubbing his eyes with his free hand,

"She's cute, isn't she?" the librarian called over to him.

"Yeah," Kirk said. His voice was thick, and he didn't meet

her eyes. He was looking over at the shelf of talking-animal books and thinking about when he was younger.

"I felt the same way about her the first couple times," the librarian said, her voice laden with sympathy. Sympathy for him, he realized, and not poor Molly. Her clothing was faded, her skin pale. He resisted the urge to film her, because at that moment he was not certain she wasn't a ghost as well, about to wink out of existence.

"But then I realized everything we see and feel—a certain song in an elevator, a flower pressed in the pages of an old photo album, a penny on the sidewalk—has that power. The power to make us feel like everything is too temporary. So I decided I'd be happy when Molly came around. I look forward to seeing her now. She comes every day." She glanced at the clock on the wall opposite her. "She was a little early today, though."

Kirk nodded. "Thanks for letting me film her," he said, his voice a clotted, froglike croak.

"Sure. Anytime."

A pressed flower, a penny on the sidewalk. Kirk held on to the railing as he ascended the stairs, realizing as he ran his hand along the smooth, familiar grooves that his palm would be left with a faint resiny smell, and his fingers would be just the slightest bit tacky, as though they didn't want to let anything go.

$$\cancel{||||} \; \cancel{||||} \; \cancel{||||} \; |$$

"Hey, kid," Veronica said, loud enough so Janine could hear her through the window that separated them. Janine was wearing her hat; the string on the left side was frayed and wet, as though she'd been gnawing on it. "Are you going to let me in?"

There were dark circles under Janine's eyes; she stared out at Veronica as though she wasn't sure if she was really real.

"I brought cookies," Veronica said, holding up the bag so Janine could see. "Macadamia chocolate chip, your favorite."

A ghost of a smile crossed Janine's lips, and she opened the door. Veronica was barely over the threshold before Janine hugged her, her gloved fingers prodding and pinching along Veronica's back, verifying her solidity. Veronica accepted the touches without comment or complaint.

"You went to Arremony's," Janine said, taking the white bag from Veronica. "I love Arremony's."

"I know, silly," Veronica said. "That's why I went there. We used to go a couple times a week over the summer, remember?"

Janine nodded, reaching into the bag to select a cookie. "I remember," she said. "I love that place."

Veronica wondered if she would love it as much if she'd

known there were no less than four ghosts in the bakery when she'd picked up the cookies—three patrons and a baker. It was the most ghosts Veronica had seen in one place before, and she wondered if the smell of fresh bread had the power to summon ghosts. Of all the senses, smell is most connected to memory, so if the ghosts were memories made visible, it only made sense that they'd be drawn to such a place.

Janine took a bite of her cookie and then inhaled deeply from the bag, as though on cue.

"I love that smell," she said, and some of the color returned to her face. "How was your date with James?"

"Oh," Veronica said, "okay, I guess."

Janine held her cookie with one hand, the other was twisting the string of her hat. "You don't really like him, do you?"

Veronica wasn't prepared for the question—she'd been expecting to get Janine talking—but she answered directly. "I guess not."

"Why not?"

"I don't know, Janine. He was kind of jerk." She wondered if Janine was going to offer her a cookie. "How about I pour us some milk?"

Janine nodded, then turned and walked into the living room as Veronica found glasses.

"You date a lot of boys," Janine said as Veronica retrieved the milk.

Veronica laughed. "I suppose so." Her laughter trailed away when she saw the photograph on the fridge of a younger Janine wearing a soccer uniform: beaming and tanned, no knit gloves or hat in sight.

She carried the glasses into the living room. Janine was sitting on the couch, her back to the television, which had been covered up with a red-and-blue afghan. Janine had decided a few weeks ago that televisions were filled with ghosts.

"I know why you do it," Janine said, taking out another cookie.

"Um, because I like boys?" Veronica said. Tired of waiting, she plucked the bag from Janine and took a cookie.

"Yes," Janine said. "But you're afraid of them. You're afraid of them like I'm afraid of ghosts. In a way."

"Really?" Veronica said. This visit wasn't going at all like she'd thought it would; she'd hoped to fill up Janine with sugar and then get her to walk around the block with her a few times; the last thing in the world she'd expected was some armchair psychoanalysis from her spirit-shy friend.

Janine nodded, licking crumbs from the stitching on the fingers of her gloves. "You're afraid that the boys will go away and leave you," she said. "So you always go first."

Veronica blinked, her crescent-moon cookie nearly slipping from her hand. What went on in Janine's haunted head?

"I'm going to go to school tomorrow," Janine said, taking back the bag. "You'll wait for me, won't you?"

"I'll wait for you," Veronica said.

⟋⟋⟋⟍ ⟋⟋⟋⟍ ⟋⟋⟋⟍ ||

Veronica thought it was a very odd thing to say.

So odd that she actually stopped on her way out of the classroom to ask Mr. Bittner to repeat it. Maybe she could understand his meaning better from the inflection and cadence of his voice.

"I said, If I had a daughter, I would wish that she was like you."

Veronica smiled at him, hugging her books and the report he'd just handed back a little more tightly to her chest.

"You're so sweet, Mr. Bittner," she said, and hurried out of class.

And creepy, and bizarre, and scary. What he'd really said was "I wish my daughter was like you." She was sure of it, which was why she'd thought it was so odd. Bittner was well known as being a long-time widower, but not the sort of widower that had the neighborhood women baking pies for him or offering to do his sewing. He radiated cold the way other people radiated warmth or good humor.

Maybe that wasn't entirely fair, Veronica thought. He had seemed genuinely interested when he'd overheard James teasing her about her birthday before the start of class.

I wish my daughter was you. Was that what he'd said?

"Oh, do you have a birthday this month, Ms. Calder?" he'd asked.

"Yes," she'd said. And then giggled when James added, "She's turning four."

"Four?" he'd asked, not getting the joke.

"Yep," Veronica said. "Leap day baby. This will be my fourth birthday."

The expression on Mr. Bittner's face was so strange. Being born on February 29 was unusual, but not so shocking that he should appear like he'd been punched in the stomach. He was actually straining to regain his composure.

"Well," he said, eventually, "a happy birthday to you, then."

She'd heard that his wife had died many years ago. Along with the rumor at school that he'd killed Mary, there was one that he'd killed his own wife. Veronica never put much stock in the rumors (another classic was Mrs. Tilden having a tail), mentally filing them in the "kids can be cruel" category.

I wish my daughter was you. Maybe he'd had a daughter years ago; she could be in her thirties now, Veronica supposed. Maybe he'd never mentioned her before because they'd had a falling out, or because she was taken in the Event.

But Veronica had never seen a picture of her anywhere in his class. She didn't think a daughter was likely. Every other word out of her mother's mouth was about some petty accomplishment of Veronica's, to the point where it got embarrassing. "Veronica went to school today! Veronica picked out clothes that matched today! Veronica can walk and chew gum at the same time!" If her mom was at all representative of a parent who'd lost a spouse at a young age and was left with a child, then Veronica would expect Mr. Bittner to have thrown in an anecdote about his own daughter every so often.

Even if he'd said, "If I had a daughter, I'd want her to be just like you," it was weird. Why couldn't he have just said "nice job" about her essay, the way a teacher was supposed to?

Walking down the hall, she ran this exchange over in her mind. Memory was such a funny thing—by the time she'd reached Pescatelli's class she was certain—absolutely certain—that what Mr. Bittner said was:

I wish my daughter was you.

Weird.

Kirk and James both looked up, like puppies hearing kibble hitting the bottom of their dish, when Veronica walked into the Fish's class. Kirk would be a lot cuter if he smiled more, she thought, whereas James would be if he smiled less. Janine was sitting at her desk with a wadded-up ball of Kleenex beside her notebook. Either she or her mother had convinced the principal to allow her to wear her hat and gloves to class, and she was flexing and relaxing her hands on her desk in some ritual of coping. Veronica said hello and gave her shoulder a squeeze.

"You okay?" she asked. "You sneezed all through last class."

Janine nodded, sniffing. "Got a cold." She looked up at Veronica and forced a brave smile, and Veronica loved her for it. "Sorry I didn't walk with you today. Mom insisted on driving."

"No worries," Veronica said, and took her seat.

The Fish actually stood up and walked to the blackboard. He found a piece of chalk on the tray and turned it over in his small, soft-looking hands, inspecting it as though he wasn't sure it would work.

"Okay," he said. "Did anyone see any new ghosts over the weekend?"

The hands of about half the class rose, many with reluctance. Kirk and James had raised their hands, as had Veronica. Janine's crept upward, and Veronica winked at her, making her laugh.

"Great," the Fish said, counting and writing the number twelve on the board. "Okay. Who wants to tell us about the ghosts they saw? Not you, Kirk. Somebody else. Janine? Holly?"

Holly Blackstone talked about a ghost she and her father had seen while raking leaves in their front lawn. A shirtless man, looking like he was pushing something from one end of their yard to the next and then back again. Veronica could picture the scene; she'd been to Holly's house, a few streets over, a number of times.

"We figured out he was mowing the lawn," she said. "My Dad did. It looked really weird, because the grass is all dead and his lawn mower was invisible. He walked right through one of our leaf piles."

"You'd never seen him before, Holly?"

"Never."

"Okay. Anybody have any ideas why the lawn mower man is in Holly's yard?"

The Fish wrote "lawn mower man" on the blackboard. His handwriting was even and straight.

"He used to own the house."

"He liked mowing the lawn."

"He hated mowing the lawn and is cursed for all eternity." This from Margi, the only goth in the class.

The Fish wrote down abbreviated versions of these theories next to "lawn mower man."

"Okay. Somebody else. Veronica."

"Um . . ." Although she wanted to talk about Brian, she said, "There's a ghost at the Jewell City Cineplex, in theater eight. He was eating from a tub of popcorn and then he disappeared."

The Fish wrote "movie guy" on the board. "Why do you think he's there, Ronnie?"

"He liked movies?"

He wrote "liked movies." "Anybody else?"

"He died in the theater."

"He saw his favorite movie there."

"He thought twelve dollars was too much to pay for one movie."

The Fish cracked a smile.

"One more. James?"

"I saw the same one Ronnie did," he said, and even though he sat a few rows ahead of her, Veronica knew he was smirking. She could hear it is his voice.

"Somebody else, then," the Fish said over the snickering. "Kirk? One?"

Kirk looked up and set down his pencil. Veronica wondered what he had been writing.

He talked about the library ghost they called Molly. The whole class fell silent, as though Molly herself were asleep under the Fish's desk and no one dared wake her.

"Why do you think she's there?" the Fish asked.

"I think," Kirk began, "that was a really, really happy moment for her. Whoever handed her that book was someone special, and the book itself must've been special. I felt like the little girl wasn't alive much longer, and that was one of her most treasured memories when she died."

The Fish looked like he was about to say something, but then stopped himself.

Kirk wasn't done talking, and there was something in his tone that made Veronica watch him more closely.

"That was one of the first times I really looked at a ghost," he said. "I mean really *looked* at it, like I was trying to understand it. I guess I'm pretty lucky because I didn't lose anyone in the Event, and I didn't personally know any of the ghosts or images that appeared because of it, so I never really stopped to consider what any of it meant. But watching her—Molly—I started to see. I started to see that this was someone who had been alive, had been living. . . ." He trailed off, clearing his throat. "I'm not saying this well."

"You're doing fine," the Fish told him. The class was completely silent.

Kirk nodded, cleared his throat again, and tried to complete his thought.

"I guess I felt like I was doing more than watching," he said. "I guess I felt like I knew her, a little. Who she was. Her treasured memory became my treasured memory. And when that happened, I felt like I understood better what it means to be alive."

Veronica smiled. Kirk looked embarrassed, like he'd just announced he was in love. He ran his hand over his damp forehead and through his thick hair. He glanced over at Veronica, and she widened her smile.

"The answers you gave," the Fish said, after a long pause, "all have to do with some aspect of memory. Molly is in the library because that was where she experienced her happiest memory. Holly's ghost remembered mowing the lawn, or we remember someone dying in a certain place or a certain way. See? All the answers dealt with memory. Except for Margi's, which dealt mostly with eternal damnation."

Light laughter rippled through the classroom, and Margi took the joke in stride.

"I know where I'll be if I die," she said, and even the Fish laughed.

"Okay," he said, "let's take a look at memory in *Hiroshima*. What was it that Toshiko Sasaki remembered most about her life prior to the bombing?"

A few hands went up. The class progressed in this way, with the Fish talking about the elusive nature of memory. He wasn't content to make the point that memories were elusive, but that *memories* of memories were elusive, fluid things, ever-shifting, impossible to grasp completely. Veronica sensed that the concept of "memory" was going to play a big part in their next test, so she took notes whenever the Fish seemed excited about his points.

When class was over, she took her time putting her things in her bag, hoping to avoid James and also to catch Kirk's attention. She failed at both. Kirk went to talk to the Fish, and James hung around her desk, waiting to walk her to her next class.

Kirk was deep in conversation with Mr. Pescatelli. They both looked back at her and fell silent.

Maybe they were discussing her.

"Hey," James said, "we're going to be late."

• • •

At the end of the day, Veronica found Janine after finally escaping James, who'd hovered around her like a rain cloud all day.

"Hi, gorgeous," she said. "How are you holding up?"

Janine offered her a faltering but brave smile.

"Okay, I guess."

"Come to the library with me."

Janine blinked liked she'd just been asked to go skydiving.

"Oh, I don't know, Veronica. I—"

"Come on," Veronica said, taking her by her mittened hand.

"They won't let me bring my Ghost-B-Gone to school anymore," Janine mumbled, allowing herself to be led.

"You won't need it," Veronica said. She knew Janine was hesitant because libraries were supposedly among the most haunted places in America. "I'll be quick. I just have to look something up."

"What?"

"Just something."

The library was almost empty: one of Montcrief's star basketball players was being tutored by a bored-looking girl; a boy was shelving books from a gunmetal gray AV cart; and the librarian was at her desk reading. All looked relatively solid.

"See? No ghosts," Veronica said. She asked the librarian where she could find the school yearbooks, and was directed toward the reference section. She went over and withdrew four volumes, beginning with the year before she'd moved to town.

"Who are you looking for?" Janine asked as they sat down.

"Nobody special."

"You're looking for that ghost boy, aren't you?"

"Mmmmaybe."

"I wouldn't, if I were you. No good could come of it."

"Uh-huh," Veronica said. The yearbooks had individual pictures of the graduating senior class and the juniors, and class photos of the younger grades. Luckily, Montcrief High was a fairly small school, so there weren't many photos to look at.

"Seriously, Veronica. You're better off not knowing."

Veronica glanced at Janine from over the top of her book; even though Janine was being a nervous ninny, it was good to hear fire in her voice.

"Why do you say that?" she said, returning to her book, turning a page.

"You just aren't," Janine replied.

Veronica flipped to the end of the book, where there were a few pages of candid photos followed by pages of notes. There was a full page that said *Mary Greer—We Love and Miss You* inside a valentine-style heart. Below the heart, in a slightly smaller font, read the headline *Montcrief High 4-Ever.*

"That's not much of an explanation," Veronica responded to Janine. After gazing at the heart another moment, she shut the book and picked up the next one from her stack. "Maybe if I knew more about him, I could help him."

"*Help* him?" Janine said.

Veronica opened the book. She couldn't remember how old Mary was when she died, but she thought she might have been a sophomore. She scanned through some pages.

"Why are you so afraid of ghosts anyway, Janine?" she said. "They can't hurt you."

She knew that Janine was getting angry. She was deliberately provoking her. There was a time when Janine had been the most feisty girl she knew. It was what had drawn them together when Veronica first moved to Jewell City.

"You don't know that," Janine said snappishly, as though her feistiness was returning.

Good, Veronica thought. Use that. "Sure I do. They just appear and fade away. They move in the same pattern, like characters in a video game."

"Not all of them," Janine said.

"What do you mean?" Veronica said. She found Mary Greer, smiling out from the middle of the front row of a homeroom class picture. Mr. Bittner's homeroom; he stood at the end of the posed rows of students, smiling benignly in a gray suit jacket. Excited as Veronica was to have found Mary, she realized that Janine was mumbling something and she didn't want to drop the thread with her friend.

"What?"

Janine's eyes were shiny, her cheeks red. "I said a ghost chased me once."

"You never told me that." Veronica had always assumed it was just the appearances of the ghosts themselves after the Event that had caused Janine to become fearful. She never imagined there had been a specific incident.

"I was walking through the woods," she said. "I saw a man. He wasn't there, and then he was, in the brush just off the path. Except branches were sticking through him."

Veronica waited. At one time, Janine had been an outdoorsy girl, before the spirits had driven her inside. She'd been a good soccer player too, far better than Veronica herself, who was totally inept at the game.

"He didn't notice the branches, but he noticed me. He was calling to me, except no sound was coming out of his mouth."

"Janine . . ."

"I was never afraid of the ghosts before!" Janine said, her voice loud enough to attract attention from the tutor and her pupil. "But he started running after me! He walked right through a stone wall, through the trees, brush, everything. His mouth opening and closing, like he was calling or gasping for air. I ran. I ran all the way home. So don't tell me that ghosts can't hurt you, Ronnie, because we don't know! We just don't know!"

Veronica waited again for her to calm down before speaking.

"That's why we have to try to find out, Janine," she said, her voice soft and soothing. We can't just pretend something doesn't exist when it does. And we have to learn everything we can about it."

Janine rubbed her eyes with one hand and twirled the tassel of her hat with the other.

"Can we just go now?" she said. "Please?"

Veronica looked back at Mr. Bittner's class photo, and saw *him*, third from the end in the back row. She found his name on the legend beneath.

Brian Delaney.

"Yes," she said, shutting the book. She stood and stacked the books in front of her. "But you should remember one thing, Janine."

"What's that?" Janine said, following Veronica back to the shelf.

"He didn't catch you."

⊥⊦⊦⊦ ⊦⊦⊦ ⊦⊦⊦ |||

"Leap day," August said. He was staring out the window of his darkened classroom at the end of the day, watching a light flurry of snow drifting in the blank sky. "She called it leap day."

"I told you," Madeline said. "Didn't I tell you? She is definitely the one."

August did not begrudge her the superior tone that had crept into her voice. Madeline liked being right, but more than that, August knew she was excited at the prospect of having their daughter back.

"They are connected by the same day," she said. "She and Eva. A day that only exists once every four years."

August nodded. Eva's death and Veronica's birth; both occurred on February 29. The way the gray wash of light was hitting the windows, it was difficult to determine if his wife was standing behind him or outside, in the snow. He didn't mention that the rarity of the date had fueled her deep depression in the months following Eva's death. "She never existed at all," Madeline would say, over and over again, during those dark days as she sat in a rocking chair she'd placed in Eva's room.

"Oh, August," she said. "We're really going to have her back, aren't we? You will be ready to deliver her, won't you?"

It had been years since he had heard Madeline sound so happy.

"I'll be ready," he said. He picked up his briefcase, crossed his classroom, and shut the door behind him.

Halfway through her shift at the concession stand, on her break, Veronica decided to see if Kirk was working. And to get tea, but mostly to see Kirk.

She waited in line behind two overdressed and overperfumed women who were having an animated discussion about the movie they'd just seen. Veronica waited patiently for them to complete their orders, which was an ordeal because their drinks were complex. The good thing was that they'd commanded the full attention of two of the baristas, leaving her Kirk. Or, hopefully, Kirk had arranged things that way. He'd looked up with a confused but happy face when she'd joined the line.

"Sounds like an interesting movie," she said when she reached the counter. "One of the few I haven't sat through yet."

"It was okay," he said, seemingly oblivious to the opening she'd just given him. James would have pounced on that one like a panther on a bunny.

Kirk asked her if she'd like the same drink she had when she was last there.

"You really remember what I ordered?" James would not have.

"Sure," he said, and told her, "Chai tea with a drop of cream."

"Impressive."

"Yeah, it's a talent. Don't they give you caffeine at your gig?"

"All the soda tastes like pink lemonade. Someone crossed the fountain lines a few months ago, and the drinks haven't been the same since. Besides, I like tea. Chai, green tea, iced tea. I'm a fiend for tea."

"I like that you like tea," he said, holding out her cup. "I . . ."

Veronica turned to see whatever it was that had cut him off midsentence: Mr. Bittner, in his gray trench coat.

"Veronica," he said, clapping his gloved hands to ward off the cold. "Out for an evening coffee?" He sighed heavily. "It is as lifeblood to me."

"I drink tea," she said, her voice small.

"What can I get you, Mr. Bittner?" Kirk said, sensing how nervous she was.

"Coffee. Black. Large. Excuse me, *venti*." He was practically bellowing, his voice at lecture pitch, and Veronica noted how few patrons there were. The women had taken their drinks and trailing scarves elsewhere.

"You got it," Kirk said.

Mr. Bittner handed Kirk a five-dollar bill and told him to keep the change. He took a long slurping drink from his coffee and smiled.

"I'm retiring this year, did you know that?"

"I'd heard," Veronica said. "I'm sure the school will be sorry to see you go."

"Go out with a bang, I always say," he said.

"Sure."

He took another sip, staring at her over the rim of his cup. His eyes sparkled, as though already touched by the caffeine.

"Good night to you both," he said, and his coat swirled like a cape as he headed for the door. The tea was warm and good, but Veronica shuddered all the same.

"What a freak," Kirk whispered, once he was out the door.

"He's been different lately," she said. "I don't know what it is. I thought he was nice at the beginning of the year. But now I think he's scary."

"Maybe it's the retirement thing."

"Maybe," she said, inhaling the steam from her cup. "This tea is really good. Just how I like it."

"Really? Then you should have gotten a *venti*!" he said, mimicking Mr. Bittner.

Veronica giggled at Kirk, at the way he imitated the tone and timbre of Mr. Bittner's voice, and she thought the Transylvanian accent was a nice touch, too. There was something vaguely vampiric about her history teacher.

"There's another thing," she said, and Kirk leaned across the counter to hear her better. "He gives me a lot of attention."

"Attention?" Kirk said, concern furrowing his forehead. "Like, what kind of attention?"

"Um, I can't really describe it. Attention. Interest."

"Like *inappropriate* attention?"

"Not like perverted, I don't think. I can't describe it. Just attention. It makes me nervous."

"Well, *yeah*. You've got to tell somebody."

"And say what? That my history teacher waves at me, goes out of his way to say hi to me?"

"Tell them he leers at you. That he tries to look down your blouse."

She shook her head. "But he doesn't. I could be all mixed up about it. He might be just a nice but weird old guy."

"I don't know, Ronnie," Kirk said. "You strike me as someone who has pretty good instincts about people and their intentions."

Their eyes met. Veronica saw concern in his eyes, and something else.

"Yeah," she said. "Do you get a break, Kirk? Can you come sit with me for a minute?"

"Sure," he said. She walked over to a couple of wide stuffed chairs clustered around a small round table and chose one while Kirk let his fellow baristas know he was taking a break. He came over without his apron. Asking him to spend his break with her was flirting, but it was also because, she realized, she *was* nervous. What if she got back to the theater and there was Bittner standing in line for yet another ticket? What if then he came to her station at the concession counter and ordered a large popcorn and another large coffee?

"Hey," Kirk said.

"Hey." Veronica was leaning back in her seat, her legs crossed, holding her cup in front of her face so the steam would reach her nose.

"So," she said, after a moment, "are there any ghosts here?"

He looked around. "What, now?"

She set her tea on the table and uncrossed her legs. "Not now. Just in general."

"I don't think so. Never heard anyone talk about one."

"Most people don't talk about them at all," she said. "Except for people like Mr. Pescatelli, who talks about them all the time."

"Right," Kirk said. He scratched the back of his neck.

"You seemed pretty interested in his class today."

"Did I?"

"Yes. Usually when he talks about ghosts you sit there with this look on your face." She showed him the look, a blank stare coupled with a contemptuous downturn of the lips. "You must've filled a whole notebook taking notes today."

"You're observant," he said, and sighed. "I'm doing an extra credit thing with him."

"Ha! I knew something was up. What is an extra credit *thing*?"

"You know, a work study."

"On ghosts."

"Yep."

Veronica leaned forward, her arms tented over her cup of tea, her chin resting in her hands. "You don't seem to be in need of any extra credit."

She watched Kirk shrug. He really was cute, in a different way.

"This doesn't have anything to do with what I said at lunch the other day, does it?" she asked.

"What you said at lunch?" he replied.

"Uh-huh."

He sighed again. "You *are* awfully observant." He looked at her, keeping his gaze steady. "It has everything to do with what you said at lunch."

"Ah. And I'm good at sensing other people's intentions, right? You do have intentions, don't you, Kirk?"

He didn't turn away. "Yeah. I do."

"You're pretty observant, too, Kirk," she said. "About most things. That's really why you are doing it? Because of what I said at lunch?"

"Yeah. And 'cause I love hanging with the Fish so much."

Veronica smiled. "That's sweet. I'm really flattered."

She realized that was the sort of thing you'd say before giving a boy the brush-off; she knew because she'd done it before. *I'm really flattered, but . . .*

She leaned over and touched his hand to show him that wasn't how she'd meant it. Even though she'd been holding a cup of hot tea, his hand felt warm to her.

"So," she said.

"So," he repeated.

"So what are you doing with the Fish?" she said. "Other than taking copious notes?"

"Fieldwork. I'm going around town filming ghosts and recording data. Only, I'm not allowed to call them ghosts. I'm supposed to call them images."

"Why?"

"The Fish, um, doesn't believe they are really ghosts. He thinks they are more like recordings."

He looked in her eyes then, as though he was worried that she'd be upset at the idea. But she wasn't; the same notion had crossed her mind hundreds of mornings when she'd watched her father vanish.

"What do you think?" she asked.

He hesitated. His reflection in the dark windows disappeared for a moment as a car wheeled into a space near the door, its bright headlights cutting the glare.

"I'm not sure," he said. "I think there is something else, something beyond just a recording. I haven't talked it over with the Fish yet. But I don't know if I could feel what I felt watching that little girl in the library if she was just a video or a photograph. There was something else. I can't explain it—not yet, anyway—but I feel something, something like an essence, when I'm with these ghosts. These *images*. It started with Molly, but it's continued with the ones I've recorded since. I'm not upsetting you, am I? You'd tell me if I was?"

"No. I mean, I'm not upset. Yes I'd tell you if I was. I think your thoughts and feelings are interesting."

"Thanks."

"Do you have any ghosts in your house?" she asked.

"Nope." He grinned. "A few monsters, though. Little brothers and sisters. Four of them."

"Awww, cute," she said. "I've got two now. Ghosts, I mean. The boy who showed up in my bathroom last week."

"Not cool."

"No, it really wasn't. That's like the one place I never wanted to find a ghost. Or an image, or whatever. He's totally disrupted my showering in the morning."

"I bet. He's not looking at you or anything, is he?"

"No," she said, but thought, That's the problem. Brian was cute. She realized that Kirk was reddening.

"You want to record him?" she said. "I mean, if my mother says it's okay. He and my Dad both appear within a few minutes of each other."

"Really? You wouldn't mind?"

"I think it would be fun," she said. "You could come over some morning. Are you an early riser?"

"Sure. But maybe it would be less shocking for your mom if I met her beforehand?"

"That's probably true. One strange boy in the house is enough."

Kirk ran his fingers through his hair. "Maybe I could come over sometime this week. So I could meet her?"

Veronica smiled. "Are you asking me out, Kirk?" she said. "Or are you just trying to meet my mom?"

"I . . . I'm asking you out. Yes. Or in."

"Good," she said. "I'll see if it's okay if you come over after school. We could have dinner with Mom and maybe watch a movie."

"Sounds good." He looked like he was about to have an aneurysm. "We could go ghost hunting."

"So I can help you with your research."

"Right," he said, grinning. "My research."

Wow, Kirk thought, watching her go, Ronnie Calder just asked me over.

||||| ||||| ||||| ||||

August watched Veronica leave the store after handing Kirk a piece of paper she'd written on. Her phone number, no doubt. Bittner sipped at his coffee, rolling the acidic liquid around on his tongue. Her phone number. He wondered if he had jumped to conclusions about her virtue. First that athletic oaf, and now the class cynic.

He had a couple of weeks. Time enough for her to reveal to him the patterns of her life, so that when the day of Eva's death and pending rebirth—leap day!—arrived, he would be ready. If the opportunity presented itself, he would take her early and keep her alive and hidden until the 29th.

"The stroke of midnight," Madeline said, and August thought he could feel her breath on his ear. "On the 28th. That would be the best time."

August nodded in agreement and then took a drink from his cup.

He watched Veronica wave through the window at Kirk. She went back across the lot with a little skip in her step. She paused at the door of the movie theater and looked up and right into his eyes. He felt a tingle at the back of his neck.

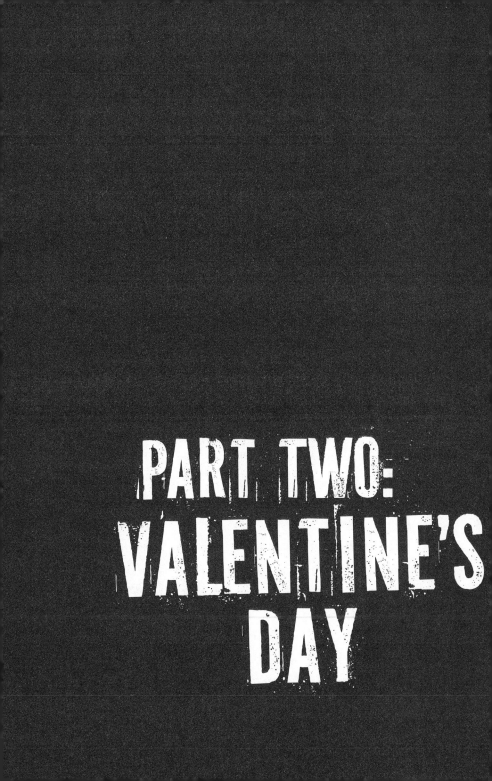

PART TWO: VALENTINE'S DAY

~~IIII~~ ~~IIII~~ ~~IIII~~ ~~IIII~~

The day approaches, time surges forward, relentless as the tide. I become visible in the bathroom, and she—Veronica—is there, warm from her shower, wrapped in a bathrobe. A towel encloses her wet hair. Steam vapor swirls within me as I make myself more solid, and she is smiling. She comes closer and reaches out toward me, her eyes intent on my reflected image.

As beautiful as she is, I do not want to be with her. What I want is to change time, to erase the past with a wave of my hand, the way she will erase fog from the mirror in order to see me better. I want to be wherever Mary is. The day approaches, the day of Mary's death, the day of Veronica's birth, the day when the veil is at its thinnest. I try to vary the pattern that I am trapped in.

My energy and my choices are finite. I need to warn her, but I am not able. My strength will grow each moment until the 29th. The thinner the veil becomes, the more I can draw from this world. I decide to wait, to conserve what little of me remains.

I disappear. My sudden exit leaves Veronica more astonished than my entrance, and she looks at her fingertips as if they have the ability to dispel the dead.

As I drift through the floor, I pray. I pray that prayer is an energy of its own, one that passes through the veil and to whatever or whoever waits beyond. I pray that waiting is the correct strategy, and I pray that I can warn Veronica in time.

I huddle at the kitchen door, no more tangible than a draft of cool air, and I pray that I can catch a glimpse of my Mary when she appears up the road.

⎍⎎⎎⎎ ⎎⎎⎎ ⎎⎎⎎ ⎎⎎⎎
|

August awoke in a foul mood. The only thing worse than his wife's nagging were her extended, acrimonious silences, as they had the tendency to drag on for days or even weeks. Quite often, these silences were not triggered by anything more specific than the fact of August's existence.

He took no joy in his breakfast of oatmeal, and the coffee had an odd taste, as though some poisonous insect had burrowed into the grounds the moment before the hot water hit them. After two sips he pitched the remainder in the sink.

He buttoned his coat, took his hat, and flung open the door.

Cold air flooded his foyer. Mary Greer was standing outside the door, the smile just forming on her face. He glanced at his watch and saw that he'd been so irritable he'd forgotten she was due to arrive.

"Go away," he said. His voice sounded warped and strange to him. "You aren't Eva. You will never be her!"

Mary smiled as though he'd finally answered a question that she'd been posing all along.

He waved a gloved hand at her. "Stop coming here! I don't want you! I want Eva!"

Did her head tilt a fraction of an inch? She looked so small, and August thought that her spirit must be cold and diminished in this chill wind. He regretted speaking harshly to her, and he reached for her tenderly, but she faded from sight before they touched.

"Damn," he said, his hand curling into a fist. He wished that he had been brave enough to embrace her, but now it was too late. "Damn."

He continued down the porch steps and got into his car to complete his weekend errands, getting gas and then groceries. He enjoyed going to the grocery store early on the weekends because that was when the produce was freshest, having just been restocked off the delivery trucks, and also because there were very few customers during those times, and so his odds of avoiding human contact were much better.

Not so on this particular day. His cart contained a single cantaloupe, and he had just begun to inspect the organic tomatoes when he felt a tap on his shoulder.

"Mr. Bittner?" he heard a soft male voice say, and in turning, saw a man in his early thirties standing before him, a canted grin on weak-chinned face.

"You probably don't remember me," the man said, but Bittner knew him immediately, even though it had been more than fifteen years since he'd seen him last. "Paul Shea. I'm in town for the weekend, visiting my parents. I . . ."

The man extended his hand, and August took it, moving and feeling as though he were in a waking dream.

"I remember you," he said. Paul Shea's hand was small and soft. He looked like he was an accountant or some form of middle manager.

"You do?" Shea said, his voice and accompanying laughter nervous. "It's been so long, I didn't—"

"You had been dating for a month," Bittner said. "Her first boyfriend."

Shea's grin went lopsided. "That's right," he said. "Eva and I, we—"

"How could I forget the boy who killed my daughter?"

Shea's eyes flicked like a small bird's, from August's face to the hand that still enveloped his own. All August had to do, he thought, was squeeze and Shea's knucklebones would grind to powder.

"I . . . I didn't . . . I had real feelings for her, Mr. Bittner. I tried—"

"I don't know what she was doing with you in that field, or—"

"We were just walking, walking and—"

August tightened his grip slightly, and Shea's words trailed off in a little gasp of pain. "—Or what you were doing to her. But I have held you responsible."

Shea began to speak, and August tightened further, feeling Shea's knuckles rolling and contracting in his hand.

"I tried to save her," Shea said, his voice strained. He tried to pull his hand free, but August squeezed. "I really did. She . . . she started gasping, like she couldn't catch her breath."

August bared his teeth at Shea. He thought that if the man didn't shut up he would sink them right into his Adam's apple.

But the look on August's face just seemed to encourage Shea, who spoke more rapidly, as though his account of the events on that unseasonably warm leap day would appease August or reverse his feelings about Eva's death.

"She couldn't breathe, and I tried to help her. I didn't know what to do. I was only a kid! I didn't know she had asthma! Please, Mr. Bittner, you're crushing my hand."

August realized that people—an old woman pushing a cart and a young man stocking lettuce, possibly a Montcrief student—were watching his exchange with Shea. He let go of his hand.

Shea took a step back, bumping into the table of tomatoes, knocking one to the ground.

"I've always wanted to apologize to you," Shea said. He looked like he was tearing up. "Honestly, I'd have done anything to save her. Eva was a really sweet girl, Mr. Bittner. I mean it. I was so sorry when it happened."

August closed his eyes. He wanted to wake up; he wanted this dialogue he was having with this specter, this nightmare within nightmare, to just end.

"Go away," he said. "Do not say another word."

A long moment later, August opened his eyes. Shea had just reached the automatic doors at the front of the store. He didn't look back as they hissed open, and he walked through them.

August looked at the stock boy, whose acne-scarred cheeks had flushed a deep shade of crimson as he put all of his concentration into forming his lettuce pyramid. August heard a dripping on the tile at his feet. He'd pulped a large ripe tomato in the hand that just moments before had been making Shea's metacarpals creak. He had no memory of picking up the tomato.

He turned to the old woman, perhaps to offer some explanation for his actions. She disappeared, her form growing translucent enough for him to make out the salad bar behind her before she faded completely from view.

IIII IIII IIII IIII
II

"The first ghost is over on the west side," Kirk said, sounding apologetic. The west side's trash-strewn neglected streets were lined with once stately homes that had been converted into multifamily units. That was where one could go to find drugs, a prostitute, or the opportunity to be involved in a more victim-intensive crime such as a mugging. Veronica had never been there except to drive through.

"You sure know how to show a girl a good time," she said. This was their second "date," if ghost hunting could be properly termed a date, since their conversation about her haunted house, and she still hadn't made good on her promise to have him over to record her father. She'd mentioned the idea to her mother, who'd said, "Why don't you wait a while and see if you still like him?"

So supportive, Veronica thought.

Kirk, oblivious, grinned. "I just hope the car is okay while we are investigating. My dad would freakin' kill me if anything happened to it."

Veronica looked out the window, suppressing a smile of her own. His invitation to go ghost hunting had been an afterthought; he wasn't as smooth as James but he was more interesting. She wasn't exactly afraid of being out and about on the west side, but she wondered why she was bothering. The idea of acting like Scooby-Doo or those goofy *Ghost Hunters* guys from that television show seemed absurd.

Kirk's enthusiasm this morning at her locker was cute, the way he'd carried himself in the Fish's class with a new sense of purpose was attractive; but when Veronica looked at him, she found herself doing so with a critical eye. Her mind was all jumbled up. She didn't think about Kirk in the quiet moments between classes; it was Brian who occupied her thoughts.

The ghost. She was fantasizing about a ghost.

"Oh, and um," Kirk said, "could you open the glove compartment? There's something in there I need."

Veronica pushed the button and the door sprang open. There was a small package wrapped in paper with a red bow sitting on a small pile of paperwork.

"Happy Valentine's Day," he said.

"Aw," she said. "You're sweet." She took the package out of the compartment.

"You can open it if you want."

She did want, and she shredded the paper. She'd never been one to carefully unwrap a gift. She didn't see the point in it. Beneath the white wrapping was a familiar metallic gold.

"Ooo, Godiva," she said. "Want one?"

"Sure. Just one. The rest are for you."

She took a dark squarish chocolate out of its nesting place and popped it into Kirk's mouth.

"It isn't much," he said, chewing, "but there's a card, too."

She took the roundest of the chocolates and was pleasantly

surprised by a sweet raspberry cream. She opened the card hesitantly, but was again pleasantly surprised by a simple, understated card that spoke about beginnings. It was a hopeful sentiment but didn't presume too much, and she liked that; she'd have been embarrassed by an overly mushy or passionate card. Especially as she didn't have one for him.

Why do I have to be so fickle? she thought. Kirk is attentive and sweet; why don't I just go with my feelings instead of fighting them all the time?

"Thank you, Kirk," she said, sincerely. And then she gave him a chocolate kiss on his cheek. He smiled back at her.

"And now for a highly romantic ghost hunt," he said.

"Mmmm. In the nicer part of town, too," she replied. She wanted more chocolate, and worried momentarily that it would be piggish to eat another. But then she ate it anyway. There was one left and she offered it to him.

He shook his head. "I guess I'll try to find a spot right on the street somewhere. There are always cops around on the west side, aren't there?"

"I wouldn't know." Two small children in jackets that were too light for the season stopped their tug-of-war over a plastic soda bottle to watch the car slide by.

Staring at the last chocolate in the box, Veronica felt guilty for fantasizing about Brian.

I'm not *fantasizing* about him exactly, she thought. More imagining what he was like, what their house was like when he lived there. His room, the room where she lived now, would be the antithesis of the simple, almost austere environment she'd created, with its few black-and-white photographs of misty beaches and lighthouses in their thin black frames. Brian's room would have had a riot of color, his walls covered with posters. He looked like a classic-rock guy. Led Zeppelin, Black Sabbath, Jimi Hendrix. Pink Floyd, Iron Maiden, Nirvana. He'd have a red lava lamp and there would be a red shag rug beneath his feet. He'd be fatherless, like she was.

Funny, Veronica thought. They passed a pizza place where a cook was standing in the doorway. Faded stains of tomato sauce like old blood on his soiled apron, and his unshaven, grayish face gave him the appearance of a zombie. When Veronica closed her eyes it was almost like she could smell Brian's room, even though the odor of garlic and dough was wafting through the car. For a moment she could feel the shag rug with her bare feet, when in reality her boots were pinching her toes.

"Would you mind turning down the heat?" Veronica opened her eyes just in time to see the pizza chef disappear. The ghosts really were out in force lately.

"Sure," Kirk said, checking a printed sheet of directions he'd gotten off the Internet. What did it say about them that neither one knew how to get to Boswell Street, only a few miles from where they lived?

Veronica closed her eyes and again was back in her room. His room. And now Brian was there, sitting on his bed, wearing faded jeans and a leather thong necklace over a faded T-shirt, his blond hair a warm pink in the glow of the lava lamp. He pushed some papers and a Frisbee off the comforter, and he looked up at her with the same expression of care and concern that he had in her bathroom this morning. She felt herself take a step forward.

There was a lurch and a scraping sound, and she snapped sideways in her seat.

"Sorry," Kirk said. "I think I cut the wheel too close. Be careful when you open your door."

She stared at him a moment, if only because his hair was a similar color to what she imagined Brian's hair to be in the glow of his lamp. Kirk, like Brian, had nice smooth skin, and for a redhead, had practically no freckles.

She opened the door, and the bottom of it dragged along the sidewalk until it hit a crack. She looked back at Kirk, who shrugged.

"No worries," he said. "We've got to walk over there. I wanted to leave the car where it was sort of visible."

She followed the trail of his finger to the mouth of a sloping street where square buildings were cramped together on small dusty lots. A patchy old pit bull struggled to his three legs to regard them from behind a low fence. He probably could have jumped in younger, leaner times.

"He looks friendly," Kirk said. Veronica smiled, but she didn't really think it was funny. She was freezing now that they were out of the sweltering confines of the car.

They walked past the yard, and Veronica kept her eyes forward, thinking that eye contact would get the dog barking. A conversation between two men ceased when they approached. One of the men shouted a single word that she couldn't make out—a word that could have been a greeting, a warning, or a threat.

"Great," Kirk whispered. Veronica saw that he had his hand tucked into his jacket, palming his camera. It almost looked like he was carrying a gun, and she wondered if that was the effect he was going for. If so, she thought that was the stupidest thing imaginable.

"Hey!" the guy called again as he walked toward them. Veronica saw that he wasn't as young as she'd first thought, his dark skin lined with wrinkles, and his head bald beneath his ball cap not because he was fashionable but because he didn't have a choice. He was wearing a blue public transit jacket with a SEAT logo patch sewn above the pocket, and his name, Larry, was embroidered in gold script. The jacket had a lived-in look, the material worn smooth and shiny at the elbows.

"Get ready to run," Kirk whispered to Veronica before answering the man. "Yeah?"

"You kids down here to see Louis?"

"That's right," Kirk answered. Louis Green was the name of the ghost they were supposed to be tracking down.

The man checked his watch. "You better hurry along. He'll be coming soon. Go down to the end of the street, turn left, third house in. They'll all be watching."

"Really?"

"Yeah," the man said. "Damn fools got nothing better to do to entertain themselves. My advice to you is, you watch, and then you get the hell out without waiting around, bothering anybody with questions."

"People watch him?" Kirk said. "Like, regularly?"

The man turned back as if Kirk were one of the stupidest people he'd ever seen. "Yeah, they watch him. Bunch of fools on the street watch him every damn day, and we get people like you coming down every so often, too. I guess you don't have anything better to do than see somebody get killed."

"It's for a school assignment," Kirk said.

"School assignment," Larry said, shaking his head. "Yeah."

He turned back to where his friend sat with an equally incredulous look on his face. The friend had a thermos, and he raised it at them as they continued.

"I didn't think anybody knew about this one," Kirk said.

"Let's go," Veronica said. "Let's get it over with."

There was a small crowd of about fifteen people standing along the street in front of the house, mostly kids ranging from six to sixteen, but there were a few adults as well, one an old woman in a satin housecoat. A boy passed them on his bike. He drew to a stop next to another boy, looked over his shoulder at Veronica, and whispered something in his friend's ear. Veronica forced herself not to turn away from their stares. Kirk took out his camera and played with the focus.

"Nice camera," the boy said. His friend, a stocky kid in a puffy jacket and wool hat with a long trailing point, laughed. Kirk aimed his camera at the house.

"Is that where Louis appears?" he asked.

"Oh, you'll see him," the boy said, getting more laughs from his pal. "You get that camera 'round here?"

"My teacher lent it to me."

"No shit?" the boy said. "Where you go to school?"

"Montcrief."

"That the one over by the baseball field?"

"No. It's off Crown Street. Where is he going to appear?"

"You just keep pointing your teacher's camera at the house," the boy said, turning toward Veronica. "You go to Montcrief, too?"

"Yes."

"All the girls there as fine as you?" he said. The kid pretended not to care that Kirk was watching him. He looked like he was about twelve.

"All of them," Veronica said, smiling sweetly. "We're fashion models, mostly."

The slyness left his grin. "What's your name?"

"Veronica. What's yours?"

"Veronica," the boy repeated slowly, getting the most out of each syllable. "Ver . . . on . . . i . . . ca. I'm David."

"Hi, David."

"Yo, David," the boy's friend said. "He gonna come now."

"Can I get your phone number, Veronica?" David said. "Maybe we can go out sometime?"

"I don't think there's any room on your bike."

Kirk looked up from focusing, shaking his head.

"Oh, I'll make room," David said.

"I don't have any paper."

David withdrew a card-sized cell phone from a deep pocket in his jeans. "I'll add you right now."

Veronica gave him a fake number, and then the crowd gasped.

Not at her. The wide window at the corner of the house burst open as a bleeding young man leaped through it and landed flat on the dirty snow. The man—Louis—scrambled to his feet. The cliché of comparing these images to a movie came to Veronica's mind, if only because the terrified expression on Louis's face was more like that of an actor in a horror movie than a real person. Terror, with a foundation of desperation.

Louis ran two steps and then his back arched and two red holes bloomed on his chest, each with a spray of blood that evaporated in the air before him. He went down, twitched once, and disappeared.

Most of the kids in the crowd cheered. David did not, but his friend pumped his fist in the air and gave a bellowing war whoop. Kirk looked up from the viewfinder with a look of total shock on his face.

"Holy crow," he said, and took Veronica's arm. "Let's get out of here."

Veronica watched two boys, seven or eight years old, high-five. A third was reenacting Louis's murder by rolling in the dirty snow, ignoring his older sister's commands to stop.

She let Kirk lead her back to the car. It was a quiet ride home.

HHT HHT HHT HHT III

They went out a third time a few days later, leaving right from school. When Kirk met Veronica at her locker she was trying to cajole Janine into coming with them, an idea that Janine, as far as Kirk could tell, found mortifying.

"No. No, no, no, no," she said, the tassels of her hat swinging with every shake of her head. "Uh-uh. No way."

"Janine," Veronica said, hints of impatience and disappointment in her voice.

"No, I couldn't. I just couldn't," she said.

Kirk had come to the conversation late, but he caught the gist of it.

"You sure, Janine?" he said. "There will be cake."

She blinked, and then she giggled. "Not even for cake."

He wasn't sure what made him happier—her smile or the one Veronica gave him for making Janine laugh.

"But seriously, Janine," he said, "it will be fine. We'll only go see ghosts that aren't very scary. There's a little girl at the library who—"

Janine clapped her gloved hands over her ears. "Ghost kids are the scariest of all!"

"Okay, okay," he said. "No ghost kids."

"It would help you," Veronica said to her. "It really would."

"I can't," Janine said, her voice dropping to a whisper. "I'm sorry."

Defeated, Veronica turned back to Kirk.

"Okay," she said. "Just me and you, I guess."

Kirk agreed to give Janine a ride home. Veronica pointed out her own house to Kirk as they drove past.

"It's haunted," Janine said from the backseat. Veronica had to stifle a laugh, and she saw that Kirk was doing the same.

Kirk pulled into Janine's driveway, and Janine thanked him as she hopped out, then she dashed across the yard.

"Poor kid," Kirk said, backing into the street. "She used to be such a tomboy."

"I think she's working up her courage," Veronica said. "I'm not going to give up on her."

"Me neither. Speaking of courage, you might need it for our first visit."

"Really? I thought you promised no scary ghosts."

"That was when Janine was coming. You," he said, grinning at her as he rolled to a stop at an intersection. "You can take it."

"Nice," Veronica said, mock punching him in the meaty part of his arm. "Mom said you could come over tonight. For dinner." Veronica had started the conversation with her mother that morning, right after her father had left them.

"I still like him, Mom," she'd said.

Her mother yawned. "Who?"

"Kirk. I still like him. Can he come over tonight so you can meet him?"

"Kirk?" her mother had said. "He's the one who wants to film your father? I suppose so."

Hearing only the results of that earlier conversation and not her mother's blasé tone, Kirk's already buoyant mood was elevated.

"Hm. So where are we going?" Veronica asked.

"First stop, Baccus Hospital."

A half hour later they were sitting in the waiting room adjacent to the Emergency Room. There were a dozen or so people there, either waiting to be treated, or for a friend or relative to be treated. Most were February flu sufferers, but there was also a woman who was holding an enormous ice pack against her forehead, and another woman holding her arm at an awkward angle. Kirk had artfully draped his jacket on the seat beside them so that the video camera was obscured, with only the lens visible. He doubted the hospital staff would appreciate his filming.

"In his book the Fish has a list of ghosts from around the town," he said. "I've seen this one we're about to see before, though. Last summer when I got my scalp stitched up after knocking heads playing basketball."

"That explains certain things," Veronica said. "The Fish has a book?"

"Yeah, that's what I'm supposed to be helping him with. He's getting it ready to send to Chicago. I don't agree with a lot of what he has to say, though."

"Like what?"

Kirk was about to answer when an image appeared so suddenly that Veronica and the lady with the ice pack cried out. It passed through the automatic doors without triggering them, moving horizontally as though being pushed on an invisible gurney. The image was of a man wearing motorcycle boots and ripped-up denim soaked through with blood. His head was turned away from the lobby, so they couldn't see his face. He disappeared just before the unseen gurney reached the check-in desk. Kirk, confident that he'd captured the shot, looked around at the living people. He thought the receptionist's reaction was the most odd, because she'd had no reaction at all. She just kept on filing and stapling, or whatever it was she was doing.

"I think that was 'point-of-death,'" Veronica whispered. Kirk bundled his gear into his coat and they left the hospital.

Not all ghosts—or images—provoked a reaction in Veronica, but the Baccus Hospital one did. The gorier ones were a more effective reminder of her own fragile mortality. She imagined the ghost as a motorcyclist who had made just one fractional error, and the result cost him his life.

"Veronica?"

"Hmm?"

"Are you okay?" Kirk said. "I was just telling you about our next image."

"Oh. I'm sorry. Is it another crisis image?"

Kirk shook his head. "Not if you believe the Fish. He would say that we are going to see an 'image of habit.' Images of habit are those that appear doing something they probably did time and time again in life, usually something routine and mechanical."

"Like the teacher who appeared in our class? Mrs. Janus?"

"Could be. But she could be an 'image of attachment.' Those are images of people who appear in places where they had a strong emotional connection, either good or bad."

Veronica thought for a moment. "So there are crisis, point-of-death, attachment, and habit images?" she said.

"If you agree with the Fish."

"So the ghost of the woman who got hit by a car on Case Street would be a crisis ghost?" she said, thinking of the horrific bleeding woman in the blue dress.

"*Image,*" Kirk said. "Crisis image. But yeah, she would definitely be one."

"And the little girl in the library you mentioned? She'd be a ghost of attachment?"

"You catch on quick."

"So my dad would be an image of habit, then?" she said.

The question made Kirk uncomfortable. "Only if you believe the Fish," he said. "Hey, we're almost there. Would you mind switching the video cassettes for me?"

Veronica reached over and retrieved the leather bag and then turned the camera over in her hands a few times before figuring out how to eject the cassette.

"I've never used one of these before," she said.

"Old-school," he said. "I wouldn't worry too much about the theories, Ronnie. The Fish has lots of nutty ideas."

"I'm not worried," she said. The cassette locked into place with a satisfying click.

"I think there may be a lot more substance to these phenomena than he realizes," Kirk said. "I think that some of these so-called images actually *are* ghosts, or ghostly, because—"

Crazed laughter filled the car, and Kirk almost swerved into the other lane.

"What the hell?" he said over the noise. Veronica shushed him.

On the tiny screen of the video camera, a young laughing girl in pajamas was poking a low-hanging bulb on a Christmas tree heavily laden with tinsel, lights, and ornaments. A pretty young woman, also laughing, also in pajamas, sat cross-legged beside her, trying to rein her in before anything could be destroyed. The video shot jerked once and then settled to get more of the tree into the frame, but still focused on the mother and child.

"Over here, Stephen," a voice off-camera said, and a moment later a man wearing sweats and a T-shirt stepped into the frame and took a seat beside the woman—his wife, no doubt.

Kirk had pulled into a gas station so he could watch as well, but Veronica wasn't even aware of him doing so until he was hunched near her shoulder, much as the smiling man in the video was leaning toward his wife. He—the man, not Kirk—stooped to kiss her neck.

"That's the Fish," Kirk said, whispering.

But the Fish like Veronica had never seen him before; he was smiling, for one—really smiling, not cynically smirking like he did in class. He had a full head of hair and didn't have the paunchy middle he sported now. Even in the slightly grainy video, she could tell that his skin was not as sallow, his eyes not as puffy.

Veronica thought of her mother, and she thought that maybe you didn't have to die to be a ghost. She doubted that that theory appeared anywhere in the Fish's book.

$$\text{𝍷𝍷𝍷𝍷} \quad \text{𝍷𝍷𝍷𝍷} \quad \text{𝍷𝍷𝍷𝍷} \quad \text{𝍷𝍷𝍷𝍷}$$
$$\text{𝍷𝍷𝍷𝍷}$$

"I'm surprised your mother is letting us do this," Kirk said.

"What?" Veronica said. "Work for extra credit?"

"You know what I mean," he said. He looked skyward at the fluffy gray snowflakes that had begun to fall from the sky, watching as they settled on the ground and in Veronica's hair. The snow that touched the asphalt liquefied on contact, but the flakes that collected on the dull green blades of grass remained, clinging for existence. "I'm not allowed to have girls over when my parents aren't home."

"I told my mother I wasn't attracted to you in the least," she said. "That helped."

"Oh?" he said.

She took his hand. "Not in the least," she said, and leaned against him. Her hair, and its scent, tickled his nose.

She unlocked the door and let him in.

"Mom isn't going to be home for a few hours," she said, tossing her key onto the table and dropping her bag on the floor.

"Oh yeah?" he said, smooth as can be. "What do you want to do until she gets home?"

Veronica shrugged her jacket off of her shoulders and hung it on a hook just inside the door. She looked back at Kirk, and there was a precarious moment where he could tell she was wrestling with a decision. His spirits plummeted until she put her arms around his neck.

"I thought we'd do this," she said, her voice just above a whisper as she leaned in and kissed him. Her lips were warm and soft against his, and her breath tasted of cinnamon as he opened his mouth to her. He pulled her closer, looping his arms around her waist and holding her tightly, and they stood there for some moments, kissing in the doorway.

She was breathless when they stopped. He didn't let go of her as much as let her float away.

She likes me, he thought.

"You want something to drink?" she asked, and before he could answer, she leaned in and nipped his lower lip. "Milk, iced tea, Diet Pepsi? Let me take your coat."

"I got it. Soda is great, any soda." He hung up his jacket on the hook next to hers, watching the twitch of her skirt as she went to the refrigerator to get the soda, and then the hike of her sweater as she reached up into the cabinet to get glasses.

She dropped some ice in each of the glasses and poured. She kissed him again, another long, lingering kiss, as she handed him the drink.

"I might need more ice," he said after they broke.

He took a long swallow and then set his glass down on the kitchen table. Veronica took a tiny sip of her own drink, and Kirk pulled her to him, kissing her on her mouth, her cheeks, and lingering on her neck.

"Mmmm," she said, her hands on his shoulders, pressing gently. "Easy. We ought to get our homework done."

His reply, thankfully, was muffled by her neck.

"What?"

"I said you are right," Kirk said. He opened up his backpack and took out a hefty chemistry book and dropped it on the table. "You are totally, totally right."

"Are you mad?" she asked.

"Hm?"

"Are you mad?"

"Why would I be mad?" Actually, he was thrilled. Kissing Ronnie was even better than he had imagined it would be.

"I don't know," she said. "I'm going to go and change. I'll be back in just a few, okay?"

"Okay," he said. She walked up the stairs. The air was hot and still in the Calders' kitchen. Kirk closed his eyes and tried to imagine what Ronnie would be taking off first, the long skirt or the soft cashmere sweater. His dreaming was answered by a muffled clunk. The boots. He'd forgotten about the boots. How could he forget about the boots?

The proverbial other shoe dropping brought him back to the kitchen. He drank his soda and allowed himself to think that she had wanted him to follow her up the stairs. The carpeted staircase beckoned him, and he almost spilled his drink setting the glass down on the slab of his chemistry book as he contemplated ascending, two steps at a time.

Then again, he'd have no choice but to kill himself if he went up there and it was *not* her intention. If he didn't drop dead right there of embarrassment.

I really, really like her, he thought.

Of course, James would not even think of such things. He'd

just walk up the stairs, and if Ronnie screamed he'd apologize and walk back down.

Maybe James had already been up those stairs, he thought.

Kirk drank more of his soda. There were a dozen notes held to the refrigerator with magnets, most of which were either cows or framed photos of a much younger Ronnie. Ronnie in a pointed party hat blowing out a candle in the shape of the number one. Ronnie in a garish dance costume pouting at the cameraman. A toddling Ronnie in a striped swimsuit holding Daddy's hand at the beach.

Kirk turned back to the table. The chair that faced the door was pulled out slightly. He felt self-conscious and chilled at the same time.

Sorry I made out with your daughter in front of you, Ronnie's dad's ghost, he thought. But really he wasn't sorry. He wasn't sorry at all. The idea of kissing and caressing Ronnie in front of her father's ghost—his *image*—was a creepy one, but Kirk could live with it.

He took the Fish's camera out of his backpack, and was struck by the thought of how quickly his scheme to spend time with Ronnie had worked. Ronnie was smarter than most of the dozen or so girls he'd been interested in, and maybe that was the difference. There was a curiosity burning within her, a tendency to question and discover, and that was what had led her, quickly, to him.

Mission accomplished, he thought. He could bag the whole extra credit thing now, if he wanted to. Let the Fish go slogging around town himself filming images.

He pointed the camera at the staircase. I've got a burning

curiosity too, Ronnie, he thought. And a great imagination.

He turned back to the table, thumbing the camera on and pointing at the seat where he imagined Ronnie's father appeared.

"It's going to be a long night, Ronnie's dad," he said, anticipating a sleepless evening thinking about Ronnie and the kiss they'd just shared.

"Really?" Ronnie said from behind him, startling him so badly he would have dropped the camera if his hand hadn't been in the strap. "I was just thinking that I wish we had more time."

"Is that the chair where your father's ghost shows up?" he asked, stuttering out the words in a lame attempt to cover his embarrassment.

"That's where he appears," she said. "Every morning at 7:13 sharp. He has a newspaper and a cup of coffee. I can't figure out the cup of coffee, because he doesn't actually touch it for part of the time. Clothes I can understand, his glasses and the newspaper, because he's touching all of those things. But the cup? Why does the cup appear when he's not touching it?"

"That is kind of weird," Kirk said, thankful that Ronnie didn't prolong his embarrassment. She'd put on faded blue jeans that clung to her like paint. She hadn't changed her sweater.

"It's the reverse of the lawn mower man. He pushes an invisible lawn mower."

"Exactly. Why do you think that happens?"

"I don't know. But my dad's cup remains."

"Did it get broken? Maybe it is the ghost of your dad's coffee cup."

Veronica's laughter was like music. "No, goofy," she said,

taking a mug out of the cabinet. It was a cheap one, and had a faded image of a smiling baby. "It's this one."

"Is that you? The baby?"

"Wasn't I cute?"

"Still are."

"Sometimes I'll drink out of the real one at breakfast when he appears, just to see what happens. I guess I keep hoping that I could change his pattern."

"Is anything different?"

"No," she said, putting the mug back into the cabinet. "The same thing happens. He reads for a while, he picks up the ghost cup, takes a sip, sets it down, and then he turns the page. A few moments later he looks up, and then he smiles."

Hm, Kirk thought. An image on the cup, the cup itself an image. He wondered what the Fish would think of all of it. The concepts made Kirk's head foggy, not unlike the sensation he'd experienced while kissing Ronnie.

"I was looking at the pictures of you," he said, and pointed to Ronnie in her frilly dress and party hat. "You look a bit older than one year here," he said. "You look more like my sister Jenny's age."

"How old is Jenny?"

"She's four."

"You're quite the detective. My dad's little joke. I'm a leap day baby. That was taken on what would have been my fourth birthday."

"Leap day? No kidding. I've never met anyone with that birthday. Hey, I just realized—this is a leap year. You actually get a birthday this year."

"Yep, in just a couple weeks."

Kirk laughed.

"Anyhow," she said, "let's not do our homework in the kitchen. There's more room on the couch."

"Okay."

"And we've still got some time until my mother comes home," she said, her green eyes smoky.

She took him by the hand and led him to the living room.

There was the jingle-jangle of keys, followed by the scrape of a lock turning. The door opened, and Veronica and Kirk heard the rustle and thump of bags dropped hastily to the floor and counter.

"Did you kids have fun?" Mrs. Calder called from the kitchen. Veronica looked at Kirk before answering; he raised an eyebrow and affected a self-satisfied smirk.

"Yes, Mom," she said. They'd spread textbooks and notebooks and loose pages around the coffee table in front of the couch in a fair approximation of diligence. They'd broken out the books about an hour ago, but Kirk had been looking at the same page of his chemistry assignment for the past forty-five minutes and still couldn't begin to guess what it was about. The other fifteen minutes he'd spent looking at Ronnie or the television, which she'd put on soon after deciding that they absolutely had to stop.

Kirk hadn't wanted to stop. Things were about as steamy as they could have been while remaining clothed. He did stop, though. Soon after Ronnie took a call on her cell phone, and he heard her say, "Hello, James." He couldn't hear both sides of the conversation, but he did hear her say "no" a lot. Before she said good-bye he heard her say, "I can't. I'm going out with Kirk that night." He smiled, because he hadn't yet asked her about any forthcoming nights.

Ronnie managed to write three pages of an essay that Mr. Bittner had assigned. Kirk was impressed by her ability to switch focus.

Then again, he thought, maybe she's just not that into me.

Mrs. Calder came in. The resemblance between her and her daughter was striking, but whereas Ronnie was in the full bloom of youth, so fresh she seemed to sparkle, Mrs. Calder looked withered.

Her smile had real warmth, though. "You must be Kirk," she said.

"Hello, Mrs. Calder," Kirk said, rising from the couch to shake her hand, which was warm but felt brittle in his. She wore a wedding band and an engagement ring with a modest stone, and no other jewelry.

"How was work, Mom?" Ronnie asked, her voice bright, as though she was excited for her mother to meet him, or vice versa. "Did Mrs. Hergstrom come back?"

"She was there," Mrs. Calder said. Kirk thought she sounded weary. "Poor thing."

"Mom has a new ghost at work," Ronnie said.

"Ah."

"Ronnie told me about your extra credit project," she said. "And how you'd like to film my husband."

"Um, yeah. If it's okay, that is."

Mrs. Calder folded her arms across her chest, a gesture that made her appear more shrunken and withdrawn, and she nodded.

"I didn't think about dinner," she said. "You are staying for dinner, aren't you?"

Kirk looked over at Ronnie, who raised an eyebrow.

"Sure," he said. "That would be great."

"I could get Chinese food. Do you like Chinese?"

"I do," he said. "Any kind is good."

Mrs. Calder picked her keys off the counter. "I'll be right back. The restaurant is only a few minutes away." She was already on her cell phone and placing an order by the time she was outside.

Kirk looked at Veronica.

"She likes you," she said, as though reading his mind.

"Yeah, I could tell."

"No, seriously," she said, crossing into the kitchen to give him a too-quick hug. "She wouldn't have invited you to dinner otherwise. She just has a little difficulty sometimes with, ah, real people."

"Is she like Janine?"

"No, not like Janine. Kind of the opposite. She'd rather be with the ghost of my father than real people sometimes."

"Wow."

"Just keep talking. She'll warm up."

He grinned. "Speaking of warming up . . ."

Veronica made a face. "She'll be back in twenty minutes. Let's get some homework done."

• • •

Mrs. Calder returned in closer to forty minutes, and by this time Kirk was pretty hungry. He hoped that Mrs. Calder couldn't hear the noises his stomach was making.

Veronica set out plates and silverware on the dining room table and then helped her mother put the food in bowls. Kirk drifted into the kitchen, offering his help, but the women shooed him away. There was fried rice, chicken and broccoli, egg foo yong, moo goo gai pan, egg rolls and boneless ribs.

"You kind of went crazy here, Mom," Veronica said, ladling out wonton soup into a small blue bowl she'd set in front of Kirk.

"When do we get visitors?" her mother answered as she carried in some of the dishes. Kirk hoped that meant James had never been invited. Boy, he thought, is he going to be pissed when he finds out. "Call it an early birthday present. You can both bring leftovers to school tomorrow if you want. Rats, I forgot the drinks. Iced tea okay for you, Kirk?"

"That would be great," he replied. Maybe their lack of visitors meant Ronnie hadn't had a string of boys over to the house. A moment later, Mrs. Calder returned with their drinks.

"Wow, Mom must *really* like you," Veronica said, sitting down next to him. Almost immediately she began rubbing his calf with her foot. "She never slices up lemon for *my* iced tea."

"Hush, you," Mrs. Calder said, finally taking her seat. "Look how pretty the food is," she said. "And it smells so good."

"We don't cook a whole lot," Veronica said. She was sitting very close to him, and he could smell her perfume even through the mélange of aromas. "Lots of salad and canned soup."

Kirk wondered if Ronnie's mother noticed how close she

was sitting, or if she'd glimpsed her daughter's toe grazing along the cuff of his jeans. "Soup is good," he said. "Nothing wrong with soup." He cut into a wonton with the edge of his spoon.

"Is your mother a good cook?" Mrs. Calder asked. "Or does your father do the cooking?"

"Mom," Kirk replied. "She's a pretty good cook."

Actually, when Kirk stopped to think about it, he figured his mother was an exceptional cook, always preparing meals seemingly on the fly for a household of seven, all of whom had different schedules, with jobs, sports, and other extra-curricular activities. He withheld the comment, though, because he wasn't sure how Mrs. Calder would react. There was a fragility to her, a woundedness that made him think any comment about his own mother's proficiency would make her feel like a failure.

Besides, he was already in love with the wonton soup. The rare times his family went out to eat was almost always for pizza or to Chez Mac.

"Do you have brothers and sisters, Kirk?"

"Three sisters and a brother," he said. "A full house."

"Five children," Mrs. Calder said, a distant cast in her eyes. "I often hoped that Eric and I would give Ronnie a sibling, a little sister, maybe, but it just wasn't to be. It must be wonderful having a big family."

"Sometimes," he said. "We don't get out for Chinese food too much, though."

Mrs. Calder laughed. "So tell me about your project," she said, not looking at Kirk, and pushing a lone wonton around her bowl with her spoon. Veronica's toe left his leg, and he wondered if that was some sort of signal; but a moment later she gave the top of his thigh a squeeze.

"Well," he said, clearing his throat, "I'm supposed to go around town videotaping images. That's what the Fish calls ghosts."

"The Fish?" Mrs. Calder asked, looking up from her soup and smiling.

He coughed. "That's what we call Mr. Pescatelli."

"Ah-ha," she said. When the light hit her eyes, Kirk could see where Ronnie got her smile.

"Anyhow," he continued, "Mr. Pescatelli wants me to videotape as many of the different kinds of images as possible. It's research for a book he's doing."

"Why do you think there are ghosts?" Mrs. Calder asked, finally cutting into her wonton.

"The Event," he said.

Mrs. Calder waited. Ronnie removed her hand from his thigh, and it was like he could think again.

"Well, of course it was the Event," he started, his throat suddenly dry, as though some strange spice had been lurking within his food. "What I mean is, the theory goes that we all have a sort of energy inside us. . . ."

"An energy?"

"Some would call it a soul, some—"

"Is this your theory, or Mr. Pescatelli's?"

Kirk looked for help from Veronica, but she was poking around at her plate. He had the sensation of being far out on the ice and hearing a sharp cracking sound.

"My theory," he said. "I've read all of Mr. Pescatelli's stuff, and some other books and articles as well. I'm just starting to really think about it for myself."

"Do you believe in a soul, Kirk?" she said.

He breathed deeply. "I do. And I believe that the soul, in life, leaves traces of its energy everywhere it goes." He thought of Molly, the little girl in the library, the look of simple, pure joy on her face as she reached for a book. "And I think there are certain things—emotions, special events—that cause more of that energy to be released."

"So how do we get the ghosts, then?" Mrs. Calder said, her voice soft, as though something Kirk said had resonated within her.

"Here's what I think. When everyone . . . died . . . in the Event, it released a great amount of soul energy all at once. The radiation from this release passed through air and matter, and it activated the images."

His soup was gone, so he started helping himself to the other dishes as Veronica passed them along. Mrs. Calder was looking in Kirk's direction, but he had the eerie sensation that she was staring over his shoulder and into the kitchen.

"The Fish is probably going to fail me for my theories," he said, hoping to lighten the mood.

She gave a slight chuckle. "Why is that?"

"He doesn't seem to believe in a metaphysical explanation at all. Most people believe in ghosts, and that the deaths of all of those people in the city opened up a bridge between this world and the next, bringing back the spirits of the dead. But he thinks the images are the result of a chemical process, one caused by the release of all of that 'life energy.' The expended life energy released stored images that were somehow imprinted on the world. So in his mind, it isn't a bridge between this world and the afterlife that is opening, but a bridge between our world and the past."

He stopped long enough to taste the egg foo yong, which had a thick brown gravy.

"If the Fish is correct, there's nothing supernatural at all about the images," he said, wishing he could stop talking and eat faster. He'd never blather on like this at home, he thought, where dinner was a race with six other hungry people and seconds were not guaranteed. "They are just the result of a rare but chemically natural process."

"And you? What do you believe? Why would he fail you?"

"I believe in the soul," he said. "He believes only in a memory."

"Interesting," Mrs. Calder said, setting the remainder of her soup aside and smiling at him. "I think I like your theory better." She put a small amount of the fried rice and the moo goo gai pan on her plate. Unlike her mother, Ronnie, thankfully, had an appetite that was as voracious as Kirk's. "You mentioned different types of images?"

Kirk nodded, getting another forkful in before listing them all off for her.

"An image of habit," Mrs. Calder repeated, focusing on the description that was the closest match to her husband. "Mr. Pescatelli's theory doesn't seem very reassuring," she said.

"I don't know, Mom," Veronica broke in, buying Kirk some time to eat. The food was delicious, and Kirk's enjoyment of it was obvious. "Many people find the ghosts frightening. They might be less afraid if there was a rational, scientific explanation."

"Is that how you would feel, Ronnie?" her mother said. "Would you be happier if someone was able to disprove the existence of an afterlife?"

She might as well have summoned a ghost, Kirk thought, as her words seemed to draw all the heat out of the room. Ronnie took a moment before answering.

"Of course not, Mom," she said. "But I don't think that finding a scientific reason for the images is the same thing as disproving an afterlife."

Kirk had to agree. After all, who wanted to spend eternity reading the same newspaper article? He cleared his throat.

"Anyhow," he said, "that's what I'm supposed to do for the project. I've recorded about twenty images so far."

"Do you have any ghosts in your house, Kirk?"

"No. Mom said our house is so noisy they're too scared to come."

The joke didn't register. "Do you know anyone who is a ghost now? Someone who died and came back as a ghost?"

"No, I don't."

Mrs. Calder lifted a napkin to her mouth and nodded, as though what he'd said explained certain things. Veronica was looking at him, but he did not acknowledge her.

"We're reading *Hiroshima* now in Mr. Pescatelli's class," he said. "He thinks the images also appeared there and at Nagasaki, and in other events where there have been a large loss of life. The Boxing Day tsunami, for example."

"Really?" Mrs. Calder said. "I've never heard about those places being haunted."

"The death tolls were considerably less than in our Event," he said. "So the hauntings were much more localized. The bigger the event, the more hauntings."

"You would think there would be more evidence," Veronica said.

"In the case of Japan, the evidence was largely suppressed. You can find stuff on the Internet, though."

"Still," Mrs. Calder said, "I'd think we would hear about these other hauntings more often."

"Well," Kirk told her, knowing that what he had to say wasn't going to go over any better than his joke about his noisy home, "Mr. Pescatelli says the images fade over time. He said that the ghosts of Hiroshima stopped appearing regularly around 1953."

"Does he think that is going to happen here? I think, if anything, there are more ghosts now than there were at this time last year. The boy in Ronnie's bathroom, and poor Mrs. Hergstrom."

"That's true," he said. "That does make our situation a little unique."

But only if you don't consider another long-held belief about spirits and apparitions, he thought, considering a subject brought up in the final chapter of the Fish's book, wherein the Fish, in the interest of fairness, discusses another type of image, which would shoot an Event-sized hole in his pet theories. He postulates a sixth type of image, one that Kirk thought more frightening than the other five combined.

The Fish indicates that the sixth image appears to foretell a future tragedy, like the banshees of antiquity, whose keening would foretell the death of the lord of the house. The sixth image could do more than just appear.

The sixth image could act.

They watched a movie that Veronica had recorded on their DVR, she and Kirk sitting side by side on the couch, without touching, while Ms. Calder sat in her recliner reading magazines. Kirk did not find the movie interesting enough to pull his attention away from Ronnie fully, but then a horde of slavering crisis ghosts could have come streaming through the windows and he would not have found them as interesting as he did Ronnie.

"Good night," Mrs. Calder said after the movie was over. "I'm off to bed. So we'll see you in the morning, Kirk?"

"Bright and early," he said, and waited until she'd disappeared up the stairs before turning and kissing Veronica.

"Bright and early," she said, mimicking him.

He stood up from the couch. "Sure would be easier if I could just stay here tonight," he said.

"Right," she said, handing him his books. "Kirk?"

"Mm-hm?"

"Did you mean what you said at dinner? About the soul?"

He laughed. "You sounded pretty skeptical. I was wondering if I was telling your mother something you'd rather I didn't."

She shook her head. "No, it's okay. I'm glad you said what you did. I think it might have helped her."

"Thank Molly," he said. "I didn't feel that way until Molly.

It isn't like I have empirical evidence or anything, but when I was watching her, I was really watching her, you know? And what I saw—it was like I was seeing something of substance, something real, not just a memory." He laughed. "I'm not explaining it well."

Veronica shook her head, and, standing above her, Kirk thought he could smell faint traces of shampoo and perfume kicked up by her movement.

"You're explaining it just fine, Kirk," she said, rising and flattening her hand against his chest, right over his heart. He wanted to hold her and kiss her again, but his arms were filled with books. "And I think I agree with my mom."

"Agree?" he said, his voice high, dazzled by her closeness and the contact.

"Your theory is better."

She brushed his lips with hers, just a faint but profound touch, and then she showed him to the door.

卌 卌 卌 卌 卌

August was awoken from a sound sleep by his wife's voice echoing in his ear, and when he didn't respond quickly enough she dug her long-nailed fingers into his ribs. Although neither sensation was pleasant, the dream he'd been having was worse, and so once consciousness returned he wasn't even angry.

"August," Madeline said. "August!" The hissed *s* of his name slithered down into the recesses of his ear canal. He shivered and sat up.

"August, I want you to check on our daughter," she said.

"What?"

"I want you to check on—"

"Veronica Calder," August said, rising from the bed. He began unbuttoning his pajama top.

"Our daughter, August," his wife said. "She . . ."

Her words were funneling directly into his brain; every sound like a permanent scratch against the eardrum. "She will become Eva," he said, hoping to drive the sounds from his mind, "at the point of her death."

"You make it sound ugly," Madeline said, "instead of beautiful."

"I think of her always, Madeline," he said. "Gasping for air. Meeting that puerile boy—a man now, or what passes for one today—was an unnecessary reminder, as there is not a day that goes by where I don't think of her . . . of, of, of her *windpipe* closing up, or her *lungs* and, and her—"

"Bring her back, August," she said. "When you bring her back, all the pain will go away."

He scratched his earlobe and then stepped into a pair of pants.

"It is too early," he said. "If we are waiting until the day."

"You have to wait until then," she said. "It is essential."

He looked back at the bed, but Madeline was indistinguishable from the pillows and bedding in the darkness.

"But you can check on her," she said. "And if you have the opportunity, take her."

August sighed. He glanced back at the bed once more before heading downstairs for his coat, his hat, and his gloves.

After her friend leaves, Veronica drifts around our house much as I do, not aimlessly exactly, but with so vague a purpose as to appear to be aimless. She walks into the kitchen and withdraws her father's coffee cup from the cabinet; she puts it back and goes through the living room to stare at an old family portrait hanging in the hallway, of her younger self sitting on her father's knee. Kirk's words have had an effect on her.

She goes upstairs and into the bathroom and stares into the mirror. I think it is me that she is looking for. Veronica Calder is an unmistakably striking girl, but unlike many beautiful girls, she isn't prone to staring at herself in the mirror for long stretches of time. Kirk is a fortunate boy, and I discover that I can still experience jealousy.

"Why are you here?" she says, gazing deeply into the mirror. "Why are *you* here?" I'm not certain whether the question is directed at me or at her own reflection. I decide that I will not attempt to manifest, and instead let her question hang on the air.

She sighs, and runs warm water to wash her face.

Sensing that she is getting ready for bed, I move away, leaving her to herself.

Why was anyone here? I think, floating down the stairs.

Maybe I will have an answer. Threat hangs in the air. I sense this as clearly as I hear the soft padding of Veronica's feet as she heads off to bed.

He is coming.

ЖЖЖЖ
ЖI

Veronica had been in the midst of a fitful sleep full of Event-tossed dreams when she heard a noise from the kitchen, a noise like a muffled clunk.

Every house had noises, of course—the settlings and sighings of a building whose wooden bones grow old and endure the elements even as humans do. When she was a little girl she often complained of a knocking she could hear behind her headboard. It had taken her father a week to figure out that the noises came a half hour after the furnace started up and that there was a pipe behind her headboard. That "ghost" had easily been dispelled by relocating her bed to the other side of the room. Now she heard the clunk again and realized what it sounded like.

A coffee mug being set upon the table in the kitchen.

Impossible, she thought. Images don't make noise. Her alarm clock read 3:33; far too early for her father to arrive. Whatever was making the clunking noise, she thought, it wasn't Dad's ghost.

She thought she heard the rustle of paper, like the page of a newspaper being turned, and she could picture him clearly in her mind—the thin, dark-haired man from the photograph hanging in the hallway, animated. A bead of sweat rolled from her forehead into her eye, and she tried to blink away the sting.

Getting up, she knocked her shin on the nightstand, but choked back her curse. She wished she'd asked Kirk to leave his camera behind.

There was another noise, one not easily identifiable, as she left her room and went toward the stairs. A thought crossed her mind—what if, in addition to making noise, the image had other abilities, such as the ability to break his pattern and rise from his newspaper, the ability to reach out and make physical contact with the living? What if he was reaching out even as she approached, and what if he wasn't really her father at all, but Something Else?

She thought she could smell coffee.

She closed her eyes and clenched her teeth. She refused to be like Janine. There was no running away from life or death.

I'm not afraid, she thought, and repeated the words in her head like a mantra with each downward step. *I'm not afraid I'm not afraid I'm not afraid. . . .*

She was at the bottom of the stairs.

The kitchen was empty.

She crossed to the door, brushing the gauzy curtain back with her fingers. Outside, the wind was making the branches of trees dance, their shadows raking over fallen leaves, which pooled at their trunks and rushed across driveways. Veronica tried to imagine that the sounds they made as they blew and scraped along the foundation of the house were like the turning of a page.

‖‖ ‖‖ ‖‖ ‖‖
‖‖ ‖

August ran almost the entire distance back from Veronica's house to his own, and only a near-tragic slip on the ice as he crossed the street caused him to slow his pace. If he fell and lost consciousness at this hour, Veronica would find his frozen corpse in the snow when she left for school in the morning.

The cold seemed to be flowing through him now; though when he left his house he'd felt immune to the chill. It was so late that the only sounds he heard were those of his footfalls and his own breathing. He expelled great clouds of vapor like a steam train or some diabolical beast as he'd boldly approached the Calder girl's house.

He still wasn't quite sure what had happened.

He'd gone to the side door, which he'd assumed led to the Calder kitchen, carefully opened the screen door, and placed his gloved hand on the knob. No one had seen him make the journey. He still wasn't sure what he was going to do; if the knob turned, would he go inside? Would he search room to room until he found the sleeping girl?

He turned the handle. Many people in Jewell City did not lock their doors, despite the unsolved crimes in the town's long history. The knob turned until he heard it click.

He didn't know why he looked up in that moment; some indefinable tickle on the back of his neck told him that he wasn't alone. And he wasn't.

He didn't recognize the boy staring back at him through the windowpane; he could only recognize the expression. He'd seen it in his own mirror that very morning as he recalled his meeting with Paul Shea; such a look of abject hatred that it made the breath catch in his throat and he stepped back.

But as he did, a hand came *through* the door, and it clamped on to his wrist with hideous strength. The hand circling his wrist wasn't large, but it held him with an unbreakable grip. August looked up at the face in the glass, and where there should have been eyes there were two slivers of darkness.

Then the hand holding him dematerialized, passing through his body like a gamma ray. August's hand felt as though it were encased in solid ice, and, stumbling back, he fled.

He didn't stop moving until he was in his own dark home, with the door locked securely behind him.

"Madeline," he called. "Madeline!"

She did not answer.

卌 卌 卌 卌 卌 III

"How'd you sleep?" Veronica said, opening the door to Kirk.

She practically glittered in the thin bands of sunlight that filtered through the curtains, and a cool cloud of soap-scented mist wafted from her as she opened the door to let him in. She was wearing a satiny gray blouse and a dark skirt, and silver hoop earrings danced brightly against her warm auburn hair.

"Like a baby," he said. "You?"

"Like a baby," she said. "One who is being raised by a family of evil clowns."

"Ouch. That bad?"

"No, but not good. Enough chitchat; you'd better hurry and get set up. Brian is usually here a little before seven."

"On my way," he said. "Why do you call him Brian?"

She shrugged, and again he caught the clean, soapy scent of her. "Funny thing. I just started calling him that because he looks like a Brian. But I found his yearbook photo and he actually is a Brian. Brian Delaney."

"Weird. We should probably try to find out what happened to him, don't you think?"

"I guess so," she said. "I guess I was enjoying having him all to myself."

"Nice."

"Mom's already up and ready," she said. "You don't have to worry about any females disturbing you."

"Great," he said.

The bathroom was tiny. Kirk grimaced at himself in the steam-free mirror. The room was a little chilly, he thought.

Mrs. Calder passed by and said hello, startling him.

"Can I make you any breakfast? I think we have some eggs."

"I'm good, thanks."

"How about some toast?"

"I'd love toast," he said.

"I'm glad you're here," she said on her way down the stairs. "It's nice to have company."

The way she said it made Kirk realize something: Mrs. Calder was very, very lonely. She was still an attractive woman, and relatively young, but he knew even though he and Veronica hadn't discussed it that Mrs. Calder did not date. He felt sorry for her.

"You love toast, huh?" Veronica said, joining him. She was holding a cup of hot tea.

"Love it," he said. "Your mom isn't seeing anyone, is she?"

"Why?" Veronica said, giving him a playful slap on the seat of his jeans. "You interested?"

"Well, she's pretty hot," he said. "But no, it's you I'm interested in. Way interested."

"She doesn't date."

"Why not?" he said, sitting on the edge of the tub. "I'm sure she gets asked out. All kidding aside, she's an attractive lady."

"I'm sure, too," Ronnie said, squeezing in next to him. "She doesn't talk about it at all."

"She should," he said.

"I know. We fight about it."

He looked through the lens. "I guess it is probably hard, with the ghost of her husband showing up every morning. Talk about a guilt trip."

"Shhhh," she said, leaning her face against his ears and sending chills racing through his body. "He's almost here."

They waited in silence for long minutes, until the LED clock in the corner of the camera's viewfinder read 7:05.

"It's five after," he whispered.

"Huh," she said. "That's weird. He's been here almost every day."

"Maybe he doesn't show on certain days of the week?"

She shook her head, her hair grazing his cheek. "No, I'm certain he has been here on a Friday."

"Hm."

They stayed a moment longer. "Should we go?" Kirk said. "I don't want to miss your father."

Veronica nodded, and Kirk helped her up by taking her hand.

Mrs. Calder was waiting in the kitchen, holding out a dish with two slices of buttered white bread cut into triangles. Kirk accepted the toast with what he thought was a winning smile, but the good humor seemed to have drained out of Mrs. Calder's face. He bit into one of the triangles.

"Get ready, Kirk," Veronica said.

Kirk stood beside Ronnie and began filming. At 7:13 Mr. Calder appeared, but all Kirk could see through the viewfinder was the newspaper, stretched out like square gray wings. He stepped in front of Veronica so he could get a better view. Mr. Calder was there. His dark hair was combed flat, and glistened as though he'd not dried it after his morning shower.

The paper's gray wings sagged as he let them go with one hand to lift the mug of coffee, and Kirk had a clear view of the faded image of young Ronnie. The ghost cup was actually less faded than the "real" cup, not having gone through the hundreds of washings that over time had diluted the image. Steam vapor shimmered off the oily black liquid before Veronica's father brought it to his lips. He set the coffee down and lifted the paper, squinting at a headline before turning the page. He read the article in the top left corner for a moment, then he turned and gazed into the camera with a directness that made the back of Kirk's skull tingle.

Mr. Calder smiled. Then he disappeared.

"Wow," Kirk whispered, and he felt Ronnie squeeze his arm.

Beside him, the ghost's wife sniffled and wiped at her eyes.

"Well, you got your image," she said, and walked swiftly out of the room.

⊥⊩⊩ ⊥⊩⊩ ⊥⊩⊩ ⊥⊩⊩ ⊥⊩⊩ ||||

Veronica's disappointment hangs on the air like the smell of burning leaves, but there is nothing I can do. I have no strength to return, not after what I had done the night before.

I'd caused him pain. I had held him and my very touch was painful to him. She will never know that he had come for her last night, and she will never know that all that stood between him and her was me. I think about this for some time, my atoms drifting above the tub where my life ended. So much of our history—collective, individual, personal—is unknown. The only one that would have any memory of my action was my enemy, but it will fade even from his mind and become overgrown with the twisted, dark roots of his soul.

But I will remember. I will remember how my touch had hurt him.

At first, I thought that in hurting him I had gained power for myself. After he fled I felt infused with a new strength, but whatever energy that I thought I felt, my ephemeral body could not contain it, and I seemed to burst apart, a sand castle swatted by a giant hand. After strength comes weakness, and despite

Veronica desperately wanting the boy she brought home to see me, I could not reassemble in time.

I know that Bittner will not remain frightened for long; I can only hope that when he appears again—and he will—that I am ready.

Ⅲ Ⅲ Ⅲ Ⅲ
Ⅲ Ⅲ

Veronica waited at the end of her driveway, waving when she saw Janine leaving her house. Janine returned the wave hesitantly, as though not wanting to intrude on Veronica's moment with Kirk.

"It was really mean the way you scared Brian away," Veronica whispered as they waited for Janine to catch up. She walked at a brisk pace, her head lowered.

"Must be the jealous type," he said.

"Don't say mean things about Brian. And be super nice to Janine or I'll hate you."

"I'm the one who should be jealous," he said. "He gets to see you showering every morning, and I didn't even get to sleep over. And I'm always super nice to Janine."

"Hey, gorgeous," Veronica said to Janine as she caught up. "How's things?"

"Things are fine, Veronica. Hullo, Kirk."

"Hey."

"Did you stay at Veronica's last night?"

"I wish," he said. "Mom dropped me off. I . . ." His voice trailed off as he tried to come up with something that wouldn't be disturbing to Janine. "I met Ronnie's father. Her parents."

"Ronnie's father is a ghost," Janine said. Her eyes were fixated on the ground ten feet in front of her, so she didn't see Veronica slug Kirk in the arm.

"Ow," he said. "Yes, he is."

"Is he a nice ghost?" she asked.

"Yeah, I guess so. He seemed nice enough." He looked over at Veronica, shrugging his bruised shoulder.

"Maybe I should meet him, too," Janine said. "We're coming close to Mary Greer."

"Who?"

"Get your camera, Kirk," Veronica told him.

"Why? Do you see an image?"

"There's one that appears on the porch of that house every morning." She looked at her watch. "Should be in just a few moments. We're a little early today."

"It's Mary Greer," Janine said, threading her gloved fingers in with Veronica's.

"Mary Greer, huh?" Kirk said, aiming the camera.

Veronica could tell that Kirk felt more than a little self-conscious aiming the camera at the house across the street. She knew he was the type to ask permission of people before filming. She thought he'd probably feel even worse if he knew that it was Mr. Bittner's house.

And then Mary Greer appeared. The sight of her bare arms caused Veronica to draw her coat in at the neck. She heard Kirk's sharp intake of breath as Mary ascended the stairs. Veronica saw that Mary skipped a little as she took the first step, a detail she'd never noticed before. She knocked on Mr. Bittner's door. She paused and then knocked again, three quick, soundless raps. She looked up and then disappeared.

"Cool," Kirk said, grinning at Veronica. "Bonus. The Fish is going to be thrilled."

"I don't think Mr. Bittner is going to be happy that you filmed his house," Janine said, releasing Veronica's hand. This was progress for her.

Kirk stuffed his camera into his backpack. "Mr. Bittner? That's Mr. Bittner's house?"

Veronica nodded. Maybe she'd let Janine walk to school on her own from now on.

"Oh, shit," Kirk said, looking betrayed. "I hope he didn't see me."

"He saw," Janine said. "He always sees. He waits by the window just inside the door and watches."

"You don't know that," Veronica said, catching herself before she added, "You barely even look up from the sidewalk." She thought she'd seen Bittner lurking beyond the curtains, too.

Janine nodded. "He's always there."

"Great," Kirk said, hoisting his bag and picking up his pace toward the school. "That's wonderful."

"What are you worried about?" Veronica said. "Even if he saw, you could just tell him about the project you are doing with Mr. Pescatelli."

Kirk shook his head. "You ever see them together? Not good friends, those two. I'd hate for them to get in a fight because of me."

"I wouldn't worry about it," she said, but saw that he would anyway.

"Who is she?" he asked. "His daughter?"

"I told you," Janine said. "It's Mary Greer."

"You're kidding," Veronica said. "You don't know who Mary Greer is?"

"Gus has Mary hanging from a tree . . ." Janine sang, her voice surprisingly clear and sweet. "He killed her."

"That's a rumor, Janine," Veronica said.

"How long has Mr. Bittner lived in that house?" Kirk said.

"My mom said he's lived there since before he got married."

Kirk nodded and looked back over his shoulder.

"Mary won't let him forget her," Janine said. She'd turned and was looking back at Bittner's house along with Kirk, which Veronica thought was odd until Janine "slipped" and nudged into him.

"Careful, Janine," Kirk said, holding out his arm to steady her, which made her smile. "It's slippery."

"I wouldn't want to be forgotten, either," Janine said, gripping his arm.

Veronica told Kirk Mary's story as they ascended the hill toward the school. The fact that the image was of a girl who had been murdered made him want to review what he'd recorded. He noticed also that Janine didn't seem to mind the story, despite its frightening subject matter. She was doing that twisting thing she always did with her gloved fingers, but she wasn't cowering or looking like she was on the verge of passing out.

"Thanks for letting me walk with you," she said when they reached the school. Kirk told her she could join them anytime.

"I guess Ronnie told you we've been doing a little . . . image recording," he said. "You could come if you want to. It might, you know, help."

Was she blushing, or was that just the effects of the cold on her white skin? "Maybe." She mumbled a farewell and shuffled away. When Kirk turned back to Ronnie she was beaming at him.

"That was really, really sweet of you, Kirk," she said.

"It was?"

"Inviting her. Most guys would be doing everything they could to make sure they were alone with me, but you put that aside to try to help Janine."

"Yeah," he said, a little puzzled, but basking in her approval. His offer to Janine hadn't been a mercenary act for Veronica's benefit at all, but if the gesture gave him fringe benefits, he wasn't going to say otherwise.

"I think we should look at that recording closely," Veronica said, nodding toward the camera.

"Definitely," he said. "After the story you just told, we'd better."

"Okay," she said. "I'll see you later, in class."

Her smile lit the whole gray hallway.

"Later," he said, and watched her walk away.

When she was out of sight, he rewound his tape, going back as far as the last seconds of Mr. Calder's image, just before his smile. After he faded, there was a blank blue screen before the video flipped to Mr. Bittner's house against the washed-out sky of morning. The audio track came back louder than he'd realized, Ronnie saying that she was a little early, and then Mary Greer appeared.

But Kirk wasn't watching her. He was looking for movement

near the bay window to her right, and he saw it—a little ripple in the curtain, and then gloved fingers.

He saw movement elsewhere in the house, a flicker between the curtains of an upstairs window. . . .

The hand clamped heavily on his shoulder with a harsh, unfriendly grip. A gloved hand.

"Mr. Lane," Mr. Bittner said, his long fingers digging into the muscle, "is there a reason why you were photographing my house this fine morning?"

Kirk turned his neck as much as the man's hand would allow. For an old guy, Bittner had a grip like iron. And he was a lot taller than Kirk had realized, six four at least. Kirk was just under five ten and he had to look up to see Bittner's face, gray beneath the brim of his black fedora. His pale blue eyes glowed with amusement and raw malice.

"I didn't know it was your house," Kirk said, and the long fingers squeezed tighter, bulging like sausages in casings of smooth black leather.

"No?" Bittner said. "Didn't Ms. Calder tell you it was my house?"

"A . . . after," Kirk said. He was peripherally aware of kids, his classmates, passing them in the hall, but the dull pain in his shoulder made it hard to concentrate. "She told me after."

Way to give up your girlfriend, he thought. Hero.

"Fascinating," Bittner said. "But that information does not answer my question. Why were you filming my house?"

"I'm filming images," he said, and tried to break free, but Bittner kept clamping down. "I'm doing a work study with Mr. P . . . Pescatelli."

Bittner released him. "Images?" he said.

"Ghosts," Kirk said, trying to lift his arm, which was numb, as though Bittner had caught a nerve that temporarily deadened his limb. "I wasn't trying to spy on you or anything. I just wanted to record the ghost."

Bittner stared at him. "Ghosts," he repeated. "And is this the camera that recorded this 'ghost'?"

Kirk wanted to mouth off, to make some flippant reply, because his arm and neck hurt, and he was embarrassed at being manhandled in the hallway for everybody to see. The injury to his pride was greater than the one to his shoulder—and his shoulder hurt like hell.

But he didn't. The icy seriousness of Bittner's gaze froze his harsh words in his throat. He just nodded.

"Ah," Bittner said, and grabbed the camera out of his hand. "You'll get this back after school. If at all."

Bittner turned and walked down the hall, and the kids who had lingered to watch the altercation scurried out of his way as he passed, his long gray trench coat sweeping from side to side like a scouring broom with each angry step.

$$\cancel{||||} \; \cancel{||||} \; \cancel{||||} \; \cancel{||||}$$
$$\cancel{||||} \; \cancel{||||} \; |$$

Pescatelli stepped into August's classroom after the second bell rang, closing the door behind him, his eyes wild.

"What the hell do you think you are doing?" he said. He was so angry he was trembling, and there was a quaver in his voice. "Shaking down one of my students like he was a . . . a . . . a thug? You could be suspended without pay for laying your hands on a student like that! Sued!"

August resisted the urge to mimic Pescatelli's stuttering. "Well, Stephen," he said. "You are lucky I did not come to 'lay my hands' on you."

He suppressed a smile as Pescatelli's bulbous eyes lowered to the desk, where August's hands had bunched into huge fists. "What the hell do think you are doing, getting one of your students to videotape my home?" August kept his voice cold and hard, and he saw the effect it had on Pescatelli, who struggled to get control of his shaking and bluster.

"You have invaded my privacy," August said, rising slowly from his chair until, even leaning over his desk, he towered over the smaller man. "I should have you arrested."

"Have . . . have *me* arrested?" Pescatelli said, his voice shrill, almost keening. "I had no idea that Kirk was going to your house!"

"Bullshit!" August said, his voice a low rumble. "The boy told me about your little project. Work study, my ass!"

"Gus, I did not know Kirk was going to your house." He was holding out his fat little hands, and they were still unsteady. "Really, I didn't."

August looked at Pescatelli. He seemed too frightened to be lying, all the anger blown out of him. But Pescatelli had made far too many cracks about him and Mary Greer since she'd started appearing on his doorstep for August to let him off easily. He lowered himself back into his seat.

"Tell me the truth, Stephen," he said. "Admit you sent him to me."

"I didn't," he said. "I gave him a list of sightings from my book. I have no idea why—"

"Your book?" August said, cutting him off.

Pescatelli's smile was nervous and embarrassed. He ran his stubby fingers through his greasy thinning hair.

"Yeah," he said. "I'm writing a book about . . . about ghosts." He gave a quavering laugh. "Want to read it?"

"Yes, I do," August said, clearly not answering the way Stephen expected. Pescatelli looked as though he'd just swallowed a lively frog. "I do want to read it, and I suggest that if you have any speculation about the poor little girl who appears on my porch, you remove it and any mention of me or my home."

"Really, Gus," Pescatelli said. "There's nothing there. I write about some of the images around town—that's what I think

165

they are, images—but I stay away from those that are on private property."

"I'll stop by tonight for a copy," August said. The 29th wouldn't wait; August wanted to ensure that there was nothing in his way.

"T . . . Tonight? Really, I could e-mail—"

"Is seven o'clock too early?"

Pescatelli looked at him, blinking. "No. No, I guess that's all right. Maybe you can give me some suggestions before I send it off to Chicago."

"I'll do that," August said. He set the camera on the edge of his desk. "You can give that back to the boy. I erased the film."

"What did you do that for?" the Fish said, taking it from his desk. "That was his extra credit work!"

"I guess you'll have to fail him."

"Why are you being such a jerk about this? What's the big deal, anyway? What do you care if he films your house for a couple minutes?"

"He didn't ask."

"I don't think there's any law against it, August."

August smiled.

"There are laws," he said. "And then there are laws."

$$\cancel{||||}\ \cancel{||||}\ \cancel{||||}\ \cancel{||||}$$
$$\cancel{||||}\ \cancel{||||}\ ||$$

There was definitely something off about Mr. Bittner today, Veronica thought.

It wasn't just the way he paused at certain points in his lecture to look at her. Teachers were always doing that, the good ones, anyway—scanning their classrooms during their lectures, gauging who was paying attention and who was drifting off into outer space. But every time Bittner paused—*every* time— his eyes stopped on her.

Sometimes, she thought, she *caused* him to pause. Normally a very smooth speaker, Mr. Bittner seemed to freeze up momentarily upon seeing her, as though confused. She was quite familiar with that deer-in-the-headlights look.

It was the same expression that people had when they saw a ghost.

"That is all I wish to say about the war today," he said, after a particularly lengthy pause. "You may open your readers and begin the next chapter."

He took his seat and closed his eyes. James glanced at Veronica, frowning. Kirk didn't make eye contact; he was watching Bittner.

There was a quiet ping as Veronica turned her reader on and advanced to the next chapter.

She lifted her eyes. Mr. Bittner was staring right at her.

He smiled.

Throughout the remainder of class, she felt as though she were in a roomful of ghosts. Ghosts standing in a ring around her desk, every spectral eye upon her. She didn't look up, because to do so, to make eye contact with just one of them, would cause her to become a ghost, too. When the bell rang, she rose from her seat and moved toward the door with lowered eyes.

"Miss Calder."

Bittner's voice froze her in midstride. She looked at him, a large gray gargoyle behind his massive metal desk.

"Come here, please."

She did. She couldn't help herself. Students moved around her—they seemed to move through her, as though she weren't really there at all.

Mr. Bittner was staring at her, waiting, until she felt like she couldn't breathe.

"Mr. Lane," he said, raising his voice and startling Veronica. "Stop lurking in my doorway and get to your next class. I wish to speak to Miss Calder privately."

Veronica risked a look over her shoulder. Kirk was standing in the doorway, concern and anger evident in his posture and expression. She loved him for it.

"Mr. Lane," Mr. Bittner said, his voice cold and rasping. "I will not ask a second time."

Kirk didn't move to leave until Veronica nodded to him. When she turned back, Mr. Bittner's eyes were intent on her.

"Every day you walk past my house on your way to school," he said. "Usually with your little friend, the one with the hat."

"Janine," she whispered, and then regretted saying her name.

"Janine, yes," he said. "And most every day, I see you looking at the ghost that appears on my porch. Do you know who that ghost was, Veronica?"

"Mary Greer."

"Mary Greer. That's right. And do you know what happened to Mary Greer?"

"She was m . . . murdered."

Mr. Bittner nodded, his eyes never leaving her face. "Yes. She was murdered, and her killer was never brought to justice. He died first. But what you might not know is that Mary Greer was a student of mine. One of my favorite students, actually. I have been in this often thankless profession for too long to pretend that I don't have favorite students."

His full, cracked lips stretched into a sudden smile. Veronica felt her heart trip as a thin sliver of his teeth became visible.

"You, of all my current crop, should understand this. You do understand, don't you?"

She nodded. The way he said "crop" made her think that he saw his students as something to be harvested rather than nurtured.

"Good. Then you must know there isn't a single day when I don't think of that poor little girl. Not one day. Even before the Event came and ruined life for all of us, I thought of her daily. I sometimes imagined it was my thoughts and my grief that summoned her back from the grave, and not that rotten business that destroyed our fair city to the south."

He paused, the strength of his gaze holding Veronica in place. Her eyes were windows that he was trying to climb through.

"I think of her every day, Veronica," he said. "But that does not mean I want to be reminded of her any more than I have to. Please tell Mr. Lane that he is not to point a camera or anything else at me or my house ever again."

She nodded.

Finally he broke eye contact with her. Veronica felt that she could breathe again.

"You may be excused," he said, and she strode away as swiftly as she could without actually breaking into a run.

Part of her wanted to march back to his desk and look into that craggy face of his and tell him that he should tell Kirk himself, but she knew that wasn't the only reason he'd stopped her. Something in his message was for her and her alone, but she was too frightened to figure out what it was.

That moment didn't last long, however. The more Veronica thought about being afraid, the angrier she became. She requested to be allowed to go to the library—with Janine—during her study hall period late in the day.

"Why did you drag me down here again?" Janine said.

"Don't be huffy," Veronica said. She plunked four yearbooks down onto the table between them. "I want you to help me." She opened the book where she'd found Mary and Brian, and then smoothed out the page with the photo of Mr. Bittner's homeroom. "Look through these and see if you find any pictures or anything about this boy here, Brian Delaney."

Janine squinted at the page. "That's the boy in your bathroom?"

"Yes, that's the boy in my bathroom," Veronica said, expecting Janine to launch into another one of her cautionary ghost rules.

"He's cute," Janine said instead. "And look, there's Mary Greer."

"I noticed her," Veronica said, surprised and pleased that the photograph of not one but two teens-turned-ghosts didn't seem to bother Janine, who was already flipping through another of the yearbooks.

Veronica hadn't been looking long when she found a large photo of Brian in the Candid section. He was standing at the front of the school on a clear day, talking to a girl. Veronica could practically see the electricity crackling between them from the years-old photo.

The girl was Mary.

"Wow," she said, holding the book out to Janine. "Look at this."

A few minutes later, Janine found a photo in her book of the pair sitting together at a school assembly.

"Oh, and listen to this!" Veronica said. "This is in the student ads. 'Brian—Thank you for an awesome year. I can't wait for summer! Your girl, Mary.'"

"I've got one, too," Janine said. "'M.G.—Let's Open Vast Eventualities—B.D.'"

"I don't get it," Veronica said.

"He's capitalized the words. The first letters spell *love*."

"Awww. He must be a poet."

Janine giggled. She was actually having fun, and between them they found three more mushy student ads from the young couple, two more photos of them together, and a few individual candid shots. They also learned that Mary worked on the yearbook committee, was in a school play her freshman year, and was a cheerleader. Brian ran track and played basketball. Janine barely even flinched when a ghost kid walked through the library cart and literally disappeared in the Biography section.

"They were a couple for a long time," Veronica said, finding another picture of them in their freshman yearbook.

"He must have been devastated when she was killed," Janine said. Veronica saw that Janine had found the big memorial heart for Mary in the most recent of the four books they were perusing.

"Oh, can you imagine?" Veronica said, looking down at the two kids smiling out at her from the center of the page. Brian was clearly younger in this photo than when he appeared in her bathroom, his hair not as long and his cheeks a little less angular.

"You know what's weird?" Janine said. "I can't find any mention of him at all in this yearbook."

"Really? Nothing? Maybe he moved away."

"Still, you'd think there would be a message or something, somewhere," Janine said. "You don't know when he died, do you?"

"No," Veronica replied.

Janine was frowning.

"What's wrong?"

"There's one message in the ads that is kind of disturbing. 'Brian D.—I hope you never sleep.' It isn't signed, and there aren't any other Brian Ds in the whole school."

Veronica felt a chill and then looked up just as the ghost boy reappeared and walked through the library cart going the other way.

"That's very strange," she said. When the bell rang, it was she, and not Janine, who nearly jumped out of her own skin.

ⲧⲏⲧ ⲓⲏⲧ ⲓⲏⲧ ⲓⲏⲧ ⲓⲏⲧ ⲓⲏⲧ ⲓⲓⲓ

In gym, Kirk was picked as one of the team captains, which meant that Coach Gleason wasn't basing his decisions on athletic talent. There were sixteen boys in his class, and Coach Gleason split them into four teams of four. Kirk was awarded the first pick, and he picked James even though there were at least two kids in the remaining pool of eleven that were better than him.

"Winner keeps the court," Coach Gleason said. "To seven. Teams one and two, get in there. Your ball, Red."

Hearing his most hated nickname, Kirk gritted his teeth as Coach Gleason passed him the ball. He desperately wanted to answer, "Thanks, Bald," but he didn't feel like spending the afternoon in detention. He was on edge after Mr. Bittner's weirdness in history class with Veronica, hot on the heels of his weirdness in the hall that morning. Something wasn't right about that guy.

He inbounded to James, who drove toward the basket around his defender and laid it up for a point. Maybe there was only one kid better than James, Kirk thought.

They were up four to one in no time, and Kirk had felt bold enough to take a shot. The ball clanged off the rim, but James grabbed the rebound and tossed it back out to him. James planted his feet, boxing out a defender, and nodded to Kirk, who took that as a sign he should try to drive around the pick. Kirk started, and was halfway there when James swung around, his elbow slamming Kirk in the back, tripping him up with an outstretched leg. Kirk went down hard, the ball squirting away and out of bounds. The sound of Coach's whistle was like a distant signal across a choppy ocean.

"Oh, sorry, man," James said, too loud, a poor actor. He bent low and picked up Kirk's limp arm, leaning in close as he did so.

"I am going to kick your ass after school," he whispered. "The soccer field. Don't miss it."

Kirk let himself be dragged to his feet. His knee and elbow were scraped up. There was a pressure at the back of his eyes, but it was fury more than anything else, and it grew worse as he saw James's smirk and similar looks on the faces of a few of his co-conspirators. He decided that he *would* meet James after school on the soccer field, and that yes, he would get his ass kicked, but it would be worth it if he could deliver one bruising shot to James's smug face.

"Better be there," James said, figuring he could cow Kirk into submission.

Fat chance, Kirk thought.

"Wouldn't miss it," he whispered back.

Coach blew his whistle again, looking back and forth between Kirk and James.

"No foul," he said. "Same team. Team one forfeits. You're all bloody, Red. Go see the nurse for a Band-Aid. Team three, take the court."

James tried to stare Kirk down as Kirk walked toward the exit, and when that didn't work, he flipped him off. Kirk took a little heart when he saw that James's pals weren't impressed anymore; if anything, they looked embarrassed for him.

I'm not afraid of ghosts, Kirk thought as he slammed open the door. Why would I be afraid of you?

After gym, Kirk went down the hall to see the Fish, who had nothing but sour news for him.

"He erased the tape?" Kirk asked.

"He erased the tape," the Fish said. Otherwise the camera was no worse for wear.

"Huh. That really sucks. I only had a couple of images on that tape but they were really good ones."

"What did you have on there other than the girl on Bittner's porch?"

Kirk didn't answer the question. "Do you think he killed her?"

Pescatelli, he noticed, didn't answer his question, either. "The police questioned Bittner, but he was never considered a suspect."

"She looked happy on his porch," Kirk said. "Why would she be appearing there? Wouldn't she be more likely to appear where she was killed?"

The Fish shook his head. "Not necessarily. You haven't been reading my book closely enough."

Your *manuscript*, Kirk thought. *Book* implies that it was actually published. He let it pass without mentioning that he had read the "book" pretty closely, but that the theories contained therein were just that: theories. Not laws, not proven truths.

"What did I miss?"

"She isn't a crisis image or a point-of-death image. We have a natural tendency to think that someone who was murdered would automatically become a point-of-death or crisis image, but that isn't the case. If she's smiling, like you say, she might be an attachment image. Plus, she died in February, and when Mary appears on Bittner's porch she is wearing shorts and a tank top."

"She looked happy."

The Fish sighed. "She had been his student. Two years in a row. She would visit him on the way to go see the boyfriend."

"Something is really weird about Mr. Bittner. The way he looks at Ronnie."

"Something is weird about him, yes. But, as I say, he was never really on the cops' radar."

The Fish was doing his level best to keep all emotion from his face. Which, for him, was like one of the creatures he was named after struggling for air on a riverbank.

"I was watching the video just before Bittner snatched it away. I saw something," Kirk said.

"Well, what was it?"

"There was some sort of movement in the upstairs window. He's got the drapes drawn, but there's a gap, and on the video you could see something moving. Flickering, almost."

"Probably just him moving around."

Kirk shook his head. "No. You could see Bittner's hand and part of his arm clearly against the curtains in the downstairs room, and this other movement was happening at the same time."

The Fish stopped a moment to consider this. "What else was on the tape?" he asked, repeating his question from earlier. Clearly, there was something he was not telling, but Kirk decided that his own questions could wait.

"It was Ronnie's father," he said.

"Ronnie's father?" the Fish repeated, his eyebrow arching high above his glasses. "Where did you get him?"

"He's at Ronnie's house. He appears there every morning."

The Fish rocked back in his chair. "Mission accomplished, I guess."

Kirk nodded, embarrassed.

"Are you going to continue with the work study?"

Kirk thought the Fish looked a little pathetic. He'd lost the button on his left cuff, and Kirk could tell he fully expected him to walk away from the project.

But Kirk still had questions, and he knew they were questions that the Fish couldn't answer for him. But there was no reason why he shouldn't still get class credit for arriving at his own conclusions.

"I want to keep going," he said.

"Great."

"Don't get mad at me."

"Get mad at you? Why would I get mad at you? I'm pleased you are going to keep with it. I think your research could be really valuable."

"Well, part of the reason I want to stick with the project is that I'm not sure some of your theories are accurate."

Contrary to what Kirk expected, the Fish laughed, nearly going over backward in his seat. "So you want to debunk me, is that it?" he said. "That's great! That's what research is all about."

"I thought it would tick you off."

"Listen," the Fish said, wiping at his eye, "I want the truth, too. My only caution is that you stay objective as you collect the evidence. Just let it happen, don't try to shade it. That's why I asked you to write a little about each image—it tests your objectivity, but the notes might also be revelatory if you find you *can't* remain objective. Intuition can be worth exploring."

The Fish took a black binder very similar to the one he'd given to Kirk, and withdrew a packet of stapled pages from one of the pockets in the front.

"This is something I've been meaning to test myself. Check out this list."

Kirk flipped through the list, which was three typed pages and had twenty numbered entries. He saw Mary Greer's name at number eight. Beside her name was MURDER BY STRANGULA-TION, followed by a location, date, day, and "estimated time of death." Beneath this line was a short description of her image and the time and place it appears. The Fish had handwritten "Bittner" with a question mark beside the image notes. Not all of the twenty entries had notes about an image.

"Were all of these people murdered?" Kirk asked.

"All died violently," the Fish said. "There are a few car crash victims, and one who died in a fire. Of the ones who were murdered, at least half are still unsolved."

"Some of these don't have images?"

"That's the piece I want you to check out. Most of these people weren't murdered where their bodies were found."

"Louis Green is on this list," Kirk said. "I saw him with Ronnie."

"Did you get him on film?"

"Yeah, He's kind of blurry, though."

The Fish nodded. "No worries. I've already got him. Three different angles."

Kirk looked back at Mary Greer's entry. She'd been found in the woods in Pequot Park, on a Friday.

"What am I looking for, exactly?" he said.

"Go to these sights and see if they have an image," the Fish said. "And if they do, record, take notes, and then we'll see what we can learn."

Kirk looked back at the list. MURDER BY STRANGULATION. MURDER BY GUNSHOT. MURDER BY BEATING. And the Fish wanted him to go to all of these sites where these people had lost their lives, their killers unidentified.

Sounded like fun.

"I'll get started tomorrow," he said.

James was already on the snow-dusted soccer field when Kirk finally made it out there, as was a crowd of about twenty students, mostly boys.

"Amazing," he said. "I didn't think you'd have the guts to show up. I figured you'd get on the bus like a little wuss."

"Yeah," Kirk said. "You figure a lot of things wrong." He tossed his bag into the snow, nearly hitting one of the bystanders. "We going to do this?"

"You bet. I'm going to kick your ass."

Kirk didn't break stride as he pushed James with both hands

in the chest. The ground of the soccer field was slippery, and James, clearly surprised, almost lost his balance. There were hoots and cries of encouragement from the crowd, who seemed as shocked as James that Kirk had come prepared for a fight. James was a couple inches taller than Kirk, broader in the chest and heavier by twenty pounds.

James's first punch clipped Kirk's ear as he tried to dodge the blow, bringing a bright hot painful throbbing. That was bad, but what was worse was that he lost his balance and slid to one knee. James was coming back with a wild punch, but he slipped and the punch hit Kirk's left shoulder. It hurt, but there was a satisfying cracking sound as James's knuckles hit the bone. Kirk propelled himself up and into James's stomach, and then they both went over into the snow, grappling for a firm purchase on each other's clothes.

The crowd had stopped cheering. James had gotten Kirk onto his back, and Kirk, panicking, tried to drive his fist into James's ribs. James tensed and tried to guard his unprotected side. Instead of pummeling him, James lifted himself up from Kirk and stepped away.

Kirk saw the reason for the sudden silence, and for James's retreat. A new member had joined their crowd, a student no one recognized, either from his shabby clothes or from his frightened, youthful face.

Kirk watched as invisible hands tore glasses from the disheveled newcomer's face, then watched as an unseen blow doubled the boy up. A moment later the boy's nose was smashed nearly flat on his face, a spray of dark blood spewing forth, disappearing once it hit the snow. The boy's legs flew out from under him, and he fell heavily but soundlessly onto his back.

"Jesus," someone whispered. "They're *kicking* him."

Kirk could see the impact of unseen boots rippling the boy's clothing. His mouth, a bloody ruin, was open and howling cries that couldn't be heard. A bruise rose up and closed a teary eye. The violence did not cease until the ghost boy disappeared.

James made only the briefest of eye contact with Kirk.

"She's a cold fish anyway," he said, rubbing his knuckles. "A tease. Good riddance."

Kirk, his clothes soaked, his ear throbbing, felt numb to James's words. Like he knows, he thought. He picked his bag up out of the snow and started on his long walk home.

꧋ IIII IIII IIII IIII IIII IIII IIII

"You saw her again, August?" Madeline said. It had been a few days since she had spoken to him; he found it pleasing to hear her voice.

"I did."

"How . . . how was she?"

"She is a beautiful girl, Madeline. I think Eva will be quite pleased."

"Soon, August? She will be home soon?"

"Yes," he said, and stood to get his hat and coat. "Very soon. I'm going to visit Stephen now. Would you like to come?"

"Stephen Pescatelli is a horrible man," she said. "And I hate to leave the house."

"I understand," August said, and turned with a sympathetic smile for her, but she had already disappeared, probably upstairs to her sewing, or to look once again at Eva's room, patiently ticking off the minutes until she arrived.

He got into his car and turned left even though the shortest route to Pescatelli's house was to the right. He wanted to pass by Veronica's house. He slowed to a crawl and looked up at her bedroom window, hoping for a glimpse of his girl. He thought that a shadow crossed between the window and the light, but ultimately he was left disappointed.

Soon, he thought, and turned right at the end of the street to circle back to Stephen Pescatelli's house.

At first he thought Pescatelli wasn't going to answer the door, and August pictured him cowering behind a brown sofa that smelled of snack chips and body odor, quivering like a cornered mouse. But he did answer, wearing jeans and a light jacket over a cotton T-shirt, and surprised August by inviting him inside.

"Be it ever so humble," Pescatelli said, waving him in. "Can I take your coat and hat?"

"I'm not staying," August said. "You have your manuscript?"

"I do." Pescatelli handed August a black binder, and he rifled through it. The last page was number three hundred and thirty-three.

"I'll return it when I am finished," August said, although he had no intention of doing so. He'd worn gloves mainly so as to not leave fingerprints, but also to avoid touching anything in the Pescatelli's home, which he'd imagined to be a filthy hovel. He was surprised to find everything neat and orderly, even the man's desk, which stood against the wall in the living room.

"Please." Pescatelli was nervous, but he was a far cry from the quaking wreck that August had dressed down in his office. August had gone to his house with every intention of terrifying the man to the brink of a heart attack, but for some reason, he himself felt uneasy. Pescatelli wore a smile that looked frozen on his face, but there was also a surge of new confidence beneath his pasty exterior.

Briefly, August wondered if he was carrying a gun or some other weapon in the pocket of his shirt. He turned on his heel, and Pescatelli's hand twitched toward the unbuttoned jacket pocket near his right hand.

August smiled at him. "You've told the boy he is not to go near my house again?"

Pescatelli licked his lips and pretended to scratch an itch on his belly, just above the hem of the pocket. "I told him," he said. "We met after school."

"Good," August said. "I look forward to reading your book. I have been thinking of ghosts too, of late."

He opened the door and walked out to his car, feeling Pescatelli's glassy eyes on him with every step.

August began reading the book at dinner, which he had out at a local restaurant named Bosco's, one of the last places in town that wasn't part of some wretched chain. He ordered a medium-well steak, baked potato, broccoli, and had a Caesar salad and rolls beforehand. Pescatelli was full of surprises today. August had imagined his prose would be as muddled and inconsistent as the author himself. He instead found that Pescatelli wrote in a very clear, unornamented style that made his points with grace. There were scarcely any traces of the hyperbole that routinely entered the man's lunchtime conversations in the teachers' lounge.

But while the writing was not disagreeable, Bittner thought the classifications of ghosts, or images, that he'd set up were completely bogus. Bittner himself did not believe that the images conformed to any set categories; he could accept the idea certainly that it was the Event that had triggered the ghosts, but beyond that he found little to agree with. In his mind, there was no question at all that the ghosts were exactly that—ghosts—supernatural entities whose form and manner had specific purpose. Mary Greer appeared on his doorstep every morning because she was haunting him, period.

He had a glass of merlot with his steak and sipped it while turning the pages in Pescatelli's binder, thinking that it wasn't a lack of imagination really on Pescatelli's part that caused him to miss the forest for the trees; it was fear. A fear of the afterlife and what it all meant; that was why Pescatelli decided to dress up these very real specters in scientific guise. If Pescatelli could convince himself that the ghosts he saw all around him were not actually ghosts but mere traces of memory caught on a sort of atmospheric tape, why then, he didn't need to think about the sorts of questions that the reality of an afterlife would lead him to ask. The existence of an afterlife implied design. It implied heaven and hell, and it implied some sort of purpose, divine or otherwise, woven into the fabric of everyday life.

Chewing, August thought about his own situation. If Pescatelli was right, and the afterlife was a myth, then all of his ghosts were of no more import than an ancient, fading Polaroid. He wouldn't need to ask himself why Eva died. He didn't need to ask God why He'd taken her from him, and he didn't need to ask why he continued to suffer.

Sawing into his steak, August imagined Pescatelli tapping away on the keyboard of his computer, using his paragraphs as one would use bricks to wall out these questions. According to his theories, the Event was not the Hand of God extinguishing millions of souls, it was merely a transference of energy. The long-dead woman in his classroom was not a ghost, she was a byte of data recorded on unseen media. Wives, children, loved ones died because hearts stopped beating, not because of a plan that had all living beings encompassed within its form.

Rot, August thought, selecting a piece of steak that still had some of the fatty rind clinging to it.

We are haunted, he thought. We are haunted and we fulfill our appointed roles. God exists, but He is not the kindly benevolent God of Christian fairy tales; He is a destroying brute and bully, and He fashioned August in much the same image when He annihilated his daughter and canceled her existence before she'd lived a full life, and then He laughed in August's face. August knew that He was laughing still.

August had seen the ghosts and felt their cool touch inside himself, on his soul. He didn't fear the afterlife.

He welcomed it.

The afterlife, to him, represented another chance to be with his loved ones. If he didn't believe in an afterlife, all he had left were memories.

He took another bite of his steak and washed it down with the last swallow of merlot. Soon he would be driving home to Madeline.

God is good, he thought, the merlot turning bitter on his tongue.

‖‖ ‖‖ ‖‖ ‖‖
‖‖ ‖‖ ‖‖

Veronica turned the water on and immediately began thinking of topics to distract herself from the fact that she would soon be walking by Bittner's house. Topics like Kirk.

Kirk is a nice boy, she was thinking as she stepped under the warm spray of water, but . . .

She squirted a quarter-sized blob of shampoo into her hand and started working it into a lather in her hair. He was smart, he was funny, he was adventurous. All week he had been courteous and kind and enthusiastic about taking her ghost hunting over the weekend.

But . . .

He was cute. He was a good kisser. He didn't chew with his mouth open, and he didn't try to grope her in public places. Or private places. She liked him.

She turned toward the showerhead and accepted the needling spray on her face before letting it hit her hair again.

But . . .

She liked him. So what was the issue?

The issue was that Kirk was falling for her. Falling fast and hard in a spiral that could only have a hard, abrupt landing. She could see it in the soft-edged, goofy way he looked at her when he thought she wasn't paying attention. She could feel it in the hundred subtle ways he deferred to her when they were together. The door was always opened for her, she was always offered the seat out of the sun. He mentioned Chinese food and she mentioned pizza, so they would get a pizza.

Attachment. Suds were cascading down her face, and she wiped them away from her eyes. She wished that the boys she saw didn't become so . . . *attached* . . . so quickly. The attachment complicated things; it brought in a level of pressure that shouldn't be there. Not to mention commitment. She didn't want to be in a committed relationship right now, even if it was with someone like Kirk.

Not someone *like* Kirk, she thought. *Kirk.*

Kirk.

She really liked him, though. Running her fingers through her hair to shake the last of the bubbles out, she wondered if there were ways to slow things down so they could still see each other without Kirk falling so headlong. Although she'd had "the conversation" with boys before, she didn't think she'd perfected it yet. Sometimes they mistakenly thought it was the "just friends" speech, and either shut down completely or worked tirelessly and pathetically to change her mind, which was as easy as transmuting lead to gold.

"The conversation" was more about attachment; it was a warning but not a good-bye. At least that was how she'd always intended it to be. Would Kirk understand? Was she willing to risk it with him?

The more she thought about it, the more she decided that having the conversation at this point was not going to work.

Emotions move at their own speed.

She checked the clock before conditioning her hair. She had just enough time to finish up before Brian appeared, if he was going to appear again.

Maybe he was like the boys she dated, she thought. Petulant and hurt that she was spending time with someone else. Maybe he'd sensed Kirk and had gone off in a huff, disappearing forever into the ether. Why should ghost boys be any different than the living?

Or maybe, she thought, his heart had been broken forever when Mary was killed. Veronica reminded herself that she needed to find out what happened to him after Mary died.

When she was done, she shut off the water and dried her eyes on the towel hanging over the curtain rod. She peeked around the curtain, not knowing what made her feel more foolish, the idea that a ghost might be able to see her, or that she cared that he did.

She still had a minute. She watch two beads of water connect on the plastic shower curtain, become one, and accelerate downward. She looked up and he was there.

He was early, and even though she'd been waiting for him, his sudden appearance startled her, so much so that the curtain slid out of her grasp and billowed away from her. She shrieked and pulled it back, but she thought that in that brief moment of exposure, Brian had glanced up in the mirror and seen her.

Her cheeks were warm as she steadied herself to look at him again. He appeared as solid as the tile walls or the porcelain sink, and his reflection in the fogless mirror was so sharp she might have been staring at an LCD screen. He hadn't cast a reflection the first couple times she'd seen him, but now his reflection was there every time.

Veronica wondered what Mr. Pescatelli would make of Brian's "image." She watched Brian comb his hair, thinking that maybe there were hundreds of images out there that had strange or unique quirks, differences that didn't fit in with typical ghost behavior.

She glanced back at the clock just about the time Brian should be vanishing. Instead he dragged his comb through his hair one last time and then put the comb in his back pocket. His eyes locked on hers in the mirror, and once again she had the very odd sensation that he was seeing her. The sensation amplified when the nonchalance he'd exhibited while combing his hair was replaced by a look of deep concern.

He turned and moved toward her, crossing the tiny bathroom in a single step, his mouth forming words that she could not hear. The warm droplets of water still clinging to her skin frosted to an icy glaze. She gasped, pulling the thin curtain shut. She closed her eyes.

She opened them a moment later. There was no shadow on the curtain, nothing blocking the light from the twin fluorescents flanking the mirror above the sink. But would Brian cast a shadow? She'd never heard of a ghost casting a shadow. But then, no other ghost had ever cast a reflection that she knew of, and she didn't know of any ghosts who broke their pattern.

Brian is different, she thought. Her heart was beating like a flushed rabbit's, her throbbing pulse warming her frozen skin. She turned toward the clock. It was two minutes past the normal start of his appearance.

Her grip on the curtain tightened. The curtain was still warm, as though whatever icy cloud the ghost had been exuding had passed right through to touch only her. She counted to herself, certain that her heart would explode if she whisked the curtain back and found him standing there, his face inches from hers.

The rings holding the curtain chimed along the bar as she dragged the liner back. Brian was gone.

She used her bath towel to wipe away the frost from her skin before going into her room to change.

Her father was already at the kitchen table when she made it downstairs. Her mother gave her a reproachful look as she rushed into the kitchen. Veronica was at the counter biting into a bran muffin just as her dad smiled.

When he was gone, her mother turned and leaned against the sink.

"You almost missed him," she said.

"I'm sorry," Veronica said. The muffin was stale, and disintegrated over her plate. "Brian stayed a little longer than usual today."

"Brian?"

"The ghost upstairs," she said. "Sorry."

Her mother sniffed, running water to wash the dishes even though there weren't any yet. Veronica realized that her mother would never go upstairs to see Brian, because she wouldn't risk missing a moment with her husband's ghost.

Veronica poured herself some tea. "Mom?"

"What?"

"Maybe you don't need to be here every morning, you know?"

Her mother turned toward her, a spark of anger flashing in her eyes.

"Where else would I go?" she said, twisting the faucet off and walking out of the room.

Veronica listened to her mother slapping magazines and books onto the dining room table as she got her bag ready for work. She sat down at the kitchen table, across from where her father had been sitting a moment before, and sipped her tea, occasionally pressing a crumb of bran with her finger and bringing it to her mouth. She stared straight ahead and tried to summon the image of her father in her mind. How different her life would be if he had lived.

She wondered if she would miss him more if his ghost did not appear every day.

꧄ ꧄ ꧄ ꧄
꧄ ꧄ ꧄ I

I feel that I am playing a dangerous game; not for myself—for whom the danger is long past—but for her. She wants attachment; she wants something and someone that she can cling to. Someone who will remain when all else fails and fades.

That someone will never be me.

But what else can I do? Time flows like a river, and I can see the point where it meets the ocean. If I do nothing, he will kill her. He will likely kill her anyway, despite my best intentions— there are too many lines of convergence, too many intersections where old patterns will be allowed to repeat.

I listen to her speaking with her mother; the conversation is a familiar one, so familiar that not only the words but the pauses and the sighs in between are scripted and certain. I wish my influence was such that I could push them to vary the script. If Veronica embraced her mother, would that somehow add a new stitch to the fabric of the universe? Would that derail the chugging train of the inevitable?

Down the road, phantom atoms coalesce to form an after-image of my beloved, my Mary. Random bits of the universe assemble to form her shorts, her tank top, the dusky tan of her skin. I can vary my pattern—I can touch Veronica, I can touch Bittner—all it takes is concentration and energy. Do I then have the energy to be able to escape this house, this yard? Would I have the energy to change the past, my present, my future?

Down the road, the memory of Mary's sandaled foot treads upon the first of three steps.

‖‖‖ ‖‖‖ ‖‖‖ ‖‖‖
‖‖‖ ‖‖‖ ‖‖‖ ‖‖

"I'm going to look at her today," Janine said. This after several days of shuffling the entire way to school with her head down and eyes averted.

"Who?" Veronica replied.

"Mary. I'm going to look at Mary."

Janine was staring ahead, grim determination evident in the tight line of her lips and the defiant tilt of her chin. Veronica had been so lost thinking about her mother that she hadn't really noticed Janine's resolve when they'd met at the foot of the driveway.

"Oh?"

Janine nodded, the strings dangling from her hat bouncing vigorously. "I thought about what you said. About what Kirk said."

"What was that, Janine?"

"I don't want to be forgotten, either," she said.

From what Veronica could recall, it was Janine who'd talked about the images and not wanting to be forgotten, but she didn't correct her. Memory was a fluid, slippery thing as it was, and she couldn't say conclusively that the concept had been all Janine's.

Janine clutched Veronica's arm as they approached Bittner's house, and she could feel Janine's fingers plucking at her sleeve as they drew closer. Her head was lowered, but Veronica could see in profile that she had one wide blue eye trained on Bittner's porch just as Mary appeared. Janine didn't hurry by, as she normally did; instead she matched Veronica's steady pace.

They watched Mary climb the steps, and they watched her lift one tanned bare arm to knock. Janine did not turn away until she'd disappeared.

"You did it, Janine," Veronica said, tugging her closer and, on impulse, pressing her lips against the band of yarn above Janine's forehead. She was surprised that Mr. Bittner had not opened the door.

"I did it," Janine agreed. "I feel much, much better, I really do."

There were notes of pride in her voice, but she did not release Veronica's arm, not until they passed through the doorway to Montcrief High School.

Veronica was cool to Kirk when he met her in the hall before homeroom, but he either didn't notice or didn't jump to a hundred different and faulty conclusions like most boys would.

"Are you doing anything after school?" he said. Maybe he was completely oblivious.

"Why?" she said, like it was strange he would even ask.

"I was going to go record a few more ghosts. I thought you might want to come," he said.

"Sure," she said.

"Ronnie?" he said. "Is something wrong?"

She paused for a moment, debating briefly with herself

whether she should tell him more about her mother. She also debated telling him that he might not want to get too attached to her, because she had an allergy to attachments.

"No," she said. "Nothing's wrong." Then, "Oh, shoot. I just realized I have to work today. Are you working?"

"Nope," he said, obviously trying not to look or sound disappointed.

"I could use a ride home, though, if you have the car," she said.

"Sounds good," he said, brightening. He walked her to her homeroom.

She thought of Brian and Mary. Thinking of them made her wonder if it wasn't Kirk's attachment to her that was scary, but *her* feelings of attachment for *him*.

She glanced at him from the corner of her eye as they walked down the hallway together. He held his head high, but there wasn't anything arrogant about the way he carried himself.

I do like him, she thought.

It was a new feeling, this assurance—one she'd been able to prevent herself from having for other boys. But with it came something else as well—she realized that she *was* a little afraid.

They passed James in the hall. A look passed between the boys that Veronica couldn't decipher. They didn't greet each other but they didn't exactly avoid each other, either. Maybe the boys she knew were maturing, she thought.

"Okay," Kirk said when they reached her room, "I'll see you in the Fish's class."

"Bye," she said. He didn't try to kiss her—something that she hated to do on school grounds—or touch her arm or even gaze longingly into her eyes. She didn't know if she was relieved or disappointed.

Oh, Ronnie, she thought. Just what are you thinking?

August was not happy.

He wasn't happy because the meddling of Pescatelli and his amateur paparazzo had spoiled his appreciation of Mary Greer. He'd been working up his courage to touch her, to take her in his arms, but he did not want to risk being filmed while doing so. Pescatelli would have had a field day with that. And today, Veronica Calder and her timid friend were there, watching. Like they had timed their walk to coincide with Mary's appearance. Except Veronica wasn't watching the ghost girl. She had been watching for him, and he'd held his breath from behind the curtain like a frightened child.

Killing her was going to be a challenge now.

A bond had existed between him and his other girls, so it had been easy to lure and lull them into an almost soporific trust. Now Veronica was suspicious of him; he'd seen her in the hallway twice today, and on both occasions he'd caught her whispering like a conspirator with Kirk.

Bittner thought that maybe he'd kill Kirk as well. But, really, he didn't want any sons.

He was also irritated to find that he was actually intrigued by some of Pescatelli's theories. He'd never gone back to the mill, or to where he'd killed the runaway, but the idea that their ghosts might return with some frequency to where they died was an interesting one. He'd love to see them again.

More, he would love to touch them again.

$$\text{卌 卌 卌 卌}$$
$$\text{卌 卌 卌 III}$$

Kirk picked Veronica up and drove her home after work.

"I must have seen a dozen ghosts," she said, and Kirk just smiled. "It's amazing how many you see when you're looking for them. You could get a whole lot for your extra credit project just in the theater."

"Really? You think so?"

"There's tons of them. One in every theater, at least." She smelled like popcorn and sugar, and Kirk hoped she wouldn't notice how heavily he was breathing. "And in one of the theaters there was a ghost *couple*, you know? It was the weirdest thing. Two young people sitting together in the back of theater four. He had his arm around her shoulders, and she was leaning into him, like they were very much in love, or watching a scary movie, or both. I don't know that I've ever seen two ghosts . . . I'm sorry, I keep saying ghosts . . . I mean *images* . . . together like that. You know?"

Kirk nodded, but Veronica wasn't looking at him. She was more interested in waving to a group of her coworkers leaving the building as they pulled away.

"All I could think was that maybe they died together on their way home from the movie. In a car accident or something.

But then later on, when I was pouring someone's soda—and Kirk, pouring soda has got to be one of the dullest jobs ever, but we get so busy that my boss needs to put one person just on sodas—I thought, wouldn't it be amazing if they *didn't* die together? Like, what if they'd died years later from that moment, separate and apart, but that was the moment their spirits chose to return to?"

"Well . . ." Kirk began, but Ronnie kept rolling. She'd been in some strange moods since he'd had dinner at her house, alternately pensive and distant and then talkative and curious.

"Those people could have died anywhere, anytime, and now they're together again in the theater. There was some stupid war movie playing, but I didn't see them until cleanup between the first and second evening shows. What if that was their last date? What if they got in such a terrible fight on the way home that they never saw each other again? What if what remains in the theater is not their ghosts, but the ghost of their relationship? I really can't get them out of my mind, it's the strangest thing."

Kirk cleared his throat. "It certainly sounds strange."

"Mmm. I don't know whether I should feel really happy for them or really sad, you know?"

"Go with happy," he said. "It makes things easier."

"Yeah," she said, her voice trailing off wistfully. "I guess."

He sensed the sadness in her, and tried to think of something to say, but it was Veronica who broke the silence.

"Speaking of happy and sad, guess what I found out?" she said.

He smiled at her. "What did you find out?"

"Brian Delaney and Mary Greer were an item." She told

him everything she'd discovered with Janine.

"That's pretty amazing," he said.

"Yeah. And oh, we saw another ghost in the library. A youngish-looking boy, kinda bookwormy."

"Libraries, schools, and theaters," Kirk said, thinking out loud. "Hospitals, factories. Places most likely to be haunted."

"Maybe it has to do with what places like that represent," she said. "Doorways to other worlds. Places to open your mind."

"That's a really interesting theory." He tapped the wheel with his thumbs. "Maybe those are all places where people enter a different state of consciousness. The Fish believes in 'psychic residue.' Some emotions and actions leave behind more of a trace, sort of like the afterimage you get behind your eyelids after seeing a blinding light. Who knows?"

They were quiet for a moment.

"Do you want to be a ghost when you die?" Veronica asked eventually.

The question made the hackles on Kirk's neck rise.

"What?" he said.

"An image. Whatever," she said. "I used to think it would be awful, having strangers staring at a piece of your life. Now I'm not so sure. Now I'm thinking it might be nice to have some part of you remain."

"I guess it depends," Kirk said. He was thinking of the image of Molly in the library.

"Yeah," Veronica said, and Kirk wondered if she was thinking of Brian and Mary. "I guess it does."

"Do you have any big plans this weekend?"

"Nothing big. Why?"

"I've got a few more ghosts to check out," he said. "I've got to warn you, though. It might get scary."

He'd meant it to sound flirtatious, but Ronnie, probably still thinking of Mary and Brian, looked unnerved.

"Oh? Why's that?" she said.

"The ghosts I'll be looking for are murder victims," he said, wishing he'd never opened his mouth. Why couldn't he have just asked her to go bowling or skating or something?

"Lovely," she said. "I should be free Saturday around three."

"Excellent. I'll get you then."

He drove into her driveway and put the car in park. She reached behind to get her backpack, and Kirk watched her stretch.

"Thanks for the ride," she said. He leaned forward and kissed her as she turned to open the door, catching her along the cheek. Surprised, she turned back and kissed his cheek in reply. Reflexively, he lifted his hand, and she placed her own hand against his. Their fingers interlaced, as though they were assuring each other that they weren't ghosts themselves. The touch seemed far more intimate than the kisses.

Once she was out of the car, Kirk didn't think she was going to look back, but she did, waving after unlocking her kitchen door.

He drove away, tingling with the memory of their contact.

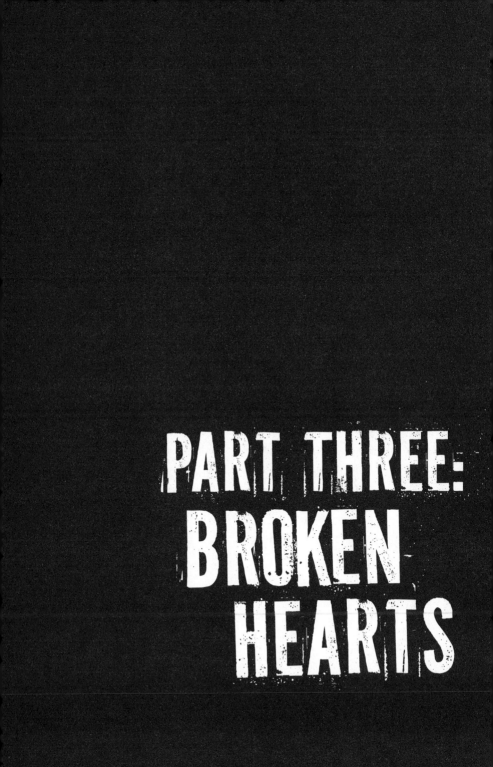

PART THREE:
BROKEN
HEARTS

||||| ||||| ||||| |||||
||||| ||||| ||||| ||||

August left his home around six o'clock. He'd killed Amber almost four years ago, sometime between seven and eight, he wasn't quite sure. Her death occurred after the Event, and there wasn't the necessity to be as precise back then. Was it really so long ago already? Years passing in leaps and bounds. It seemed like yesterday that she'd breathed her last breath on his face. The memory made him smile.

His disposition had improved considerably since the school week had ended. Pescatelli had avoided him completely but had stopped by his room after the last class had let out.

"So, Gus," he'd said, as though they didn't loathe each other. "Did you get a chance to read any of my book?"

"Some," August replied. "I had reports to correct as well."

"Well?" Pescatelli said, a little expectant, a little hostile.

"The section I read was . . . interesting," he said.

"Interesting?"

"I haven't read it all yet."

"Interesting."

"For the most part. I'm not sure that I can accept all your theories, though."

Pescatelli smiled, as though he'd lured August into a trap.

"That's why I need Kirk to shoot the films," he said. "I need to shore up my points in the book. I gave him a list of every ghost I knew of in town."

Idiot, August thought. Pescatelli is an idiot. But he nodded, content to let Pescatelli think he'd won a valuable hill in their war of wills.

"As you say," he said, latching his case. "Maybe I'll get to the rest of it this weekend."

He took his hat and coat from the closet and was surprised to see Pescatelli still slouched in his doorway.

Pescatelli licked his lips and stepped aside.

"Have a good weekend, Gus," he said, all the air gone out of his voice.

"Take care," August said, and his good mood returned, just like that.

That was yesterday. It was now officially the weekend and he still hadn't read any more of Pescatelli's foolish manuscript.

He drove downtown and left his car in the commuter lot by the train station. The trains were running again, but with the city no longer a stop on their route, they seemed rather pointless—a gesture of nostalgia, or worse, defiance. Whoever—or whatever—had orchestrated the Event was unlikely to be impressed by such a minuscule display of pluck or perseverance. What good was a commuter train when there was nowhere but other towns as forlorn and suburban as their own?

He'd killed Amber, his third and most recent victim, in the basement of the thread mill. She had not been a student of his. They'd met at the homeless shelter downtown, where, ironically, August had begun volunteering to try to work off some of the guilt that had been accruing since he'd killed Mary. Madeline began talking to him about Amber the moment he'd started volunteering, around the holiday season, letting him know that February 29 was only a few months away.

The mill was a short walk from the shelter—through the town and then along a road overgrown from disuse. Across the railroad tracks. August had killed Amber there after convincing her that the mill was a popular place for homeless people to camp in the winter. They could do an especially good deed, he said, by delivering a box of winter coats to the people who sheltered there. Amber, like Mary before her, was too pure of heart to expect anything but the noblest of intentions from a kindly, well-known history teacher. With Madeline whispering in his ear the entire time, he'd asked Amber if she was frightened to go to the mill. And, irony upon irony, she'd replied that she wasn't afraid of anyone when she was with someone as big as him.

A northbound train had rumbled outside the mill after she was dead, shaking dust down from the exposed wood beams in a gray rain that collected in the brim of August's hat. At the time he'd thought it was God descending. Amber's body was discovered three days later by a homeless man recently released to society after the state mental hospital closed its doors. Darryl Kosoff admitted to having committed the crime, if only because incarceration meant he would be better fed, cleaner, and more well rested than he had been in years, the prison being more comfortable for short- or long-term stays than the mental health facilities. The police never bothered to search for anyone else, as Mr. Kosoff had a history of violence, and had assaulted a young nurse while undergoing psychiatric treatment at the state hospital. Against Mr. Kosoff's wishes, his intrepid young attorney argued that the impressions and bruises made on the young lady's throat could not have been made by Mr. Kosoff, who, it turned out, had small hands. The attorney gathered some of the best forensic experts in the field to make his case, and good thing, because the rats from the river down below had already been at the poor girl. But Kosoff was shot dead after a trip to court by the girl's father five months after being arrested, thus saving the state a long and protracted trial. The father killed himself not long after. Bittner felt bad about that.

He remembered Amber's death vividly. He'd choked her with both hands, until her struggles grew faint, and then he held his flashlight up to her face with his left hand while ending her life with his right.

He tried to imagine what her last moments were like for her, as he crouched above her, trying to catch a glimpse of Eva dancing in her eyes. She would have been blinded, her vision filled with his light, as though it were beckoning her forth.

It must have been like being born, he thought.

He couldn't wait to see her again. To touch her. Touching her would give him vitality; it would lace his blood with electricity. He would try to touch as many of them, his daughters, as he could. Their force would pass into him and give him strength for what he had to do, and perhaps having them within him would help him draw his Eva from the other side and ensure that she would flow from there into Veronica's body.

He was certain he was going to find her here; she'd never

visited his home, like Mary did. But he was sure because Madeline told him he would. She knew about such things.

"Kiss her for me, August." It was the last thing she'd said before sending him out the door. "Kiss her for me."

Just a short walk, a little less than a mile, all told. Traffic was sparse, the halogen bulbs of the streetlights were just beginning to hum. His gloved hands were thrust deep in the pockets of his coat, and he flexed them until his knuckles popped.

He started whistling an aimless tune.

‎‎‎IIII IIII IIII IIII
IIII IIII IIII IIII

"I can't believe I let you talk me into this," Veronica said, and she really couldn't. "Isn't it illegal to be out here?"

The crumbling brick facade of the mill came into view. People used to discuss making it into an office building, then they'd considered converting it to condominiums. Now when people talked about it, if they talked about it at all, they talked about demolishing it.

"Probably," Kirk said. "I don't think we'll get arrested or anything. Least, I hope not. My parents wouldn't post bail."

"My mom would," Veronica said. "For me."

"I had the impression that your mother liked me," he said.

Kirk parked the car at the far edge of the lot under an overhang of branches. He noticed Veronica raising an eyebrow at him.

"Getting ideas, Mr. Lane?" She had to admit, the illicitness of what they were about to do was sort of exciting, as was the fact that Kirk didn't even look nervous.

"I always have ideas," he said. "But right now my only idea is to keep the car from being spotted. No need to tempt fate." He killed the engine.

Veronica looked back at the mill, to the brick, faintly luminescent in the moonlight. Most of the windows were boarded up poorly, revealing an impenetrable darkness behind the gaps in the slats. If any building was haunted, the Slader Thread Mill was.

"Looks spooky," Veronica said.

"I'm sure it's filled with ghosts," Kirk replied. "Then again, the whole town is filled with ghosts. The whole country, maybe."

"So comforting."

"You can't really be scared. You live with two of them. You're even related to one."

They pushed their car doors closed rather than slamming, but even so, the sound was like gunshots in the stillness of the night. A main thoroughfare was only about half a mile up a curving access road, but the occasional noise of traffic was far away.

They were quiet as they walked across the lot toward the mill. The moonlight disappeared, as though God had flipped a switch. Veronica looked to the sky expecting to see a big cloud swallowing the moon, but all she saw was darkness.

She counted a half dozen "No Trespassing" signs, a few of which promised prosecution to violators. At least two of the signs had bullet holes in them. Kirk tried the doors, but they were locked.

"Nobody home," Veronica said. "Let's go."

"There's got to be a way in somewhere," he said. "If a drunken hobo could find his way in, I'm sure sharp teens like ourselves can."

"Maybe he had better motivation."

"You aren't really scared, are you?" Kirk said, playing his light along the facade of the building. The windows had all been smashed out and boarded up years ago, and on the second floor there was one window where the plywood had come completely away from the wall.

"Of course not."

"I wonder if I could climb up there."

"Not even if you were Spider-Man," Veronica said. "Seven o'clock and it is black as ink out here. I swear February is the darkest month. We won't even be able to see the image if it shows up."

"It is kind of overcast. Let's walk around to the back," he said. "We'll find a way in."

"Nice of Mr. Pescatelli to help you commit crimes," she said, following him down a hillock of crumbling rock.

"Maybe he'd bail me out. Especially if I named him as the criminal mastermind."

"He's a teacher, dummy," she said. "He couldn't afford it."

"Good point."

The back of the mill faced the river, which was at the bottom of a steep slope just beyond the railroad tracks. Veronica took a moment to gaze at the black and stagnant water. Farther down it glittered, reflecting the city lights. A single boat chugged upriver, a bluish light at its prow. She turned back to tell Kirk to be careful with his flashlight, but he'd already switched it off. He was standing beside a chest-high window where the planking had been torn away.

"I'll help you in," he said. She was still wearing the long skirt she'd gone to school in.

"Great. What a gentleman. How do we know there's a floor beneath?"

"The floor looks okay. Tell you what, I'll check it out."

"I wonder who took the plywood off," she said.

"Hoboes. They're everywhere. Either that or teenagers." He boosted himself up and leaned over the ledge until he could get his left leg up and over. His light cut through the darkness, revealing only a dusty plank floor and thick wooden columns spaced out every thirty feet or so.

"*We're* teenagers, dummy."

"Hoodlum teenagers," he said. "Kids who come out and drink and do drugs and . . ."

And have sex, was what he was going to say, but Veronica's look cut him off. He swung his other leg over and dropped beneath the sill. His light went out.

"Kirk?"

He popped up, startling her.

"Floor's fine," he said, grinning.

"Idiot. How are we going to do this?"

He sat on the window ledge and slid back down to the ground beside her. "I'll cup my hands, you step into them. I'll hoist you up far enough to get a leg over. The floor is higher inside, so going out is going to be a breeze."

"Great."

She got it on the first try, and he followed. Once inside, she sneezed twice as the dust hit her nostrils.

"Spooky," she said.

"Yeah," Kirk said, switching on the light. "Good thing, though, about all this plywood over the windows, because if it was just glass, people would be able to see our light."

"What are we going to do if there are people in here?" she said. "Like, real people?"

"Hoboes, you mean?"

"Whatever."

"Run, I guess. I'll go slow. Or maybe I'll speed up and go get help."

"Ha. I could outrun you any day."

She held his hand as they shuffled through the warehouse.

"We're looking for stairs going down. He killed her in the cellar."

"The cellar, beautiful," she said, hugging herself. The air in the mill was cold and dry, the tang of wood dust filling her nostrils.

"I wonder where Bittner was when Amber was killed."

Veronica looked at Kirk, but his expression was unreadable in the gloom. Was he deliberately trying to frighten her?

"What makes you say that?"

He shrugged. "I don't know. Amber was strangled. Mary was strangled, her neck broken. I wonder if Amber was one of his students. Do you remember when that happened?"

"I remember."

"I don't, at all. I'd forgotten about it completely until I saw her name on the list, and even then when I read about Amber I didn't connect that it only happened four years ago."

"You aren't a girl," Veronica said. "Maybe we notice things like that more."

"Maybe."

"He's really frightening me, Kirk."

"He really freaked out about us filming Mary. Guilty conscience, you think?"

Veronica squeezed his hand, but the movement was bereft of any romantic spirit. "What if he did, Kirk? What if he killed her? And Amber, too?"

"According to the files Fish gave me, Amber was killed by some crazy homeless guy who gave a full confession. He was shot and killed by her father, coming out of the courthouse."

"Really? I didn't remember that."

"Scout's honor."

"Even if Bittner didn't do it, there's something wrong with him. Seriously wrong," Veronica said.

She had a very uneasy feeling, the sort she'd get just before a ghost would appear. "Is this really going to be enough light to see her by?" she asked. "I'm guessing the basement, when we find it, is going to be pretty big. We'll have a lot of ground to cover."

"They found her in the northeast corner," he said. "Which would be the on the river side, by where we came in. All we'll have to do is orient ourselves from wherever the entrance to the basement is."

"Well, I guess you've just thought of everything," she said. "We've got a two-hour window for her to arrive?"

"Two and a half," he said. "Starting in thirteen minutes. That was the closest that the police could come to estimating time of death. She'd been dead for a week or so when they found her."

"Ick."

Veronica checked the time on her cell phone. She was about to say something else when Kirk announced that he'd found the stairs.

"See them?" he said. "Someone took the door off the hinges."

They walked to the edge of the stairwell. Freezing, moist air came from below, like breath.

"Ladies first," Kirk said, smiling.

Veronica took the challenge and stepped out onto the creaking wooden stair.

August felt his good mood evaporate the moment he saw the light darting along the crumbling foundation of the mill. He was beginning to feel thwarted, as though some dark, divine hand was purposefully interceding to keep him from communing with his ghosts.

Whistling no longer, he moved to the side of the path and into the underbrush to get a closer look. The light fluttered like a hummingbird, and August could see that there were two figures moving along. He squinted, taking care to make as little sound as possible. The other was a girl. He realized that it was Kirk and Veronica.

He spat into the dirt, slow anger burning hot in his veins. The amateur ghost hunters on yet another errand for Stephen Pescatelli. Was he still supposed to believe that the filming of his house was just some random accident? The theory may not have been stated in the pages of his book, but it was clear that Pescatelli was an armchair detective who suspected August of committing crimes.

Crimes that he had, in fact, committed.

He wasn't sure what made him more angry, Pescatelli's meddling, or these situations putting Veronica's virtue at risk. August would bet hard money that the backpack the boy was carrying just happened to have a blanket in it, and when he found a place that was secluded, with maybe a few slivers of moonlight peeking through hastily nailed window boards, he'd spread it out and ask Veronica if she'd like to take a break from hunting spirits. With boys, there is always only one goal.

The branch August had been gripping snapped with a loud crack, which echoed in the night. He looked down at it, wondering when he'd picked it up. Certain he'd been discovered, he looked up in time to see that Kirk and Veronica had moved around to the back of the building.

There was a wide open space of scrubby land between where he stood and the mill, and he hurried across it as soon as their light was hidden from view. They were headed for the basement, no doubt on a tip from Pescatelli. He knew a quicker way—he'd been here before, after all, and intended to be there, in the dark, before they arrived.

"I've got a blanket," Kirk said, reaching into his backpack.

Of course you do, Veronica thought, watching him spread it on the slab floor. He set the flashlight on the blanket.

"I figure we could hang out here until she shows," he said. "Or doesn't show, whatever the case."

Veronica smoothed a corner of the blanket down with the toe of her sneaker.

"And what do you propose we do until she appears?" she said. "Tell ghost stories?"

"I brought a couple drinks, too," Kirk said. "Iced tea for you. We can tell ghost stories if you like." He checked his camera before setting it gently on the blanket beside him, and patted his shirt pocket.

"Extra batteries," he said. "For the camera. And for the flashlight."

"Great."

"Aren't you going to sit down?"

"Oh, I guess so."

Kirk looped an arm around Veronica's shoulders, hoping to warm her. Two hours was an awfully long time to wait, but he had some ideas about how they could occupy themselves.

"I should have you read some of the Fish's book. He's got a chapter on 'old-time' ghosts and ghost hunting. He said people used to believe that ghosts drew electrical energy from appliances and batteries and stuff to get the energy to manifest. That's why people always had an excuse for not being able to get any actual physical evidence of a haunting, because when the ghosties finally did appear, they sucked the power cells of the cameras and tape recorders dry. Cell phones and watches would croak, too."

"We're going to have a hard time finding our way out of here if that happens," Veronica said.

"It won't happen," Kirk said. "Pescatelli tells these stories to debunk the traditional ideas of ghosts. Think about the images you've seen: do they seem to do anything like suck energy? Your dad? Do the lights flicker, or does the coffeemaker go on the fritz? Nope. Nada. The images don't have any physical effects at all. They are like movie projections."

"Brian makes the bathroom cold."

Veronica could feel Kirk staring at her, although she couldn't see him because he'd pointed his light over to a flat patch of flooring in front of an oversized furnace, which was where the Fish's notes told them Amber had died.

"Really?"

She nodded, and then said yes when she realized that he couldn't see her in the gloom. "He defogs the mirror. And when I go over to where he was standing, I feel a cool tingling on my skin."

"Seriously?" Kirk said, shifting his weight against her.

"He casts a reflection, too."

"Too weird. I really need to sleep at your house so I can see him."

"Or you could just give me the camera," she said. "Or I could use my own."

Kirk must have turned toward her then, because Veronica could feel his spearmint-scented breath on her cheek.

"That's no fun."

"Says the guy who brings his date to a grimy abandoned warehouse where a teenage girl was murdered."

"Hey," he said. "*This* is fun."

He leaned in and kissed her. His mouth was warm.

August Bittner could hear every word they said, even though they were whispering. He could even hear the sound of them kissing.

Damn him, he thought.

He was standing behind a battered wooden workbench not twenty feet from where they sat. He watched their flashlight do a tight, slow roll, its faint glow cutting a round hole in the darkness.

The one question in his mind—should he kill her now? It would not be the 29th for a few days, and he'd never killed one of them ahead of schedule. Or should he instead just kill Kirk and subdue her? Could he keep her here for days without anyone knowing?

Twenty feet. He could run the distance and be on the boy before they could react. Or he could drift in slowly and not take the chance of alerting them in any way. The boy he would beat to death, bashing his brains out on the concrete floor. But Veronica . . . Veronica he would have to capture. He couldn't risk killing her early, he decided.

Part of him wanted to forget the whole thing, but the anger he felt was such that he knew it would only be cooled if he took action.

Twenty steps. He took two, treading with care. The light had stopped curling, but the couple was still kissing, or maybe worse. Eighteen more steps and he could strike the boy. But what if Stephen knew that they were here? What then? Would their bodies be discovered quickly? What if he were to hide them? The boy's death was sure to be a bloody one, even if he took care. August would have to dispose of his coat and gloves, at the very least, if he was going to kill him that way.

Sixteen steps. August stopped as his shoes rasped against something, a screw or piece of metal on the stone floor. He stopped, but the young couple was oblivious. He could see their legs and shoes in the glow of the light.

Fourteen steps.

But how else could he dispose of the boy? He hadn't come prepared for murder, nor had he planned for it, as he had for

Amber. He could strangle him. But he knew that choking him until air had ceased would make him a part of his family, and he did not want him for his child; just the girl. And how could he kill both at once? Strangling required effort; it wasn't as simple as pulling a trigger or inserting a knife. Struggle was involved, and strength. They said that Mary Greer's neck was broken, and he supposed that had happened, but even so she'd taken a good five minutes to die.

Twelve steps. Eleven.

His fault Mary had taken so long, mostly. Could he get Veronica out of the mill and bring her home? Not on foot. He could carry her, but his car was too far away. He'd just have to act and trust that things would work out the way he needed them to.

Eight steps.

Such a pretty girl.

Seven.

And then she screamed, and the rafters trembled and shook with the echo of her voice.

Later, Veronica would remember hearing the flapping, like the wings of a hundred bats, or whipping sails in a tacking breeze. Kirk would tell her that the sound was a passing train. But that wasn't what she'd heard or felt; she'd felt a wing graze her cheek. She saw something scrabbling backward in the glow of Kirk's flashlight.

"Shit!" Kirk said, and Veronica realized her scream must be ringing in his ears, even above the typhoon of wings. He reached for his flashlight but put his hand on her stomach instead. Her leg flailed out and sent his flashlight rolling away, and in the spinning light she saw Amber.

She was two feet from where they'd sat and was on her back, pushing herself with her hands and feet. Veronica caught just a glimpse of her face, at eyes that were bulging, at a tongue that was extended fully from an open mouth. She tried to untangle herself from Kirk, and in the process felt her shin collide solidly in the last place he wanted to be hit.

"Sorry!" she said.

The light went wild, but there was a bluish glow, like a black light painting, of the girl, who was still moving backward, her jerky movements like the scuttling of a crab robbed of a few of its limbs.

Then the light winked out.

She heard a nearby clatter that could mean he'd dropped his camera. She heard him curse as she scrabbled for the flashlight in the darkness.

Finally, she found and stuck it with the palm of her hand a few times before trying the switch. She almost cried out with relief when the light turned on.

She aimed the light and saw the ghost. Although the ghost's attacker was not visible, it was clear she was being strangled. Her bare belly was indented as though a weight was pressed upon it, and Veronica could see her neck constricting like a sponge. The girl made an attempt to remove the unseen murderous hands, but lost hope quickly and tried some faint punches.

The girl, her eyes like Ping-Pong balls as she managed to lift her arm, was pointing. Right at Veronica.

Veronica tried to hold the light steady while she screamed for Kirk.

August ran when Amber pointed at him. When she first appeared, he was confused, he was exhilarated; but when she pointed at him he was actually frightened. And so he ran.

Someone was shaking him, someone was saying his name. His breath came to him with a sudden rush.

"Kirk?" Veronica said. "Kirk, are you okay?"

He groaned, trying to focus in the dismal light.

"Kirk?"

"What . . . what . . ." He knew he was babbling, but couldn't help himself. He'd been slugged, he was almost sure of it. Something was bothering him, something beyond the knock he took.

Veronica sagged with relief. "We're still in the basement, Kirk. At Slader Mill. You fainted."

"Fainted, my eye," he said, rubbing his jaw, which looked red even in the spectral illumination provided by his flashlight. "You clocked me one. Two, if you count the kick in the groin."

"I'm sorry, Kirk," she said. "I'm sorry. I felt myself hit you once. In the, um, soft parts."

"You nailed my jaw, too."

"Really?" She played the light on his face, gasping when the power cut without warning to half the illumination.

"Yeah, really." He ignored the faded light. "Was it something I said?" He clicked his jaw from side to side.

"I'm sorry," she said again, kissing him where a bruise had begun to rise along the bone. "Poor baby."

"Mmmm. Thanks."

"So," she said, releasing him and handing him the light. "Did you get her on film?" Calling the image "her" brought back the harrowing image of the girl being strangled, the fear-mad eyes, the accusing finger.

"You're joking, right? I barely even saw her." He slapped the flashlight as though trying to coax more wattage into the bulb.

"It was horrible," Veronica said. She looked like she was having trouble breathing herself. Kirk watched as she brought her hand to her own throat. "Please, let's get out of here."

"Good idea," he said. It wasn't until they were outside that he realized what was bothering him.

"Ronnie," he said. "That isn't my flashlight."

Veronica looked down at the light, gripping it as though it were a living thing that could twist around and bite her wrist.

ⲓⳁⳁⳁ ⳁⳁⳁ ⳁⳁⳁ ⳁⳁⳁ ⳁⳁⳁ ⳁⳁⳁ ⳁⳁⳁ ⳁⳁⳁ |

August waited for twenty minutes in a convenience store down the road from the mill until the boy's car passed by. The thin man at the counter watched him with arms folded, and August bought two Table Talk Pies to allay his suspicion. As the man bagged up his purchases, one blueberry, one apple, August realized it was exactly this type of situation that enabled law enforcement officials to capture criminals. *Yes, officer*, he thought, *tall man with gray coat, black gloves, and black hat. He came in twenty minutes ago; all alone. Bought two pies.*

August wondered if Kirk or Veronica had seen him in the confusion. Certainly Veronica had not, so intent was she on watching a replay of a life ending that she had no fear for her own. The boy might have. Might have. August didn't think so, however. His fist had shot out with such speed and accuracy, coming in from the side as Kirk was patting around for his camera, that the boy had no opportunity to defend himself. Maybe he'd wake up remembering the stinging kiss of the leather glove, but then again maybe he would reason that it was Veronica's sneaker connecting with his jaw.

August knew that if he was going to get another opportunity to kill Veronica he'd have to make it on his own. The problem was that he'd always relied on providence to provide him with a daughter; either that or he relied on Madeline's constant urging. Some planning would not be a bad thing, though. He could solve the little conundrums of how to cover the mess and dispose of the evidence, etcetera, that way. And he could focus on the girl—his girl—and not have to kill the boy as well. Killing the boy would be just wasted effort.

An effort he would have made, surely, if it hadn't been for Amber's ghost.

How strange the mixture of sadness and elation at seeing her again. He hadn't really allowed himself to believe that she would still be there, repeating her death; he'd been fortunate enough just to have Mary. . . . But there she was, just as she'd been in their final moments together.

With one difference. That night, she hadn't pointed.

He was sure of it. That night, there had been light from parking lot lights, long since smashed, filtering through the boards and the gaps in the foundation where the casement windows had been kicked out. When Amber realized they were not on a mission of mercy, she tried to scratch August, to claw at his eyes, but he'd slapped her hard, and her struggles grew weaker. She'd managed to push with her legs, enough to propel herself a few feet, but then he had his knee on her stomach and held her still.

She hadn't been able to lift her head off the floor, toward the end, much less her arms. She did not point. He was sure of it. They were alone in the basement. There was nothing to point at.

It had startled him, her pointing. He had just been about to clamp his hands around Veronica's neck, and then Amber had to go and point at him. Veronica, thankfully, had not turned around. He began backing away as soon as he'd seen the accusing finger.

Was it really accusing, though? Or was it *beckoning*?

She had frightened him, but at the same time he'd wanted to touch her again. His daughter. His original purpose had not been to murder, but to see Amber again and touch her and to feel her coolness on him as she vanished. He wanted to let her know that he still thought about her.

Mary was denied him this morning, Amber this night. He was denied killing Veronica; denied, denied, denied. Denied everything but pie. Pie he would not eat. How much denial can one man take? Not much, not nearly this much.

He walked back down toward the town with his pies, thinking how strange it all was. When he got home, he did something he had not done in some time—he went upstairs into the study where his wife had hung herself from the ceiling fan, and where she was hanging still.

August watched her, a dark form in a dark room swaying slightly, as though tossed like a leaf by the whirl of wind created by the fan's spinning blades. He felt no such wind, because fifteen years ago, when he'd tried to untie her, the fan and body both came crashing down from the ceiling. He'd never replaced the fixture, and so the rope that now held Madeline aloft was tethered to nothing; it just hung in empty space.

"You failed," she said, her words thick with bitterness and recrimination, her head nearly at a right angle to the floor.

He walked to the drapes to make sure they were closed snug and tight.

"I have not been a good father to our children, Madeline," he said, looking up at her. He was nearly sobbing. "I have not held them. I have not held them and told them not to be afraid of the dark."

"You are less than a man," she said, ignoring his pain, the way she always did. Her feet spun in a wider arc than her shoulders.

"Not suitable for fatherhood," he said. "I have not held them, as I should have held you." Looking up and spreading his arms wide, he stepped into the path of her dangling torso, closing his arms in an embrace as the icy sensation made the hairs on his arm stand up, even though he had not yet taken off his gloves, his coat, or his hat.

"Do not touch me," she said. "I loathe you."

He stood there, holding the memory of her, for some hours.

꜀꜀꜀ ꜀꜀꜀ ꜀꜀꜀ ꜀꜀꜀

꜀꜀꜀ ꜀꜀꜀ ꜀꜀꜀ ꜀꜀꜀

||

Some days, I can see her. My Mary.

Everything takes effort, everything takes energy. I know this is true for the living, but for the dead, effort is required literally to hold one's self together. Without the effort, we begin to dissipate. I can feel myself going like a pill dropped into a glass of water. I wonder sometimes if that is the fate of all of us who don't cross the bridge, an existence of slow erosion and decay.

I'm strongest where in life I was weakest. I return there, to the bathroom where I ended my life, when the cost of exertion has been too much, after I've spent myself.

I saw Mary after following Veronica to the door. Grief clung to the walls like a new coat of paint that day; Veronica and her mother were both crying as they watched the shade of her father—who is like me but not like me, like them but not like them—fade away. Veronica was crying but her mother had no consolation for her because she could not find any for herself. I reached out for Veronica, but my hand passed through her hair, doing no more than causing her to shiver as she headed out the door. It slammed as I pressed myself into one of the panes of glass, where an observant eye could have seen me as a reflection of light from an invisible source.

Veronica was joined by her nervous friend at the foot of her driveway. I believed her affection and devotion to Janine might be evidence of a greater good. My intention was to cling to this sentiment, to draw strength from it, when I saw something that caused that trace of feeling to bloom within me.

Mary. I watched Mary appear at Bittner's house, at the foot of his steps. She turned toward my house as though she knew she would find me at the window. She was smiling. Then she began to ascend the steps, and she was lost.

I pushed through the door. I could feel the sunlight coursing through me as I sped, determined that I would not lose her, not again. But it wasn't the sunlight that was coursing through me, it was my own energy fissioning away in accelerated half-life. I had bled myself out of existence before I'd reached the driveway.

I reassembled days later, and at the appointed hour I saw her, and again I tried to keep Mary from continuing on her path. I was exploding like a sun, and this time Veronica must have heard my cry of rage and pain, because she turned at the moment. Mary never did. Mary kept walking.

I don't know if she is like me, or if she is like Veronica's father at the table. I don't know, precisely, if there are any like me. I've seen a young man in the tree that shades the driveway across the street; he arrives just after midnight and remains visible for no more than a handful of seconds. I don't believe that he has ever been seen by anyone still alive. Can it be called a haunting if the only one haunted is a fellow ghost?

My death has brought me an entirely new vocabulary. I've given up most of my memories; perhaps memories were atoms that I cast off. I don't ever remember thinking about what death meant when I was alive; maybe if I had, I wouldn't have done what I did.

I don't remember much of my life anymore.

Except for Mary.

If I could leave this house, this yard. If I could touch her shade, if only for a moment, I would be free. The bridge would open for me, and I would take her hand and we would cross together.

Unless, as I hope, she has already passed over, and the girl who smiles at me from so far away is really just a memory. I would rather that be the case than imagine her trapped, as I am, in between.

Veronica's mother is standing beside the kitchen table. She reaches out to the air where his image appears, tentatively, as though she expects to be burned. Her hand flutters. Her expression makes me think she is the one in between.

I dwell upon love. It is easy for me to do so, having just seen both Mary and Veronica. I imagine love and contemplate and feel it until the point that I *am* it; it is all I can do. And Veronica's mother, she can feel it as I drift through her. She draws a sharp breath as I leave her, and for that moment she feels love, thinks it is him, and I carry out with me another piece of her grief, a tiny nugget of sadness etched from the wall of her soul. It is all I can do. For now, it is enough.

It costs me. I'm spent. I'm spiraling away. But even as I scatter, I sense new possibility, because I have acted, and have reached out from the in-between, and again my spectral touch has altered the course of a day.

And then, I'm nothing again.

ⅡⅠ

Ⅲ⊦ Ⅲ⊦ Ⅲ⊦ Ⅲ⊦
Ⅲ⊦ Ⅲ⊦ Ⅲ⊦ Ⅲ⊦
Ⅲ

Veronica woke up early even though her matinee shift was still hours away. She'd fallen asleep quickly, and her dreams were replays of what she and Kirk had gone through the previous night. Except it wasn't Amber scrambling backward in the sawdust, her fingernails etching trails in the grimy planks. It was her. And the assailant with his hands on her throat was unseen no longer; he gazed down upon her as she was dying, with a gray light in his eyes and an expression of perfect love on his face.

"Bittner," she'd said, whispered it, actually. She'd said the name out loud to Kirk last night, and this time he had not disagreed. He'd driven her home, and on the way brought his mother's car to a crawl as they passed by Mr. Bittner's house, his Cadillac conspicuously absent from the drive.

"What are we going to do, Ronnie?" Kirk had said.

She was terrified beyond belief. She'd felt Bittner's hands on her throat even then, and the feeling filled her with rage.

"Evidence," she'd said, her voice a dry croak. "We need to get the evidence. He's not going to stop."

"Ronnie . . ."

"We have to go back, Kirk," she'd said. "He'll kill me if we

231

don't get something on him."

Kirk didn't know what to say after that. He hugged her, saw her to the door, and drove home.

That night, once the sound of Kirk's car had faded into the distance, Veronica spent some time on the Internet looking for Brian Delaney. There wasn't much to find, just a few articles on the *Jewell City Sentinel* Web site concerning his exploits on the junior varsity basketball team: "Delaney Scores Twenty in Loss to Oakvale" was the first hit the search engine retrieved for her. She found what she was looking for halfway down the page.

His obituary.

Much like the ghost himself, the obituary didn't reveal much. Or rather, it revealed as much by what it didn't say as by what it did. It was only two paragraphs long, with no photo, but Veronica had to read no further than the first part of the first line: "Brian Kenneth Delaney, 16, died unexpectedly. . . ."

He'd committed suicide. She knew it as surely as if Brian were standing at her side, whispering in her ear.

She'd held her face in her hands and wept.

And now she was in the shower early enough to see Brian, if he was planning on coming. He did, and he arrived just as she secured her towel around her. He looked into the mirror, looked at her through the mirror, combed his hair, and left, almost as if he were too ashamed to see her after her discovery. She was disappointed.

He hadn't turned around or approached her, hadn't done any of the little things that had signified a break with the pattern she'd observed the other day. She wondered if it was at all possible for a ghost—an image—to have two separate patterns, or more. She suddenly found herself wishing that she could read the Fish's book.

But if the images didn't have more than one pattern, why didn't they? Why weren't they tied to more emotional or more exciting life events? There had to be more interesting things in Brian's life than his morning hair-care ritual—no one is that narcissistic.

Veronica took her time getting dressed, deciding at last on a plain white skirt, a sweater, and shoes with low heels. When she went downstairs, her mother did not even turn around from washing the dishes.

"You missed your father," she said.

"Oh," said Veronica. She felt a strong compulsion to respond to the accusation in her mother's voice, but chose not to. "I'm sorry."

"I scrambled you an egg," her mother said. "And made toast, but the toast is cold."

"Thanks, Mom," Veronica said. She'd debated telling her about Mr. Bittner, about how strange he was acting, but she didn't think her mother was in a mood to hear it. Her tone, the way that she washed the same dish over and over again . . . everything about her was spoiling for a fight.

"Kirk can bring me home from work tonight," she said, thinking that she was lightening her mother's burdens.

"You're spending an awful lot of time with that boy," her mother said, not looking up from her scrubbing.

"'That boy'? I thought you liked Kirk."

"You are a little young for a serious relationship, that's all."

Veronica's mouth opened in surprise. "What?"

Her mother's shoulders rose and fell. "I'm just saying you are spending a lot of your free time with him. And this whole chasing ghosts business. I don't think it is healthy."

Veronica wanted to laugh—that trying to find answers about why the ghosts were here and what had caused them was somehow unhealthy, but making sure you are standing in the kitchen at the appointed moment to get a glimpse of your long-dead husband was the mark of sanity. She almost said something to that effect, but then her mother turned around to face her.

"Mom, do you know who the ghost upstairs was?"

Her mother folded her arms across her chest, a cold light in her eyes. "The house had been empty a few months when we bought it." She looked over at the spot where her husband appeared, as though hoping to summon him back for a second time. "I have no idea who he was."

Veronica felt a sinking feeling in her stomach. Her mother was lying to her.

When her mother unfolded her arms, Veronica noticed how thin she was. The cuffs of her blouse were pulled back, and Veronica saw her bony wrists and shaking hands, and her irritation gave way to worry. When she spoke, she tried to make her voice sound soothing and apologetic.

"Mom, if this is because I wasn't here to see Dad—"

"It has nothing to do with you not seeing your dad!" her mother shouted, eyes blazing. She turned back to the sink with an inarticulate cry, upsetting the world's most spotless dish from the counter ledge. The dish completed a single somersault before landing with an abruptness that split it down the center.

Veronica bit into her cold, butterless toast as her mother gripped the edge of the sink with both her hands, her skeletal shoulders shaking with rage or grief or both. Veronica counted slowly to ten in her mind before responding.

"Mom . . ."

"I'm sorry, Veronica," her mother said, lifting a bony wrist to wipe away the tears that were already coursing down her face.

Veronica knew she was probably supposed to get up and hug her mother, or at least get a dustpan and sweep away the broken dish.

"I think you need to talk to someone, Mom," she said. "I think you need to get some help."

Her mother sniffed. "I'm going to a psychiatrist today," she said. "It's my first appointment with her."

Veronica blinked. That bit of news was even more unexpected than her mother's sudden rage.

"Mom, that's great."

"Is it?" her mother said, laugh/crying. "I'm afraid of going. I'm really, really afraid."

Veronica did get up then, to place a reassuring hand on her mother's shoulder.

"You don't need to be afraid, Mom," she said. "She'll help you with this."

"Help," her mother repeated, shaking her head. "I'm afraid that 'help' is going to mean she'll tell me to forget him. I'm scared she's going to tell me to change my routine so that I'm not here at 7:13 every morning, that I'm not here waiting for him to turn the page, and to squint, and to . . . to . . . to smile at me. I'm afraid she's going to say to forget him!"

Veronica rubbed her mother's back, and it was hard for her not to look at the ridge of her spine or the sharp angles of her shoulder blades. Why did it seem her mother's weight loss had been such a sudden thing? Was Veronica really that unobservant?

"She won't say that, Mom," Veronica said, but really she wasn't sure. She had no experience with grief counseling, but it seemed plausible that a psychiatrist would tell her mother to avoid the thing that was making her unhealthy, even if that thing was her father's ghost.

Her father's *image*.

"I don't want to forget at all," her mother said. "I'd rather see him every morning, like I do now. I'd rather he break my heart one thousand times, like he does every morning, than go through a day where I don't see him or think about him."

Veronica pulled her mother closer to her.

"I don't want someone to take that away from me," her mother said. "Even if it's supposed to make me better, I don't want that."

Veronica kissed her mother on the temple. "Maybe the psychiatrist won't say that, Mom. Maybe it will be something different."

"I don't want to forget," her mother said. "I don't."

＃＃＃＃

＃＃＃＃

||||

Kirk pushed through Pescatelli's front door. The man was still in his pajamas, a ratty bathrobe drooping over his shoulders, a mug of coffee in his hand.

"What aren't you telling me about Bittner?"

"Come right in, Lane," the Fish said, blinking blearily. "Make yourself at home."

"Who killed Mary Greer, Fish?" Kirk said.

The Fish cocked his head at an angle and scratched his stubbly jaw.

"*What* has gotten you so fired up this morning?"

Kirk was pacing; he couldn't help it. "We saw Amber. We saw her at Slader Mill."

"You did?"

"Yeah. We saw her, and somebody else did, too. We came out of there with a different flashlight than the one we went in with."

"What? What are you talking about?"

Kirk didn't know what to do with all his nervous energy, so he punched the wall. It didn't help.

"You aren't telling me everything you know about Mr. Bittner, are you?"

Pescatelli sipped his coffee. "What do you mean?"

"Was he a suspect in these killings or not?"

The Fish sighed. "I don't believe he was ever questioned about Amber Davis. She wasn't a student of his. Kosoff confessed before the body was even cold."

"What about Mary?"

"He was questioned about her death, but the police already had their suspect. They thought her boyfriend did it."

The Fish was lost in his story now, and had no idea that Kirk's jaw had dropped nearly to his chest.

"I never believed it," the Fish continued. "Those two were in love. Mary and her boyfriend. You'd see them after school, holding hands. They must have held hands every day, walking past Bittner's house. They were both in his class."

"Brian Delaney," Kirk whispered.

"That's right," the Fish said. "How did you know? Been doing some research."

"Ronnie has," Kirk said. "Ronnie lives in . . . the Delaneys' old house."

The Fish blinked rapidly as he processed what Kirk was saying. "So the image in her house . . ." he said, trailing off. "Wow."

"Yeah, wow."

"He killed himself there," the Fish said. "Slashed his wrists. They found him dead in the tub. I'm sure he was distraught when Mary died, and then to be accused of her murder? The poor kid."

"You're sure he didn't do it? Brian, I mean?"

"I *know* he didn't do it. It was Bittner."

"Then why . . . why didn't you *do* anything about it?"

"What could I do?" the Fish said, spreading his hands. "This is a small town. Quiet. In both cases the police had their murderers in a week—justice is served. I had no evidence, nothing."

"Evidence."

"There's nothing about Mary's ghost that incriminates Bittner. There isn't really anything I can say to interest the police. They knew she was his student, and that he tutored her, but there's nothing new to offer."

Kirk had the list of Jewell City's murder victims; he took it out of his notebook and looked at the notes he'd written.

"The bodies were both found in early March, right?" Kirk said. "Amber's and Mary's?"

"Right."

"And they both died in a leap year?"

"Yes," the Fish said, drawing out the s, almost hissing.

"What day did Bittner's daughter die?"

The Fish blinked. "She died in February."

"February 29th," Kirk told him. "What if he is killing them on the 29th of February every leap year?"

Fish sat up, taking the list from Kirk, his hands shaking. "I've got to check this."

Kirk looked at him with disgust. "Check it? Why don't you have him arrested?"

"It isn't that easy."

"I don't care how *easy* it is! In case you haven't noticed, he seems to have developed some sort of obsession with my girlfriend. And this is a leap year. And the 29th is her frickin' birthday!"

"I know, I know," Pescatelli said, punching the keys on his keyboard, his face awash with the spectral light of the monitor.

"You know," Kirk said. "You've suspected all these years, and you've never even tried to catch him! Why not?"

The Fish frowned, gnawing at his lower lip as he straightened some files on his desk.

"Isn't it obvious?" he said. "I'm terrified of ghosts."

"All these years, you've been working on this project. The ghosts. For what?"

The Fish looked away.

"Your wife and daughter, right?" Kirk said. "It isn't really about you; it's about them, right?"

The Fish's voice, when he answered, was no more than a whisper. "I wouldn't . . . I wouldn't want them to think I'd forgotten them."

Kirk nodded. "Of course not. Of course you wouldn't want them to think that—that's why you are researching this thing, that's why all the study and thought."

"They never . . . they never came back," the Fish said. "They were gone, after the Event. Gone."

Kirk nodded. "So these things that we see can't be ghosts. They can't be conscious. That's why they're just images to you, right? Because—"

"Because then my family can still be somewhere," the Fish said.

"Mr. Pescatelli," Kirk said, "if there really is another world after this, you would want them to think you did the right thing, isn't that so?"

The Fish nodded.

Kirk slapped his hand on the desk. "Ronnie is alive, Mr. Pescatelli. She's still here and she needs our help. Isn't caring for the living the best thing you could do for the dead?"

The Fish looked like he wanted to cry but didn't have any tears left.

"I miss them," he said, his voice hollow. "You don't know what it's like."

"I know I don't," Kirk said. "It has got to be terrible to lose someone, and worse to lose them and sense that they are just out of reach. Honestly, I think this book you are working on is the best thing you could have chosen to do if you wanted to torture yourself. If you wanted to remind yourself, every day, that they are gone and you are here, all alone, you picked the right thing."

The thought had obviously occurred to the Fish before. Tapping a nervous rhythm on the edge of his desk with his knuckles, he looked like he was caught between screaming at Kirk and throwing him out of his office or bursting into a loud and tearful confession.

"You aren't wrong," he said, his voice throaty and gruff.

"I don't want to feel what you are feeling," Kirk said. "No offense or disrespect intended. I don't want to lose her. We've got to do something," he said. "Ronnie is convinced that Bittner is going to try to kill her."

"She's probably right."

"Well then *help* us. She wants to go back to the mill!"

The Fish drummed his fingers on the table. "You can't let her go. But you need something."

Kirk shook his head. "You've got to help us," he said. "You've got to."

The Fish kept drumming, unable to meet Kirk's eyes. Finally, he stopped.

"Okay," he said. "This is what we'll do."

Kirk picked Ronnie up a half hour later.

"Hey," she said, filling his mother's car with her clean floral scent. "Thanks for getting me."

"You bet. How'd you sleep?"

She leaned against his shoulder as he backed out of her driveway. "Like you'd imagine. We're really going to go back tonight?"

"Yeah," he said. It was the first lie he'd told her.

After changing out of her usherette uniform, Veronica left the theater. There was no sign of Kirk, but her mother was parked at the curb.

"Hi, honey," she called.

Veronica looked around, scanning the lot for Kirk's car. She didn't see it. She walked to where her mother was parked.

"Mom?"

"Hi, Ronnie," she said. "Kirk called and said you needed a ride. I guess he wasn't feeling well and went home sick."

"He did?" she said. "That's what he told you?"

"That's what he said. Get in. I thought I'd treat you to some ice cream after your long day. How would that be?"

"Great," Veronica said. The door handle was ice cold beneath her fingers. Sick? Or just a coward, she thought, sliding into the warm car.

Or . . . ? No, she thought. He wouldn't.

But he did. She was sure of it.

An hour earlier, Kirk changed in the employee restroom, throwing on a pair of Levi's, track shoes, and a well-worn dark sweatshirt over a clean T-shirt. He pulled on his jacket and slung his duffel bag over his shoulder, said good-bye to his coworkers and walked out to his car under the glow of the streetlamps, thinking about ghosts.

Starting the car, he realized that what he was about to go do was perhaps not the smartest thing in the world, but he was compelled by something that he didn't understand. Quite simply, it was something he needed to do. He couldn't stop thinking about them.

Totally normal for a boy his age to spend his day dreaming about girls, to zone out while pouring coffee and collecting cash. Thinking about their curves, their smiles, the way light reflected off their hair. Only, he knew his obsession wasn't quite normal, because the girls he'd been thinking about lately— except for Ronnie—were all dead girls. He was going back to the mill to capture the ghost that he and Ronnie had seen the previous night.

There was something there, he thought, something that might help him and the Fish make sense of why they all appeared in the first place.

The walk to the mill was not as nerve-racking as it had been when he was with Ronnie. Part of it was the familiarity, but beyond that was the realization that he'd felt somewhat responsible for her safety. Even though he was by himself, walking

243

on a cold night to the haunted mill under a full moon, he was oddly calm. A peace had settled over him, the idea that he was where he was supposed to be.

Some internal spidey sense told him to douse his flashlight before approaching the mill, and the feeling changed the moment he reached it. The feeling was beyond a general sense of rightness—it was now one of destiny.

The thought chilled him, but he continued forward. He was considering trying to find an entrance to the building on the south side, closer to where he knew the stairwell was, when a flash of light within froze him in his tracks.

He squinted and saw it again, a fleeting white blur visible through the cracks in the window planking. He wondered if this was the illumination provided by some new specter. Sometimes ghosts cast a faint radiance, sometimes they did not.

The idea that there could be hundreds more of them, invisible in the darkness, made him uneasy. What made him even more uneasy was that the illumination was not that of an image. What he suspected was far more frightening; that the glow that danced across the boarded windows was being cast by a human being.

It was Bittner.

He couldn't identify why he knew that, any more than he could identify why the night felt charged with destiny. If what he saw was the light of a flashlight, it could be anyone in there. A policeman. A hobo looking for warmth. Kids like him, searching for answers, or not like him, searching for thrills and/or trouble.

Bittner. It was Bittner. He killed that girl and now he was

returning to the scene of his crime.

Kirk knew this in his heart and he went forward anyway.

The light—which shone only for the briefest of moments—had disappeared. Kirk could picture Bittner walking down the stairs to the basement and moving with purpose toward the far corner and the boiler.

Kirk stopped and withdrew his camera from his backpack, then climbed in through the unboarded window.

He could feel the difference the moment he stepped onto the dusty bare floor of the mill. The difference—a slight gradient in temperature, or a change in the air quality. The mill, for lack of a better term, felt *inhabited.*

Then again, maybe the boards that he'd pried and forgotten to replace last night just allowed a current of air, laden with moisture from the river below, to sweep through the building. Either way, he took his time moving from the window to the south corner. The floor beams were thick enough that he didn't have to worry about them creaking like the floors of his home.

Kirk kept his light off, navigating instead by the shards of moonlight that cut through cracks in the window boarding. He'd begun to sweat, although the mill was not warm. The air tasted like sawdust; his armpits were damp and he could feel a trickle behind his ear, which ran down under the collar of his sweatshirt.

Once near the stairwell, he heard a shuffled step echoing from below. Bittner was not being careful in traversing the basement. Kirk palmed the camera and then remembered that it made a tinny chiming noise when turned on, so he stepped back out of the stairwell, pressed the camera as best he could into the folds of his clothing, and thumbed it on. The resulting noise was like the tolling of a church bell, and he held his breath and listened for some sign that Bittner had heard. He stood still, looking through the night-vision lens at the stairwell. He was reasonably sure that he could outrun Bittner if it came to that, as long as he got a decent head start.

He waited until three minutes had passed on the camera's display. If the ghost was punctual, Kirk only had another four minutes until she arrived. He descended.

Bittner still had his light on—and yes, it was Bittner—far across the nearly empty basement. The gray silhouette of the man, a tall figure in a belted trench coat and fedora, was visible as he held his flashlight before him. He was far away, but the flashlight projected a wide cone of illumination.

Kirk leaned out to peer around the corner. There was about ten feet between him and what looked to be the twisted ruin of a thread machine, a haphazard pile of splintered wood and rusty metal. If Bittner heard him, all he'd have to do is sweep his light over and he'd see him. Kirk figured he'd still have enough of a head start, as long as he didn't freeze like a deer in headlights.

He stepped out, willing himself to be invisible, to bend light to his needs. The nature of light was something that he resolved to study a bit more once he got back to the library. Why didn't light pass through ghosts? What did light hit to give ghosts color and shape? It didn't make a whole lot of scientific sense.

He still had a few steps to go when Bittner, as though sensing his thoughts, swept his flashlight across the basement. Kirk crouched and dove.

Had he seen him? He didn't dare lift his head, as Bittner was still playing the light on the doorway he'd just left. He backed up against the wreckage of the thread mill, wondering if Bittner was coming toward him.

The light lingered a moment, then withdrew.

Kirk looked around the corner. Bittner was still far ahead. Kirk gasped as the ghost appeared.

Sitting, she pushed herself along the basement floor with her feet. Bittner crouched, setting his light on the floor, and then he lashed forward with a motion like that of a striking snake. Kirk filmed.

Bittner's thick body blocked much of the light, but when he reached out for the ghost, falling *into* her, she began to glow with a soft violet radiation. Bittner, his coat obscuring most of the ghost within its folds, reached forward with hands that clasped through the girl's neck. Kirk brought him in close-up focus, and the expression on Bittner's face could only be described as one of ecstasy. It was an expression he wore the entire time that Kirk filmed.

The ghost—all Kirk could see of her was her face, her eyes bulging—flickered before disappearing entirely. The violet aura was around Bittner now, and he seemed to be panting, as though the act of strangling the ghost had taken a great deal of energy from him. As the large man began to rise, though, he did so the way a much younger man might have, without effort or protest, which made Kirk wonder if the act hadn't taken but given energy to him.

Kirk was still filming. Bittner appeared to be looking right at him, and when he lifted his light, Kirk knew that he was.

"Who's there?" he called, his voice echoing. Kirk ran for the stairwell, feeling as much as seeing the light as it washed over him.

"Stop!" Bittner called, but Kirk was already hurtling up the stairs. It wasn't until he was halfway across the empty mill that he nearly broke his wrist.

It was the mill's emptiness, or rather the sudden *lack* of it, that caused the injury. Kirk had managed to get his flashlight out while charging up the stairs, and he'd identified two or three support posts that could impede his progress. The open window was in sight, but Bittner was closing in fast.

And then there was a thread machine, the operating sibling of the ruined hulk below, directly in his path, and he couldn't stop in time to avoid running into it.

But he tried. Stumbling, he spread his hands out before him to brace against the impact, but there was none. Not from the machine, at least. The impact came a moment later, when he hit the floor.

His right hand was still cupping the camera, held there by the strap, and he screamed as he landed, his wrist bending back farther than it was supposed to. The flashlight went flying out of his left hand, and his forehead bounced off the dusty floor hard enough for him to see stars when he lifted it.

That wasn't all he saw. The mill was filled with activity; dozens of people were tending to the rows of machines that had sprouted like violet luminescent mushrooms. Ghosts—images—there were at least fifty of them, all engaged in keeping the dead mill alive.

He tried to push himself off the floor, and he had to stifle another scream as a spike of pain shot from his wrist up his arm. The machine he'd fallen through had disappeared, as though dispelled by his contact. Unstrapping his hand and flexing his wrist, he got to one knee and realized that one of the ghosts, a young woman in a shabby dress and bonnet, was pointing at him, wide-eyed. She was pointing with her middle finger, as her index finger was missing to the knuckle. Other ghosts turned from their work and seemed to be staring at him in slack-jawed fascination.

Kirk, wincing and blinking away tears of pain, looked around at them, and they began to fade, their machines fading with them, until they were only outlines. When the outlines were gone, only a hazy violet mist remained.

He could see through that mist to where Bittner stood. He couldn't see the man's expression, but Bittner had stopped at the doorway to the stairwell, so Kirk could only assume he'd been stunned by the mass of ghosts that had appeared. Never before had Kirk seen or heard of anything like what he'd just witnessed, a manifestation of large physical objects as well as people. Of a *place*.

But he didn't waste time thinking about it. He started for the window, his hand and his ankle throbbing with each hurried step.

He was at the window when he heard Bittner running across the empty mill.

I'll never make it, Kirk thought as he squirmed through the window. He considered, briefly, picking up one of the boards lying on the ground and waiting to nail Bittner as soon as he came through the window. Maybe he'd get lucky and knock him out with a good swing.

He discarded the idea and ran for the woods. Bittner looked large and strong enough to be trouble in a close fight, but there was no way he'd have the wind for a long chase, even with Kirk gimpy. On the other side of the woods was a fairly busy road, and if Kirk could just make that, he should be all right.

At least until the next day of school.

꧁ 卌 卌 卌 卌
卌 卌 卌 卌
卌

August was wheezing by the time he'd reached the window. His lungs felt constricted, and he leaned over to hock a phlegmy mass onto the dusty floor. He cursed aloud.

He looked down at his hands, which tingled from the contact he'd made with Amber. It had been a moment of sheer bliss for him, feeling her energy flow into him. He felt like he had when he'd taken her life. He flexed his hands into fists, the wide hairy knuckles popping as he squeezed. His hands tingled, but they also ached—ached for the boy's throat.

He thought the boy had had a camera.

Climbing through the window, he thought of the possible repercussions of that fact. If the boy had filmed him—and why else would the meddlesome brat be down there again, without Veronica to paw and grope?—then what would be the end result were the tape to become public? Which, he thought, it certainly would. Teens today were the most prurient and public generation ever, even more so than the pre-Event teens with their YouTubes and Facebooks and Myspaces and bloggering and whatever else. The insipid solipsism of the Me generation had given way to the You generation of today, whose only goals it seemed were to catch their neighbors in the act of doing something filthy, something wrong.

Much like Kirk had caught him.

He scanned the trees, thinking that he saw a bobbing light far ahead. There was no point in chasing after Kirk now. At best, all he'd manage was a heart attack and a gasping lonely death in the fallen leaves.

He breathed into his hands and then put his gloves on. He still tingled all over from his contact with Amber, and the fact that his moment of joy had been caught on video, as much as it disturbed him, also filled him with a guilty thrill. The tape, on its own, proved nothing. It wasn't as though he could be arrested for having choked a ghost. Pescatelli could use the video to humiliate him at school, but likely the worst that would happen is that he'd be encouraged by the administration to leave before his full year was up. They were a spineless bunch, from the superintendent right down to lowest person on the admin totem pole. August would only have to hint at a lawsuit and they would rush to ensure that he was mustered out with full benefits and pension. Pescatelli would likely be silenced under threat of termination. The administration was as vigilant against scandal as they were against actual education.

The worst thing that could occur is that a viewing of the tape might make murdering Veronica Calder difficult, if not impossible.

There was a man standing on the sidewalk, just beyond the gap in the trees where the mill road began. Startled, August opened his mouth to say something, but then the man disappeared.

• • •

Ghosts were everywhere on his drive home. Before the drive home, even. Just walking back to his car, August spotted two more after the man at the edge of the path; an old woman who peered out from an unlit second-story window and vanished by degrees, her image rolling up slowly like a window shade; then a child riding down the hill, the wheels of his phantom bicycle hugging the center line. The boy evaporated the moment he reached the crossroad, where a brand-new stoplight had replaced a quartet of stop signs.

August was sweating inside his overcoat long before he reached his car. The quick sprint after Kirk had been the action of a foolish, guilty man. All it had done, perhaps, was to afford the boy a good look at his face. He'd had about as good a chance at catching the fleeing figure as he did resurrecting the bodies of the girls he'd murdered.

He drove out of the municipal lot, cranking the heat to remove the gravelike chill that had settled in his vehicle. His skin was clammy, and sweat rolled from under the brim of his hat into his ears and eyes. A ghost of a woman was calling soundlessly to a person only she could see.

The shops were just beginning to close on Main Street, although Dunkin' Donuts still had some customers, a number of whom were clustered on the sidewalk in front of the store, steam rising from large Styrofoam cups. Waiting for a light to change, Bittner looked over at them and watched one of them disappear. Across the street, a policeman turned transparent and then was gone. August blinked twice and did not realize that the light had changed until the driver of the car behind him leaned on her horn.

Putting the car into motion, August turned toward the ramp for the interstate. He didn't want to go home, nor did he want to go to one of the many bars that lined the streets downtown. He had visions of sitting on a stool, drinking a glass of beer, as the fellow patrons disappeared, one by one, until only he and the bartender remained. He'd ask for another drink, and the bartender would smile, and then he—August—would disappear.

There were few cars on the highway at this hour. August gunned his vehicle past a lone semi headed north. There was no one ahead of him as far as he could see.

Turning, he saw a flicker of movement from the corner of his eye to the right. When he glanced back, what he saw nearly made him lose control of his car, and he had to bank hard on the wheel to keep from hitting the median guardrail.

The first girl he'd murdered, a runaway he'd picked up in New York City, was peering in at him from the passenger window, the trees and highway signs flying by behind her at seventy miles an hour. She stepped into the car through the closed door as August jerked the wheel, overcorrecting.

His heart was hammering in his chest. She was looking at him and smiling, wearing the same drab coat and smeared lipstick she'd worn on the night he'd killed her. She flickered out and then returned, and flickered out again.

She leaned in, as though resting her head on his shoulder, as she'd done so many years ago, but he'd driven a compact car then, so now she slouched toward him but was still a foot away.

August was sweating and his mouth was dry. I'd had a different car, he thought. There was nothing to attach her to this vehicle, and the empty stretch of road he now traveled was not the one that he'd driven her down before taking her life. There was nothing at all to anchor her to this spot, at this time. But here she was.

Unless, August thought, unless *I* am the anchor.

He turned to the ghost slouching beside him, and in that moment she lifted her head and laughed, although he heard no sound. She seemed to settle, and slouched once again, her eyes closing.

Bittner lifted her hand to graze her cheek, and his fingertips passed right through her. There was a crackle of energy, like the release of static, and an electric charge spread through his body as she faded away, leaving him shuddering.

‖‖ ‖‖ ‖‖ ‖‖
‖‖ ‖‖ ‖‖ ‖‖
‖‖ |

She's looking at my reflection in the mirror. She's behind me and leaning against the tile wall. She's wearing her bathrobe and has her arms folded across her chest, and she's crying.

I want to comfort her, but I'm only a memory. A memory that she never had. A phantom comb passes through my phantom hair, and my image does not turn to look at her. I'm conserving my strength because the day when the veil is thinnest is nearly here, and I do not want to expend what little energy I have. How much comfort can a memory provide, anyway?

Not enough. My image fades from her view, and she rubs her eyes and replaces me at the sink. She's not crying over me anyway. I can read her thoughts, those most forward in her mind—they hang like mist in the air around her. She's frightened. She's feeling betrayed and lost, and these feelings have something to do with the boy who came over the other day. Maybe it is easy for me to read these feelings because they are similar to feelings I'd had before I trapped myself in this room.

Mary had been coming over to my house to see me, but she made a stop along the way. A single stop that turned out to be her final destination.

Grief and fear are useful only to a point. I try to gather the girl's emotions to me like flowers, leaving only one that is a small blossom barely in bloom. I pour my own energy into this bloom, nurturing it, encouraging it to fully flower.

I feed her anger with my own. I may not be able to comfort her, but maybe I can provide strength.

She has stopped crying, and the helpless look in her eyes has been replaced by a much steelier emotion. It is a small gift I have given her, and one that increases her chances only slightly, but there is no refuge to be had in despair. This I know all too well.

I wait a moment to watch her splash water on her cheeks, and the sight of her simple action is so natural, so beautiful, and so *human*, it is almost painful for me to watch.

I need to prepare for the coming day. Making her a little stronger has made me a little weaker, and so I allow myself to fade completely away.

⧄⧄⧄ ⧄⧄ ⧄⧄⧄ ⧄⧄⧄ ⧄⧄⧄ ⧄⧄⧄ ⧄⧄⧄ ⧄⧄⧄ ⧄⧄⧄ ‖

She saw him first, standing by his locker. He must have heard the swift tread of her heels on the tile floor, because he turned just as she approached.

"Ronnie . . ." he said. She could see the words forming on his lips.

She slapped him.

"What happened, Kirk?" she said. "Weren't feeling well, were you?"

She made to slap him again, but he turned her arm aside. He had a brace on his wrist. People were watching, but she didn't care, balling her hand into a small fist, hitting him on the shoulder.

"Ronnie, stop it!"

"Had a tummy ache? Is that it?"

"Ronnie," he said, grabbing her wrist with his uninjured hand. "I went back to the mill."

She twisted her wrist free, looking at him.

"You went to the *mill*?" she said, like she was surprised, even though his answer confirmed what she'd suspected.

He smiled at her. "I got some evidence, Ronnie. I think we've got it."

Whatever "evidence" he had couldn't have been too impressive, because she and Janine had waited behind a parked car until she'd seen Mr. Bittner drive away from his house this morning. He'd stepped out onto his porch and into the ghost of Mary Greer, throwing his arms wide, as though he were being given an invigorating jolt of electricity. He didn't look like a haunted man. He didn't look like a man about to be made to answer for his past. He looked ecstatic.

She punched Kirk just above his heart, twice.

"You think that makes it better?" she said. "You left me behind while you went and put yourself in danger. You think that makes you a hero? It doesn't. It just makes you a jerk."

She considered hitting him again, but that wasn't going to make him understand anything. Nothing was.

"I don't like being left behind, Kirk," she said. He started to protest, but she lifted her hand, silencing him. "So I'm going to leave you behind instead."

She lowered her hand and walked away.

"Today is your test," Mr. Bittner said. "Today is your chance to become a part of history."

It was his little joke, one he'd made before every test he'd handed out for the last thirty years. Very rarely did his little witticism elicit a laugh, and today was no exception.

But today *was* a little different because the joke had other layers of meaning. He was staring at Veronica Calder as he said it.

She stared back at him, an almost defiant look in her eyes. "Some of you will pass, and some of you will fail," Mr.

Bittner said, dropping a test onto Kirk's desk. Then, turning back to Veronica, "And some of you will never die."

Kirk failed completely, not even trying to do the essay. As soon as the bell sounded—after a quick glance Veronica's way—he went down the hall to find the Fish.

"Did you watch it?" he said. He'd dropped off the broken camera—and its wonderfully intact cassette—before the morning bell.

"I watched it."

"So what do you think?" Kirk said. The Fish rewound the video and watched it yet again.

"What do I think?" he said, more to himself than in answer to Kirk's question. "I think he murdered her."

"Well, yeah," Kirk said, bending his wrist, flexing his hand into a fist. The brace, one he'd bought at Walmart last year after hurting his hand playing basketball, creaked with each flexion. The movement was painful, but he considered himself lucky he hadn't broken it. "I kind of figured that. But why'd he go back?"

The Fish shook his head, rewound the video, and played it frame by frame. "Look, there it is again."

"What?" Kirk said, leaning in. The Fish took a screen-cleaner wipe from a round plastic tube and gave the screen a quick dusting.

"Look closely."

Kirk did, even though the girl's expression—her bugging eyes, especially—made it difficult to watch. Bittner scrabbled on his knees to catch up to the crab-walking girl, and when he reached forward with his gloved hands, Kirk saw it, just as Bittner made "contact" with the girl.

"Did you see the flash?" the Fish asked, turning toward him, the awful image of the girl's death reflected in his glasses.

"I saw it," Kirk said. "A flash, a spark almost, of purple light all around them when he touched her."

"A corona," the Fish said, turning back to the screen.

"What is it?

"I have no idea," the Fish said, shaking his head. "I've never seen anything like it before."

Kirk sat back and sipped from a can of soda. "Never? Do you have other ghost videos on your computer?"

"Hundreds," the Fish said. "None of them have anything like that, not even the ones where someone touches an image. Look."

He brought up a video on his computer, a smiling toddler walking toward an equally beaming older woman, his grandmother perhaps, who had crouched down low as if to receive him. The Fish slowed the video just as the little boy reached out for the woman, going frame by frame as the boy's arm passed right through her chin, and over he went. She disappeared a moment after he'd hit the deck, at which point he started crying.

"No flash," Kirk said.

"Here's another one," the Fish said, bringing up an image of an urban road race on a sunny day, a flock of sweating joggers rushing past a sidewalk filled with cheering spectators. A figure in a soaking trench coat and hat stepped into the frame, entering the road as though he couldn't see the runners bearing down on him. The closest runner, unable to stop, threw his hands in front of him and stumbled as he went through the trench-coated figure. Once the trailing pack had barreled on through him, the figure took one additional step and disappeared before reaching the other side of the street.

"Nothing there, either," Kirk said. "Could it just be because it's so dark in the basement where he killed her?"

The Fish rewound the film of the runners and watched closely as they passed backward through the trench-coat image.

"I don't think so," he said. "Why would it happen at the *exact* moment that Bittner's hands came into contact with the image? Maybe the contact triggered it somehow. Maybe some chemical process . . ."

"This is all great fun. But what do we do with this now? He's a killer. He's obviously a killer."

The Fish sighed. "Not to a court."

"What are you talking about?"

"This would fall under the category of 'spectral evidence,' which is not admissible in court. No one will arrest him because of this video, as compelling as it may be." The Fish pinched the bridge of his nose between his thumb and forefinger.

Kirk threw his hands up. "We need to go to the police."

The Fish shook his head. "We've got nothing but circumstance, Kirk. Circumstance and spectral evidence. Nothing that ties him directly to the crimes."

"But, the dates . . . the video! Can't we at least tell them about—"

"They won't do anything, Kirk. There's nothing that could be done."

Kirk was as angry as he was frightened. "You won't . . . you won't even try? She thinks he's going to kill her. Soon! Tomorrow is the last day of February!"

"Then you should be with her, not with me."

"Ronnie," Kirk said. "Ronnie, don't walk away. I've got something that you've got to see."

"I just bet you do," Veronica said, and when Kirk tried to touch her she shrugged him away. "Just let me go to lunch, please."

"He kills every February, Ronnie. On leap years. You're like his perfect victim. You—"

"Go away, Kirk. *Go.*"

"Please, Ronnie. Just watch the video." He held out the camera to her, the little playback window extended to the side.

"I don't want to watch the video, Kirk."

"He killed her, Ronnie. You can see right on the—"

"I know he killed her. Just leave me alone."

She turned away.

"Ronnie, please," Kirk said, hurrying to catch up. "You've got to see it. When he touches her, it's like—"

Veronica stopped, so suddenly Kirk nearly ran into her. "It's like what, exactly, Kirk?"

"It's like . . . it's like he's *absorbing* her."

He saw the fright in her eyes, mixed with anger. She opened her mouth to answer, but then a deep voice cut her off.

"Miss Calder. Mr. Lane," Bittner boomed. If Bittner's voice was like thunderheads earlier, it was like an atomic weapon in the cavernous acoustics of the school corridor, a noise of

Event-like proportions. Veronica gasped as though she'd realized her hand was on a hot stove, and Kirk, upon hearing his name, flinched.

"Good morning to you both. How did you do on your test? Did you give performances worthy of history?"

Veronica couldn't form any words. Kirk took a half step in front of her, and however angry she was at him, she was grateful for that.

Mr. Bittner leaned toward them. "Or did you fail to study? Is it because your weekend was as thrilling as mine? Filled with chills and adventure?"

In his long overcoat he almost looked like he was gliding above the scuffed floor, the flaps trailing like the tattered robes of a banshee on the moors.

"I will make you wish that you had taken up a different hobby," Bittner said, bending down over Kirk, who was trying his best not to shrink back. Veronica could feel her teacher's anise-scented breath on her cheeks. She was aware of other students in the hallway, walking past them in a wide arc and staring with fascination at the spectacle of a newly insane history teacher accosting two kids. But it was like they were passersby at a ghost appearance—no one stopped to help.

Almost no one, that is. Veronica became aware of another figure drawing Bittner's eye away from them.

"Is there a problem, Gus?"

Mr. Pescatelli appeared out of the passing stream. Veronica thought he looked as scared as she was.

"Oh yes, Mr. Fish," Bittner said, none of the dark humor going out of his smile. "There is most certainly a problem."

Mr. Pescatelli nodded. "There is, isn't there? One that we could solve. We could really solve it pretty easily, I think."

There was a moment when Veronica thought that Mr. Bittner actually looked confused. He was a man who was so imposing that he didn't need to bully people; people were just naturally cowed by his size, his presence, and his steel-gray eyes. Mr. Pescatelli—Mr. Fish Pescatelli, of all people—was standing before him and not backing down. Quaking, shaking, with a quaver in his voice, perhaps, but not backing down.

Mr. Bittner straightened to his full height, and Veronica expected him to throw a punch that would knock the Fish's head clean from his body. But no punches—just words—were forthcoming; words that were drained of all emotion until they sounded almost bloodless.

"Yes," Bittner said. "Very easily."

He turned and retreated to his classroom.

Mr. Pescatelli was blinking furiously behind his glasses, and his hand shook as he brought it up to stroke his chin. Kirk and Veronica exchanged a look, and both of them reached out at the same time to steady him.

Kirk spoke first. "Mr. Pescatelli," he said. "Thank you."

"Don't thank me," he said, wiping his forehead with the back of his hand. He looked toward the ceiling and whispered a prayer—or perhaps a greeting—to an unseen companion.

ЖΓ ЖΓ ЖΓ ЖΓ
ЖΓ ЖΓ ЖΓ ЖΓ
ЖΓ III

The confrontation between the Fish and Bittner seemed to have triggered some sort of image explosion, as images old and new began to appear all over the school. At lunch there was a phantom lunch lady in a drab gray uniform dispensing uniformly gray ghost beans. There was a young boy crouching beneath one of the desks in Veronica's next class, a memory from the 1950s. Eileen Janus showed up again in Mr. Pescatelli's class, along with two new ghosts, and did not leave until the bell sounded. The Fish gave a pause-free lecture without glancing at either Veronica or the images. The two new ghosts were clearly of different eras, a little girl in a blue wool sweater and a plaid skirt that went all the way down to her scuffed shoes, and a tall T-shirted boy whose afro was bushy enough to hide test answers in. The boy disappeared first, after laughing at a joke no one had told.

"This is crazy," Kirk said, waiting for Veronica to get her things from her locker after the final bell. "I don't understand it. I think I've seen seven new images today. There was a naked girl in the boys' locker room."

"That must have been thrilling," Veronica said, without laughing. All of the new images had put everyone on edge.

"No, really," he said. "She was crying, wet, and shivering. Trying to cover herself, like someone had yanked her towel away."

This made Veronica think of Brian, and this time it was she who shivered. Kirk wasn't getting the hint that she really didn't want to talk about this, but when she turned toward him she saw a hulking figure over his shoulder, running full tilt, right at him.

"Kirk! Look out!"

Kirk turned just as the figure, a huge boy in full football regalia, ran into—and through—him. The ghost continued on his path down the hallway, passing through a half dozen students on his way.

"Ugh," Kirk said, and shook as though someone had dumped a gallon of cold water over his head. "Let's get out of here."

Veronica wanted to say no. She wanted to say, *Let's just stop with the images or the ghosts or whatever they are, and ignore them.* In the back of her mind she thought that maybe all the attention Kirk and the Fish, and especially Mr. Bittner, were paying them was causing this new activity, as though the images were somehow feeding off of it.

She opened her mouth to reply just as an older teacher she didn't recognize walked out of a classroom. The teacher look right, looked left, straightened his bow tie, and then disappeared.

Veronica closed her eyes.

"Okay, Kirk," is what she said.

They went to the library, and Kirk played her the tape. When it was over he asked if she needed a replay.

"No, I don't need to see it again," Veronica said. She was cold all over, as though the wind had found its way from outside into the library.

"Pretty crazy, huh?"

"That's one word for it," she said.

"This is proof that Mr. Bittner killed her," Kirk said. He pressed a button on his camera and the image went away.

"I'd say that's pretty obvious." Veronica was thinking of the song, the nursery rhyme that had existed prior to her attending Montcrief High.

Gus has Mary hanging from a tree . . .

It was like everyone had already known he was a dangerous man, that he had killed, and they ignored the evidence right in front of them. Kirk was right; the way the ghost flashed and seemed to fold into Bittner at his touch—all Veronica could think was that Bittner was some large black parasite, absorbing what little was left of that poor girl into himself.

"He's obscene," she said. "What is Mr. Pescatelli going to do?"

Kirk snapped his camera shut and hauled his pack onto the table to put his gear away. "I tried to get him to show the tape to the police," he said. "There's never been a case where 'spectral evidence'—and that's an actual term, used a couple times in court—has been admissible. I was hoping he could at least drum up some interest in reopening the investigations."

"Do you think the police will listen?"

"No. He doesn't either." Kirk sighed, cinching his bag closed. "I don't even think he's going to try. We could go, but I don't think anyone would listen. Nobody ever listens to the kids when they try to warn the townspeople that the monster is coming."

He reached for Veronica and touched her on the elbow.

"Are you all right?"

Her laugh was harsh but she saw no reason to sweeten it.

"Am I all right?"

"You're still mad at me, aren't you?"

"Yes. I'm mad at you."

"You're really tense. Your arms all folded, and . . ."

"Kirk. I'm terrified! I'm absolutely terrified! You show me that monster m . . . murdering that poor girl and you expect me to be, what, relaxed?"

"I know, but—"

"You think I want to see this stuff? Do you think I want to see him with his hands around her throat, squeezing the life out of her?"

Veronica closed her eyes, and the girl's face rose out of the darkness, and for a moment she could imagine it—being breathless for all eternity.

"I thought you'd want to know."

"Gee, thanks."

"What was I supposed to do? Not tell you? He's dangerous."

"Well obviously he's dangerous!"

Kirk held up his hands and looked around the library as gray heads rose from old books. "I mean to you," he whispered.

"Yeah, thanks again."

"Why are you mad at me? It's my fault that he's a psycho? It's my fault he might have a thing for you?"

"Yes," Veronica said, although she didn't really believe it. "We should have just left it alone."

"What the hell are you talking about? We—"

"Don't raise your voice at me."

"We can't ignore this."

"Everyone else did. For years. And from what you are telling me, we still don't have any actual evidence he did anything."

"I can't even believe you're saying this."

"Of course not."

"Ronnie, he's after you. Don't you realize that?"

She could see in his face that not only had she bent his brain, she'd broken it. If only real boys were like Brian; all smiles, no demands. Brian didn't need anything from her except to show up in the mornings. And he didn't complain if she didn't.

"I'm worried about you, Ronnie."

Veronica laughed. "Sure. All you did was make him more angry."

"Ronnie," Kirk said. He could have argued the point, but didn't bother. Veronica's arms tightened around her as though she were trying to hold her true self inside her body.

"Since you're already mad," Kirk said, after a moment, "you might as well know the rest of it. About Brian."

"What about Brian?" she said. "Why don't you just leave him out of this?"

"He was the cops' number one suspect for Mary's murder."

"Shut up, Kirk." Veronica knew what he was going to say next—the thing that she had kept as her own secret—and she felt her heart frosting over. "He didn't kill her."

"Probably not," he said. "But Brian couldn't take the accusations. He killed himself. Opened himself and bled out right on your bathroom floor."

"He was in love with her, you ass," she said.

"Ronnie," Kirk said, his tone half apologetic, almost whiny. He had the audacity to look surprised, as if he had no idea that what he was saying would hurt her. He reached out for her again, but she jerked away, as though his hand were a fanged and poisonous snake.

"I hate you, Kirk. I never want to see you again," she said. "Ever."

|||| ||||| ||||| |||||

||||| ||||| ||||| |||||

||||| ||||

That went well, Kirk thought.

He pulled into his driveway and sat behind the wheel with the engine running. There was a flutter of movement within his house, at the great bay window—a short, stubby-fingered hand ruffling the blue curtains. The curtain pulled back and his youngest sister smiled out at him.

Veronica was possibly the moodiest girl he'd ever met, and Kirk felt he had a right to that opinion, living with three sisters and one mother; even their two cats were female. There were times where he and his brother would lock themselves in their room and read comic books rather than venture out into the estrogen-rich atmosphere. No wonder his dad worked all the time.

Against Veronica's wishes, no doubt, Kirk followed her home in his car after school. Pulling out of the school lot, he noticed that Bittner's car was still parked. Even though Veronica only lived a mile away, Kirk thought it was important that he at least see her safely home. He watched her from a respectful distance. She walked with Janine, who was chattering away about something, with Veronica barely saying anything in return.

When they got close to Mr. Bittner's house, Kirk thought he saw movement in the upstairs window. What if Mr. Bittner had left early that day, and walked home so as to allay suspicions? Kirk found himself gripping the wheel of his mother's car, wondering if there was a tire iron or a jack in the trunk, in case Bittner came running out of his house, at Veronica. The image of Bittner tearing across the snow, his coat flapping and the gleam of madness in his eyes, was as palpable in Kirk's mind as any ghost image he'd ever seen, and he blinked his eyes rapidly to get it out of his head. Veronica didn't even glance at Bittner's house. Her head down, she kept moving, the way you'd move past an angry barking dog, avoiding even the possibility of eye contact.

When she reached her door a moment later, Kirk hoped she would at least glance back at the car. He knew she was aware of him following her, and he thought that his concern might at least warm a tiny piece of her heart toward him. But no.

She walked through the door and closed it behind her.

Lock it, Veronica, Kirk thought. He turned around in someone else's driveway and retraced his route, once again driving past the school, where Bittner's car sat unoccupied. He drove home thinking of Veronica.

Moody, he thought. Maybe not. Maybe she's just sick of me.

I hate you, Kirk, she'd said. *And I never want to see you again.*

He sighed and leaned forward until his forehead touched the steering wheel. He couldn't get her out of his mind; it was like she was walking around in his head like a ghost.

Veronica grew sick of people pretty quickly, he'd noticed. Boys, especially, but neither James nor any of the other guys fortunate to have dated her spoke of her in vulgar terms, and oddly none of them seemed to have any bitterness toward her after she moved on. Even now Kirk's disappointment was more about himself than her, even though it was her attitude that had prompted him to lose his temper.

He saw his mother walk by the kitchen window, and upon seeing his lights, she stopped to peer out at him. He gave her a quick wave and cut the engine.

Ronnie was like a girl who had a thing about new shoes, he thought. She liked trying them on, wearing them around town for a week or two, and then boxing them at the bottom of her closet. It wasn't really that she didn't like the week-old shoes, and it wasn't that they were poorly made or scuffed or particularly uncomfortable. It was just that she liked to get new ones.

And right now Kirk was two weeks old, a pair of leathers that had lost its luster.

He opened the car door and hauled his backpack from the seat next to him. It felt like it weighed a metric ton with the laptop and the camera and, oh yeah, a quartet of books all of which he should look at tonight.

His little sister Jenny opened the front door and screamed, her little face squinching up behind the glass of the storm door as she let loose. Cackling, she slammed the door, and Kirk could hear his mother yelling at her to be quiet.

Jenny had looked just like a ghost, Kirk thought. A little ghost. He realized there was movement at almost every window of the house; his mother cooking, one of his sisters brushing her hair in front of her vanity upstairs, the little ones running and jumping.

He paused and slung his backpack down so he could get Mr. Pescatelli's camera. He winced, forgetting for a moment the pain and stiffness in his wrist. He pointed the camera at the house, going from window to window. His mother, camera shy, waved him away like she would a pesky insect, and stepped away from the kitchen window in order to avoid the camera's gaze.

Ghosts, Kirk thought. Seen through the camera's eye, the house looked like it was full of ghosts. Jenny behind the glass, a flutter at the curtains, a shadow as she turned away.

There had been so many of them today—in the school, in the library, on the streets. Ronnie's perfume lingering in the car when he drove home. The ghosts of Hiroshima in the Hersey book in his backpack, another billion in the heavy history text that stayed in his locker. His cat Skitty appearing in the bay window, walking along the unseen back of the sofa, her long gray tail flicking.

Kirk lowered the camera and decided he wanted to be done with ghosts for a while. He'd felt like he'd been on the verge of some great new discovery the first few days of carrying the camera around. Talking to the Fish and Ronnie about what he'd seen, creeping through the black air of the mill basement, he'd felt like an explorer, a chronicler of things unknown, and it had been a strange and wonderful feeling. But that was before his adventures had led to him hurting Ronnie. Staring up at his house, at the bustling scenes of life behind the glass, at the gutters that needed cleaning and the siding that needed power washing, he felt that he hadn't discovered anything new at all, only what had been there all along.

No such thing as wasted time, he thought. And in truth, he wasn't at all bitter about any of it, including and especially his brief fling with Ronnie, which he knew with certainty was over. Rather than feeling rejected, he was amused, as if the universe itself were gazing down at him with a wry smile.

Laughing, he decided that he would go inside and kiss his mother and offer to help her with whatever she was cooking. He'd tie Curtis's shoes if the laces had come undone, and he'd ask Samantha if she wanted a drink even though she'd refuse, fearing the addition of foul-tasting contaminants. He'd look in on the baby and even change her diaper if need be, and he'd hug Jenny to him, and he'd smell her hair and she'd be real. They'd all be real and warm, with sniffles and contrary ideas and irritating quirks. He'd do these things, and they'd all look at him and think, He's weird. They'd whisper in his wake about what had gotten into him—*why is Kirk acting so weird?*—and he'd know.

He'd hug them and touch them and smell them and he would know.

PART FOUR: LEAP DAY

He really was handsome, Veronica thought.

She was watching Brian from behind the shower curtain, and she smiled as he lifted a hand as though to fix his already perfect hair. His fingertips brushed his cheek, scanning for an invisible blemish.

Quite handsome.

Handsome enough to make her forget about that toad Kirk for once and for all. Her anger had blazed into a white-hot fury. She should have known he was like the others. Always there when they want something, but never there when you need them.

Brian's reflection was visible in the mirror, and then it wasn't.

Veronica took the towel from the bar and began to dry herself. The steam was already beginning to dissolve in the tiny bathroom.

Kirk had left her high and dry, and was so cowardly that he'd brought her *mother* in on his cowardly act. Why did he do that? Why did he have to leave her when she needed him the most?

It wasn't that, though. She could forgive his leaving her and returning to the mill, because in her heart she knew he wasn't being cowardly at all. But she wasn't sure that she could forgive him for the way he'd broken the news of Brian's suicide, like it was an event of no great importance. Like his suicide wouldn't have any emotional resonance for her.

His suicide.

There was a ghost theory that they had never discussed; it was one that was never discussed by anyone other than religious fearmongers. Some people believed that ghosts were the spirits of those cast out of, or denied entrance to, heaven. The souls of the damned, in other words.

Veronica wiped a tear from her eye. Maybe she wouldn't go downstairs to see her father today.

Brian turned on a phantom faucet and ran his hands under the phantom stream. He was hanging around longer than usual today. Was he being punished?

His reflection appeared in the mirror again, and he glanced at Veronica, as though he could read her thoughts. She pulled the curtain back, and he smiled. It looked like he was smiling right at her, as though touched by her concern.

"Oh, Brian," she sighed, "if only you were real."

She let her towel half slip, and then she let it fall to the floor.

Maybe the ghost's eyes widened, and maybe they didn't.

He stepped toward her.

Madeline was floating down the stairs, her arms slack, her toes pointed down. The path of her descent was not linear, but as though she were a balloon being tugged by air currents. August closed his eyes as she drifted into and through the banister like the car of a drunk driver crossing the median. The angle of her head in relation to her neck was not natural or pleasant.

"Today," she said.

"Yes," he said, wincing at the twinge in his shoulders as he pushed his arms through the sleeves of his coat. "Today."

"Do not fail us," Madeline said. "Again."

He lifted his briefcase and pulled the brim of his hat low.

"No," he said, and waited for his daughter to appear.

I dissolved.

If only I could touch her, really touch her, and if only she could feel me as something more than a cold mist on her skin. She was so close, but I became immaterial rather than touch her because I didn't know if I'd ever be able to make myself whole again.

He's after her. And now she knows that he is, and there is nothing I can do to help her. Nothing. I have tried to go beyond the confines of the house we share, but I can do no better than drift, as the snow drifts, halfway across our yard before my consciousness begins to scatter. I pushed forward until I broke apart, like a lost ship on an unforgiving reef. The sensation was painful to me. But I gathered again eventually, somehow reassembling in the bathtub where I died.

But before I had broken apart, I could see his house. The house where Mary had stopped on her way to my house.

Bittner's house.

Traces of me follow Veronica downstairs, trailing after her like the scent of her perfume. Her mother is angry; the image of her father has been here and gone. I try whispering in her ear, telling her that she should stay. But she cannot hear me over the sound of her mother's nagging. He is going to kill her. He is going to kill her like he killed my Mary, and there is nothing I can do.

I watch her leave our house. I watch through the window as she moves closer to her destiny.

⊥⊦⊦⊥ ⊥⊦⊦⊥ ⊥⊦⊦⊥ ⊥⊦⊦⊥
⊥⊦⊦⊥ ⊥⊦⊦⊥ ⊥⊦⊦⊥ ⊥⊦⊦⊥
⊥⊦⊦⊥ ⊥⊦⊦⊥ I

"Happy birthday!" Janine said.

"Hmm?"

"I said, 'Happy birthday!'"

"Oh. Thanks," Veronica said. "Sorry. My mind must be elsewhere."

She smiled at Janine, at the little worry lines around her mouth. She could notice details like that about her now because Janine did not walk with her head down all the time.

"I have a present for you," Janine said. "But I forgot it at home."

"No worries."

"Did you have a date last night?" she said.

"What? No, no date."

"I like Kirk," Janine said.

Veronica laughed and almost told her that she could have him.

"I don't think I'd be scared of ghosts if I had a boyfriend like Kirk."

"Why is that?" Veronica said. She knew that she sounded snappish, but she couldn't help it. She was furious at Kirk, and she was irritated at the implication that having a boyfriend would somehow empower her or make her less afraid to face life.

But Janine's answer surprised her, and made her think about her reaction.

"Because he would never forget me," Janine said. "No matter what happened, he would never forget me. Kirk is like that."

They walked a few moments in silence—or rather, Veronica did. The newly chatty Janine was asking her if she could come over some morning to see her father's image, when suddenly her voice grew tight and rose in pitch.

"Look," she said, pointing. "Look at Mary."

Veronica looked. Mary had already knocked on the door and stepped back, and Mr. Bittner was just leaving his house. He took one step forward, into the center of the ghost, and seemed to take a deep breath, as though trying to inhale her.

"Did you see that?" Veronica whispered.

"Yeah," Janine whispered back. "He stepped right into her."

All they could see was the bottoms of Mary's stick-thin legs. The rest of her was swallowed up by Bittner and his voluminous coat. A tiny hand darted out from his side for a moment, like that of a drowning victim.

They had stopped walking, and Veronica found herself leaning into her friend.

"Not that. The flash."

"What flash?"

"That light. That violet light."

Janine shook her head, and Veronica realized she was scaring her. Mr. Bittner was still on his porch, his arms wide, his barrel chest expanding. His eyes were closed, his face raised to the sky, and he wore an expression of beatific satisfaction that was more than perverse. He looked like he would inflate to the point that his feet would leave the earth and he'd begin to float away.

"Ugh," Janine said.

"Look at him," Veronica whispered.

The word she thought of but didn't want to say was *feeding*. At some point she'd grabbed Janine's arm and was clutching it tightly, as tightly as Janine used to hold her.

Mary disappeared.

A moment later, Mr. Bittner turned toward them. "Miss Calder," he called, his voice a thunderhead. It cut through the gray day and echoed, seeming to warp in and out among the houses and yards lining their quiet suburban street. "Happy birthday."

The simple words took Veronica's breath away. Unable to speak, she nodded at him.

"Would you like a ride?" he said. "My gift to you on such a cold day."

You already gave me a gift, she wanted to say. *The gift of terror.* Janine winced, Veronica was squeezing so hard. Veronica opened her mouth but no sound came out. A ride. Where was Kirk when she'd wanted a ride?

"Miss Calder?" Bittner repeated, his mouth wide and full of yellow teeth. It was an insane grin, one that bespoke not only of knowledge but pride in the abomination he'd just enacted. "I will warm it for you first, if you like."

"R . . . Ronnie?" Janine said.

"N . . . no thank you, Mr. Bittner," Veronica said, noticing that his invitation did not include Janine. Mr. Bittner's grin made her wish she had not worn a skirt, or perfume, and that her hair was not long and stylish. Even across the street, from two houses away, she could feel something terrible emanating from the man; something oily and viscous, something that would stain the skin in a way that no amount of washing would clean. "I like to walk."

Mr. Bittner's expression did not change, except in that it seemed to intensify.

"Very well," he said, triggering the automatic car starter. "I will see you in class."

"Walk with me," Veronica said, her voice a harsh whisper.

"You're crushing my arm," Janine replied, and Veronica released the pressure a little. They began to walk, moving with tentative steps, as though the sidewalk were a thin sheet of ice above a dark and empty lake.

Bittner watched them—her, really—as his field of vision did not seem to include Janine at all, as though she were already a ghost. Veronica waited until they were halfway up the street before turning back, but he was still standing there, grinning at her beside his car as it coughed wave after wave of exhaust into the air.

"He's weird," Janine whispered.

"You think?" Veronica answered. They began to pick up the pace, although the boots she'd worn didn't lend themselves very well to running.

"I mean really weird. Like rabid-dog weird."

"I think you are right."

Veronica was having visions of him getting into his car and tearing off after them, angling over the curb and onto the sidewalk, laughing as he gripped the wheel tightly with his gloved hands.

"It was like he was eating her," Janine whispered.

Veronica wanted to hit Janine for saying it out loud, but, turning, she saw how angry Janine was beneath her goofy hat.

"He's bad," Janine said, her tiny hands balled into fists.

"Come on," Veronica said. "Let's try not to think about it."

Mr. Bittner passed them when they reached the corner, slowing down just enough to wave at Veronica with his huge gloved hand.

Kirk tried to talk to Veronica in the hallway, but she was not interested.

"Ronnie, please," he said. "I shouldn't have said what I did. I—"

"I don't want to talk to you, Kirk," she said, bringing her books close to her chest and slamming her locker shut.

"I know. I know you don't, but—"

"You're going to make me late for history."

Kirk stood in front of her, struggling for something to say. He couldn't believe she was really going to brush him aside so she could rush to Mr. Bittner's class.

"Ronnie . . ." he started, but then a hand clamped down on his shoulder. The grip was tight, but the hand was too small to be Bittner's. Kirk turned, and there was James scowling at him. He looked like a cat who had been waiting patiently for hours for a bird to alight on a nearby branch.

"She said she doesn't want to talk to you, jerk."

Kirk, in the next five seconds, considered about half a dozen ways to react to James, the outcome of the large majority of them ending with a bloody nose. He shrugged James's hand off.

"Be careful, Ronnie," Kirk said. "Please."

"*You* be careful," James said, and then looked disappointed when Veronica turned on her heel and left the boys standing there. Kirk shook his head and followed her off to class. He almost collided with a red-faced girl in a big blue parka, but the girl disappeared and her coat faded away a moment later.

"History, some say, never repeats itself," Mr. Bittner was saying. He was standing at the window, looking out, his large hands clasped behind his back. He was still wearing his coat even though homeroom and half of his first class were over. There were three ghosts and a dog in the field; Veronica could tell that they were ghosts because they didn't leave tracks in the snow.

"Mark Twain said that 'History never repeats itself, but it does rhyme.' I always liked that one. But then Santayana counters, 'Those who cannot remember the past are condemned to repeat it.' If I cannot remember, does that mean I am doomed to repeat the past? Does that seem reasonable to any of you?"

Veronica watched as the dog, a large black Lab, leaped into the air and disappeared at the height of its jump. Ghost animals; that was new.

"But are there really patterns to be found? Are there patterns or . . . intersections? The intersection of significance and random chance—how much of what we know of the world today would be different if one single individual who died an untimely death had avoided their fate and gone on to live, love, and create? Or if one terrible person who overstayed their welcome had perished before his horrible deeds had come to fruition? It is easy for us to focus on the Events of the world, those cataclysms that shed human lives like fleas off the back of a dying dog, but I am left wondering if it isn't the comings and goings of single, solitary souls that mark the real tragedy in our lives."

"He sounds like the Fish," someone said behind Veronica, a whispered remark that elicited a muffled giggle.

"Single, solitary souls," Bittner repeated. He wasn't even trying to find the source of disruption in his class. His eyes were focused on Veronica.

JHT JHT JHT JHT
JHT JHT JHT JHT
JHT JHT II

Madeline had hung herself from the ceiling light in Eva's bedroom a year after Eva's death. August had come home from school and found her there, above the soft lavender carpet, still in her housecoat, both slippers dangling from her toes but not falling off, by some miracle of gravity.

He'd killed for the first time three years later. He'd driven to the city, hoping to outrun the depression that he knew would come in the days prior to the anniversaries of his daughter's and wife's deaths. Madeline had been driven mad by the absence of the 29th of February. He was fearful at its approach. His plan was to have a week of distraction, a holiday surrounded by people. People were everywhere in the city; even when one was locked safely behind a hotel door their presence was seen, felt, and heard; with sounds from the halls and streets echoing all around. Cooking smells, diesel smells, and others permeating the room. A million or more people were just outside the window no matter where you were in the city, and August had thought that being surrounded by all of that life would keep his mind off his pain.

It was a good strategy, and one that might have worked had Madeline not joined him on his trip.

She'd appeared beside him in the car as he was at a dead stop in traffic on Interstate 95, that most hated of roads. She whispered his name, and although her voice was low and hoarse, as though abraded by rope, he was so happy to hear her, tears sprang readily to his eyes.

"Madeline," he said. He could only see her as a reflection in the side mirror, but he could feel her presence, a warm electric charge in the car with him. "How I've missed you."

"I've been with Eva," she said. "She wants to come home."

The sound of her voice made his own throat dry, and he wished he'd brought a thermos of water or coffee. He angled his rearview, but even with the mirror positioned to reflect the passenger seat, she was at best a gray-brown blur.

"You've seen Eva?" he said, his heart filled to bursting with emotion.

"She departed on a special day, August," she said in her croaking voice. "A day when the veil between this life and the next is at its thinnest."

"I don't understand, Madeline. She . . . she died. Like you."

"You can bring her back," Madeline rasped. And then she told him how.

What Madeline proposed was too horrible to contemplate. He could, she said, open a door that Eva could walk though, but only on the anniversary of her death. Dates and anniversaries had meaning, she said, and in some ways it was very fortunate that Eva had died on a day when the veil between worlds was thin anyway. The problem was with the "door" that she encouraged him to open.

"You have to kill a girl Eva's age," she'd said. "At the moment the girl dies, the door opens. The girl steps through to the afterlife, and then our girl—Eva—can step through back into yours. We're all energy, August, and when Eva's energy returns she will live again in the other girl's body."

"No," August had whispered. The knot of traffic before him had begun to unravel, and he was able to put his car into gear. When he glanced in his rearview mirror, Madeline had gone.

She didn't return until he saw the runaway.

He'd been walking along a crowded side street, searching for bookstores and a good meal when he saw her. A few days had passed since his conversation with Madeline; he'd mostly written the incident off as an episode of stress and grief, but there had been many times while walking that his eyes rested a fraction too long on a passing teen, and he wondered, was it true? This girl was young-looking and wearing a battered army jacket. She was blond, whereas Eva's hair had been dark. She looked cold and hungry, and she was holding a sign stating that she was trying to raise bus fare to a town three states away.

Suddenly Madeline's voice and breath were like hot steam hissing in his ear.

"Look at her," she said. "Squandering what our Eva was cheated of. The world would not miss her!"

He winced and looked around him, but Madeline was not to be seen.

"Open the door, August!" she said, her voice loud and shrill in his ear. Finally he saw her reflection in the window of a parked taxi, an indistinct brownish mass hunching over his left shoulder. "She's our daughter!"

August closed his eyes and nearly doubled over, his insides clenching with pain and nausea. He felt a light pressure on his arm, and, thinking it was Madeline, he nearly cried out.

But when he opened his eyes, it was the girl who was touching him.

"Are you okay, mister?" she said.

"I'm . . . I'm fine," he said. "Thank you."

The cardboard sign she held flapped in the wind. She was wearing layers of clothing, each with a few tears that revealed the next layer beneath. She was shivering, either from the cold or from some type of withdrawal.

"She's weak," Madeline said, causing August to flinch. "She's perfect."

"The town you want to reach is very far away," he said.

She nodded. "I know. I've got an aunt there."

His throat was dry. "I have a car," he said, his voice constricted.

"I can't pay you," she said. "With money."

As though he were the sort of man who would want such a transaction from a girl not yet out of her teens. He had been much younger then, but thinking about her even now made the heat rise to his face, and his grip on his umbrella became so tight his leather gloves creaked against the strain. But he'd said yes and smiled, and they walked together the two blocks to the garage where he'd parked his car. Lord knows how many hundreds of people had seen them that day, something he'd sweated after her murder, wondering if her body would be found and traced back to him. He'd fed her, stopping at an off-ramp fast-food drive-through, and at her request he bought her a toothbrush, some toothpaste, and a stick of Teen Spirit at a convenience store. His next stop was a wooded commuter lot off the highway a few exits down from Jewell City—where he'd taken her sleeping body out of the car and into the woods—and there he killed her by wrapping his hands around her throat and squeezing, almost gently, with continued pressure until the life left her body. She'd woken up near the end, and he'd had to hit her, but even after her meal, she did not have a lot of struggle in her.

There was enough light that he could see the moon reflected in her eyes as he squeezed, and at one point he thought the light split in two.

"Eva," he said. "I'm here, Eva!"

But the girl died, and Eva did not come through. Kneeling in the leaves beside the girl's cooling body, August wept.

This time the reassuring hand on his shoulder was Madeline's.

"You failed," she whispered. "But there will be other chances."

He dragged the girl—Shelly, her name had been—beneath a hollow made by a rotted and fallen tree, and then gathered brush and leaves to further hide her. Years later, on a beautiful summer day, the city where August had sought life and solace was swept clean of those things and everything else by the Event, an irony that he thought of quite often.

The girl's body was never found.

He failed twice more over the years, with Mary and then Amber, and thus far he had failed to catch Veronica Calder. But there would be no hesitation this time, August thought. No hesitation and no last-moment appearances of spectral visitors to shake him from his course.

He parked in front of Pescatelli's house without bothering to see if anyone was watching him. There was no point in subterfuge, no point in covering his tracks, as he'd done so successfully over the past twelve years.

Pescatelli's car was in the driveway. August had waited in his classroom for a few moments after the final bell, until the mad din of the students had subsided to a few sneaker squeaks on tile. Even the ghosts had gone home. He sat at his desk and thought about what he would say to Pescatelli.

What he would do to Pescatelli.

He hadn't thought that he would kill him; it really wasn't what he was planning. Threaten him, yes. Physically harm him, yes. But not kill. The impulse to kill him didn't materialize until August had exited his parked car and started across the lawn.

He could feel strength coursing through him. Each embrace of one of his girls seemed to flood his system with power; he'd felt suffused with energy all day since holding Mary that morning.

There was an old man kneeling on a board in front of the snow-dusted hedges. The man wore a straw hat, grass-stained khaki pants, and a short-sleeve shirt that was so white it almost shone. He leaned forward to clip at the hedge, and long-needled branches passed through his clippers and into his chest when he leaned. The Fish, apparently, did not care for his shrubbery as the man once had.

The man disappeared. Without knowing why, the sight of those branches passing through the ghost filled August with a hot fury that begged release, as though the energy he'd drawn from his girls was about to explode.

The Fish answered on August's first knock.

"I've been waiting for you," he said, opening his screen door.

He was holding a gun.

卌 卌 卌 卌

卌 卌 卌 卌

卌 卌 III

"Are you okay?" Janine asked Veronica.

"I'm fine, Janine."

"You seem upset."

"I'm not upset."

"Really, because—"

"I said I'm not upset!"

Janine sighed. "Okay, okay. You aren't upset. Are you sad because you're fighting with Kirk?"

"Janine, I—"

Janine laughed, and Veronica turned toward her and saw there was something in her eyes that Veronica didn't often see—confidence and good humor.

"Sorry," Veronica said. "I'm a little on edge." Even though she'd watched for Bittner's car to leave the school lot, and watched him drive away down Fire Street in the opposite direction of their houses, she was nervous. She didn't think he'd try to get her during the school day, or so close to home.

Just live through the day, she thought. Everything will be fine if I can get through the day.

"Sure," Janine said. "Can I bring your present over later?"

"You can bring me presents whenever you want."

They were nearing Bittner's yard. The snow around his house was a bright white, the house itself dark and closed. Veronica thought she could see fluttering from an upstairs window.

What if it isn't me that he's after? she thought. What if he already has a girl trapped in his house and is just waiting for the right time to kill her?

She peered up at the house; there definitely was something moving upstairs.

I could just walk away, she thought, trying to see. I could just walk away, go home, and lock the door tightly behind me.

And maybe then Mary wouldn't be the only ghost forever climbing the steps onto Bittner's porch.

She looked up and down the street, then stepped off the plowed sidewalk and into the slushy street.

"Ronnie, what are you doing?" Janine said.

"Wait here," she said. "I want to check something out." Bittner's car wasn't in the driveway.

"Ronnie," Janine said, her voice a shrill whisper. "That's Bittner's house!"

"You go ahead, if you want. This will just take a minute," Veronica told her, nonchalant. "I'll be along in a bit."

Walking across the street, she withdrew her cell phone from her jacket. What would she do if she got to the window and saw bound feet, or a chained figure with a bag over her head? Would she have the courage to do something about it?

She heard her name whispered, harshly, but did not turn back.

IIII IIII IIII IIII
IIII IIII IIII IIII
IIII IIII IIII

I wait at the window like a faithful puppy. I see her enter his yard and I am confused, because it is not her appointed hour, and I realize it is not Mary I see but Veronica. Veronica, who is still among the living.

Veronica, who will not be among the living much longer if I am recognizing the signs correctly. I would scream if I had a voice.

She moves swiftly across the street toward his yard, as though she has a right to be there, as though she has a right to walk without fear. Mary was the same way. She'd liked our history teacher, thought him a kind man. She didn't know.

Veronica should know. Maybe what she knows is incomplete.

I cannot scream, but I can pray.

You go ahead.

Veronica had said it with confidence, but that confidence had nearly deserted her by the time she'd made it halfway across the road. The temperature seemed to be dropping with each step, the wind like icy fingers trying to claw through her coat. She squinted up at the window and saw it again, the flickering. She couldn't shake the feeling that someone was tied up in that room. There was a slight gap, just a few inches wide, where she thought she might be able to see in if she had the right angle.

She turned and saw that Janine was still standing there on the sidewalk, puffs of vapor rising from her.

Veronica waved mittened fingers at her, and smiled against her fear. She took a step into Bittner's snow-covered yard.

Screw you, Mr. Bittner, she thought.

There was a glare as she looked up at the window, but it was gone in a few steps. And then through the gap in the curtain, she saw the shoe. It was dangling from a foot that was suspended in midair.

Veronica brought her hand to her mouth in the same moment that Janine screamed.

"Ghost!"

Veronica turned, thinking Janine had somehow seen the shoe from all the way across the street. Janine was off and running, moving with a speed her slight frame seemed incapable of. Stunned, Veronica watched her slip and go sprawling. Without looking back, Janine picked herself up off the ground and continued to slip and slide in a mad dash to get away from whomever—or whatever—she'd seen.

Frightened, Veronica backed away a few steps, and saw why she'd run.

She'd expected Bittner, as though he'd somehow teleported home from school. Instead she saw that it was a familiar ghost that Janine had been frightened by—but it was acting in a completely unfamiliar way.

Mary Greer was in the act of descending the porch steps,

which alone was a divergence from the pattern Veronica was familiar with. Mary went down the steps, her bare feet leaving no mark on the snow at the edge of the walkway. Her neck was broken so badly that her cheek nearly rested upon her shoulder, and her eyes were wide and staring right into Veronica's soul. Her mouth opened and closed, but no sound came out.

Veronica tried to back away, but she was rooted in place. Like a statue. Like a ghost caught in its pattern. To the right of Mary, in the empty driveway, a young blond girl appeared from nowhere, her body unfolding as though she were stepping from an unseen automobile. She was wearing a drab green army jacket that would have been no protection against the chill, if she could have felt it.

The second girl walked toward Veronica, but did so with a strange, hobbling gate. She was thin to the point of emaciation, and her jacket was ragged at the cuffs. She blinked in and out of existence every two or three steps. She walked with her chin lowered, her blond hair shading her eyes from Veronica's view.

The two girls moved toward her, and Veronica couldn't even scream. She didn't know what was worse—the lopsided, idiot grin that Mary Greer wore or not being able to see the blond girl's face at all.

Shaking free from her paralysis, Veronica turned to run, but stopped short, watching as a third figure rose out of the ground, its arms and legs in a crablike posture. It was Amber, the ghost Veronica had seen at the mill. Amber stood, unfolding like a marionette jerked by its strings, and stared up at Veronica with bright, expectant, almost hopeful eyes—and again Veronica didn't know which specter she feared the most. She turned back with lowered eyes, wanting to see how close the ghosts were, but too afraid to look at their faces.

Veronica was saying a prayer in her head—not a prayer, really, more of a plea—*Please, God. Please, God. Please, God.* She cast her gaze skyward, hoping to speed her prayers to heaven, but she found that looking up had been a mistake.

A woman came through the window as easily as she would the surface of a swimming pool. She was hanging from a rope, a rope that passed right through the aluminum siding, a rope that was attached to the sky. The slipper dangling from the woman's foot slid off and disappeared in the air before Veronica's face as the woman began to descend, lowered by the rope as though she were the bait on some unseen fisherman's pole.

Veronica, with effort, pulled her eyes away, but the moment that she did so, the ghost of Mary Greer passed into her. There was a sound, a brief burst of static, but the noise was all in Veronica's head. The girl's memories flooded through her, making her instantly nauseous, her spine and brain aching. There was another shock to her system as she felt Amber's chill touch along and then in her spinal column. Her body gave a shuddery convulsion just as the blond girl raised her head and stared into Veronica's soul with empty eyes; and then she too stepped into Veronica.

Veronica wanted to throw up, but her body would not let her as the girls' lives flashed before her. The agony was intense; she couldn't breathe. She tried to straighten, but the woman with the rope was there, hovering just above her. And then she was inside of her.

At once, Veronica knew. She knew it all.

Her scream shattered the window the ghost had floated through, and a sharp rain of glass fell to the ground below.

⸻ ⸻ ⸻ ⸻

⸻ ⸻ ⸻ ⸻

⸻ ⸻ ⸻

"Have a seat, August," Pescatelli said, motioning to the sofa with his gun.

August looked at him, very surprised that the man's hand was not shaking. August knew nothing about guns. It looked small and ineffectual, like the man himself.

"Aren't you going to offer to take my hat and coat?" he said, smiling.

"Just sit down. And keep it buttoned. Put your hands in the air."

"Stephen . . ."

"Sit down, August," Pescatelli said. The hammer was back on the gun, August noticed. He sat.

"You came here to kill me," the Fish said.

"Don't be a fool," August replied. "I came here to tell you . . . to ask you to leave me alone."

"I can't do that, August," Pescatelli said. "Not now."

"Can't, or won't?" August wanted to keep him talking. He realized that it was quite likely this myopic runt, this half man, might actually pull the trigger and kill him. Why not? What did he have to live for beyond a life, quite literally, of chasing phantoms.

"You murdered those girls, August. Both of them."

"What girls, Stephen?" August said, noting that Pescatelli's arm was steady when he made the accusation. He was standing about ten feet away. A low flat coffee table, nearly the entire length of the sofa, was between them, pressed into the deep pile carpet by a half dozen stacks of books.

"You know, August," he said. "I've seen the tape."

"Tape?" Pescatelli would shoot him in the time it took to flip the table over. He didn't think kicking it would be enough.

"Don't be coy, August. We both know what I'm talking about. Mary Greer. Amber Davis."

August watched Pescatelli wet his lips. "Ah," August said. Maybe he could shock Pescatelli, get that gun quivering in his tiny, pudgy hands. Maybe he'd get an opening. Or get shot, but what did he have to lose? "Those girls."

"You're admitting it?" Pescatelli said, and then his gun arm did shake. And why not? What else did the Fish have in his pathetic little life but the thrill of discovery? At least August had his memories.

"Why shouldn't I?" August said, pleased with how agitated the Fish appeared to be getting. "You say you have a tape. And you are pointing a gun at me. What else can I do?"

"You're being coy again."

"Are you going to shoot me?" August said, and then Pescatelli made a mistake.

"I'm not going to shoot you," he said. "I'm going to call the police. I want to see you in jail for this."

"Call the police?" August laughed. "And what will happen then, when they gently pry the gun away from your fat little fingers? Am I supposed to confess?"

That really riled him, August thought. But he didn't think Pescatelli had the nerve to shoot him. He almost said as much.

"You'll confess. They'll see the image and you'll have to confess."

August made a great show of shrugging. "As you say."

The other man's shoulders seemed to droop. The gun wavered.

"Why did you do it, Gus? Why did you kill them?"

August smiled. "Why, indeed."

He almost laughed out loud at Pescatelli's expression: it truly was fishlike. The gaping mouth that opened and closed, the eyes wide and magnified behind the thick lenses. His hand was really shaking now.

"They are returning to me, Stephen," August said. "My girls. The first one has come back to me. She climbs into my car and we ride off together into eternity."

Pescatelli stared, his mouth working as though trying to capture words that were floating past his face. August made a point of looking him directly in the eyes. The table was just below knee level.

"You can send the boy 'round to my house," he said. "Have him bring his camera. You can film our embrace."

When Pescatelli finally found his voice, it was like a strangled cry, an anguished word meant to be called up and released in a final breath.

"Why?"

"You really want to know?" August leaned forward and lowered his voice to a whisper.

Pescatelli, idiot that he was, leaned forward as well, nodding. "Yes," he said, his voice, his whole body, vibrating. "I really want to know."

"I'm just like you, aren't I?"

"What . . . what do you mean by *that*? I'm no murderer."

"This silly little book of yours," August said. "It is how you are trying to resurrect them, isn't it?"

Pescatelli shook his head. "I don't—"

"Don't pretend. It's your way of trying to bring them back to you. Your dead wife and daughter. Isn't it? Well, that's what I am trying to do, too. Bring back Eva."

"How? How does killing—"

"You are a man who looks at pictures, Stephen. Images. That's what you do. You sit and you observe and jot down notes and pretend you are going to change the world."

Pescatelli looked mesmerized, an image frozen in a still photograph.

"I act," Bittner said. "You observe, I act. There is a veil between this world and the next, as you state in such a puerile fashion in your book. The veil may be crossed permanently, once a suitable vessel is found."

Pescatelli's gun hand wavered. "I don't understand what you are trying to say."

"I'm saying that they can be brought back, Stephen," August replied. "I'm saying that I saw Eva—her spirit, her soul—in their eyes as they drifted away. She was there, just out of reach. But I know how I can reach her."

Pescatelli wet his lips. "You think that she can, what, *possess* the body of someone you kill? Is that what you mean?"

"What I mean is—" August reached for the edge of the table with both hands and yanked, sending books and papers and photographs and the heavy wooden table upward and outward, propelling himself forward with both legs, literally leaping up from the couch as the table flipped and struck the Fish in the knees. The gun went off, and August was on Pescatelli before he hit the floor, driving him down into the shag carpeting with the full weight of his body. The gun spun away, and August's hands were around the Fish's throat.

"You shot me!" August screamed, and he could feel it, a hot red stripe along his side where the bullet had struck. "You shot me!"

He pressed his thumbs into Pescatelli's windpipe, and already the man had begun to choke. He looked more like a fish than ever, his eyes bugging, their gaze flattening as August's concentration narrowed to a single point on his throat. Pescatelli's tongue protruded from his open mouth, and he made a sound like a cat in agony.

August lifted Pescatelli's head from the floor and brought it swiftly down, twice, even while applying increasing pressure on his throat with his thumbs.

"You know why I killed them, Fish-man?" he shouted, bringing Pescatelli's head up and down, squeezing, squeezing. "You want to know? So I could keep them!"

He was shouting, he knew, dimly hoping that Pescatelli did not have nosy neighbors who cared about him. Spittle dripped from his mouth and spattered on the left lens of Pescatelli's glasses, but the dying man did not blink.

"So I could keep them," he repeated. "So I could keep them forever."

He punctuated every other word with another slam to the floor. At some point Pescatelli's eyes rolled back in his head.

August knew he was dead, but he kept squeezing anyway. The pain in his side was like a hot iron being pressed into him by devilish hands.

"The way I'll keep you," he said, although Stephen Pescatelli could no longer hear.

August saw movement from the corner of his eye. He turned, and there was Pescatelli sitting at his desk by the wall, staring at a blank computer screen, drinking from an invisible mug.

August actually had to make a conscious effort to will his hands from the dead man's throat, and even when he stood, his fingers seemed to retract into crabbed claws within the black leather gloves. He looked back from the ghost to the piece of meat cooling on the beige shag carpeting, and he laughed.

"The way I'll keep you," he repeated, hurling back Pescatelli's chair with one hand, sending it flying against the wall, where it punched a hole in the Sheetrock and sent a framed picture crashing to the floor. The ghost, still bent in a seated posture, did not seem to notice, not even as August stepped forward and into it.

The feeling in his gut after he laughed was a ripple compared to the wave of nausea and pain that washed over him as he merged with Pescatelli's ghost. It felt as though someone were raking hooks slicked with a noxious chemical through his insides, and he cried out in pain. Groaning, he saw himself reflected in the glasses of the dead man, and the face he saw staring back at him was old and tortured, a fiend with no trace of the young teacher and husband and father he'd been, so many years ago. He fell onto his back, away from the image.

The Fish stared down at him. He was smiling. Then he was gone.

August closed his eyes, and he could see himself, a pale, slavering revenant pacing the hallways of an empty school long after the children had all gone home. There wasn't much time.

August struggled to sit up. His trench coat was dark with blood a few inches above his right hip, and there were stains on the carpet as well. Not much time at all, he thought.

She had to die. Now.

He got to his feet.

卌 卌 卌 卌
卌 卌 卌 卌
卌 卌 卌 |

Kirk went in his mother's car. He was kicking himself for not having followed Ronnie home, but he'd watched Bittner leave immediately after school and drive in the opposite direction from his home, looking like he had an important errand to run.

Kirk knew he couldn't allow things with Ronnie to end where they now stood; not unless he wanted to be haunted for the rest of his life by the fading memory of kissing her.

One more day, he thought. If she could just make it one more day, then maybe she'd be all right. Maybe then Bittner would prove himself to be nothing more than some weird old bachelor, and the deaths would be nothing more than coincidences puffed up into a conspiracy by the tired and haunted mind of Stephen Pescatelli.

One more day.

Before backing out of the driveway, he looked up at his little sister, sticking her tongue out at him behind the dusty surface of an upstairs window. He returned the endearment and started backing into the street.

His cell phone rang. *Private Number*, the display told him. He stopped the car, half in and half out of his driveway, to answer it.

"Hello?"

"There's something else," a male voice told him.

"What?"

"Bittner's wife. She killed herself in February." It took Kirk a moment to realize it was the Fish.

"She did?"

"She hung herself at home. In Eva's room."

"She . . . she hung herself?" Kirk whispered. He hadn't realized she'd committed suicide. Was that why Bittner strangled them?

"Eva's room."

"What day?" Kirk said. His mind was racing, and it was difficult to hear the Fish. He sounded like he was transmitting from the other side of the world. "What day did she do it? Was it a leap year?"

"Eva's room. She hung herself in Eva's room at midnight on the twenty-eighth of February."

"Eva? Eva is their daughter?"

"Eva."

"What? Listen, was it a leap year?"

"Not a leap year. Eva was the leap year."

"Are you saying *Eva* or *Evil*?"

"Catch. Catch her breath."

"You aren't making a lot of sense, Mr. Pescatelli," Kirk said. He couldn't tell if the phone was echoing or if the Fish was repeating himself. "Can we go to the police—"

"No."

"Go to the police. If we go to the police they could—"

"No. He is killing her."

"What?"

"He is killing her. Now."

Kirk dropped the phone and pressed his foot down on the accelerator.

‖‖‖ ‖‖‖ ‖‖‖ ‖‖‖
‖‖‖ ‖‖‖ ‖‖‖ ‖‖‖
‖‖‖ ‖‖‖ ‖‖‖ ‖‖

Veronica's hand rose involuntarily to her throat. That's how he'd killed all of them.

Shelly Bonder was a young blond runaway who was trying to go to an aunt in Ohio. When the ghosts touched Veronica she could see their lives playing like a movie in her head. But it was more than a movie, because she could feel herself—her consciousness—slipping back and forth between the players in the dramas as they unfolded before her. First she was Bittner, then Shelly, then August again—he was a prematurely old man muttering to himself on a street corner, she was a runaway teen, strung out and hungry. Veronica relived the moments leading up to her death, the empty lot off the exit ramp, the sensation of being carried through the woods on a cold winter's night. She was Shelly when she breathed her last, and then she was August as he hurried to hide her. There were tears in his eyes when he walked back through the woods; her body was cooling under a decaying oak, but his car was still warm.

My daughter, he thought, after she was hidden away. And once she existed only in his memory, she became more fully his. *My daughter my daughter my daughter.*

Two others. Mary and Amber.

When Mary's ghost had touched her, Veronica saw a girl taken completely by surprise by her teacher—a man she'd trusted and liked, one she'd visited with some frequency on the way to her boyfriend's. Sometimes just to say hello, sometimes to bring him cookies or a brownie from the batch she'd made for Brian. He was a lonely man growing older, and she was a girl with some problems at home, and for a while they cast a little light into each other's dark places.

But the anger was still in him, the anger and the madness that comes from loss. Mr. Bittner began to believe that his wife was calling to him, telling him to "take care" of their daughter. Mary had no idea what he was doing right up until the moment that his hands began to squeeze.

Then Amber, four years later. The image of Amber scuttling backward like a crab in the dust of the mill basement, trying to escape him, was already etched permanently in Veronica's mind, but now she saw it from the perspective of Amber herself. A wash of feelings, of fear and betrayal, came over her as huge hands reached for her throat.

But the most powerful jolt to Veronica's system had come when Madeline's ghost touched her. All of that poor woman's smashed hopes and crushed expectations flooded into Veronica's brain.

Veronica could hear Madeline Bittner's voice as the specter of the hanging woman settled into her the way one would settle into a new coat.

She was a rare child, the voice said. *Born after I'd miscarried twice. There were complications, for her and for me. Her lungs were underdeveloped; I would never have children again.*

Veronica could see a crib; she floated above and looked down; the baby within was red-faced, her cries choked and gasping

I never left her side. I felt like I was the one holding my breath. But what she lacked for in strength, my beautiful Eva made up for in spirit. She survived infancy and grew. There were scares in her young life, close calls that, were it not for the extra inhalers cached like rainy-day money in purses, pockets, and glove compartments, might have meant an even earlier death for poor, frail Eva. But she weathered all of those scares bravely and sweetly. She never let on that she was afraid.

Veronica felt a darkness cover her like a shroud.

She lived until she was sixteen. And then, despite her spirit, her throat closed up like a frozen drain on a frigid February afternoon.

Veronica could feel her pain, the totality of it, a cold crushing weight pressing in on her.

I was sick, the voice said. *And I could not get well. The loss of my daughter was not something I had the strength to overcome. August tried to help me, but I froze him out. My suffering was a wall that I hid behind, one he could not break through. He was attentive, concerned—even though he was suffering himself—but I would not come out, and I would not let him in. He faded from my view, a ghost himself.*

My depression gave way to mania. I became obsessed with the day of her death . . . February 29. I would look on the calendar for that date . . . and it would not arrive. It did not exist. And if the day did not exist, then my daughter did not exist.

315

Veronica tried to reply, but couldn't, not verbally. What she could do was project her feelings: her sadness, her empathy.

Madeline Bittner's tone seemed to soften as she continued.

I wanted my daughter. I wanted to hold her. To love her. But Eva was gone. She was gone.

Veronica was aware that she was lying in the snow. From a distance, she could feel the cold and damp numbing her skin. But she was elsewhere as well, a strange in-between world where she had no solid form.

She was gone, but I wanted to be with her. And so I tried to join her. I timed my passing from this world to the next to happen at midnight on the 28th. I thought the timing was important. It was not.

Veronica then felt a wave of emotion that was completely overpowering, one that erased the distant feeling of cold. It was a wave of complete happiness and joy, an almost overpowering wave of affection.

The timing wasn't important at all. But Eva was here. *She was* here.

Veronica felt the wave of joy transform—it ebbed and was replaced by other feelings equally as powerful—guilt, remorse, shame.

But August was not. My suicide broke him; he was already so fragile from the loss of Eva and my year-long silence. Like me, he began to obsess about the 29th—the day that appeared infrequently, like a faerie gate. But his obsession took him down a far different path than mine.

I tried to speak to him. Even before the Event, when the veil between the realm of the living and the dead was at its thinnest,

316

I tried to speak to him. My whispers, like my actions, I fear, only served to feed his madness. He believed I was asking him to kill those girls. The voice he listens to is not mine. The image of me he sees is not me.

He believes I asked him to kill you.

The next wave of guilt and sadness that washed over Veronica's mind was too great for her to bear.

But not before she heard Madeline one last time.

He's coming.

Veronica opened her eyes.

Her own hands were resting on her throat, and she was having trouble breathing. Not, she realized, because of self-strangulation, but because Janine was standing over her spraying great clouds of potpourri-scented Ghost-B-Gone from the cans in each of her mittened hands.

"Get out of her!" Janine was shouting. "Out! Out! Out!"

Eventually, Veronica sat up, coughing and waving powdery clouds away from her face.

"Ronnie?" Janine said, spritzing again. "Are you all right?"

Veronica's voice wouldn't come—she was choking on the awful powder—so she nodded. She didn't know how long she'd been lying in the snow beneath Bittner's living room window—she didn't think it had been long, but the snow had melted in a two-foot radius around her body. Her back and bottom were soaked. Her cell phone was on the ground beside her. She tried to turn it on, but it was dead.

"I'm sorry I ran away," Janine said. She was soaked to the skin after her multiple pratfalls in the snow. "I went to get my spray. They don't let me carry it in school. I came back and saw the ghosts touching you. Why did they do that?"

Veronica answered with a shake of her head. She knew the answer to that question, but what she didn't know was why the ghosts were able to do what they did; what enabled them to break out of their pattern and touch her. Nor did she know why their touch brought knowledge.

"Let me help you home," Janine said.

Veronica didn't argue, and allowed Janine to hold her arm for the short walk to her house. She tried to keep her eyes focused straight ahead, on her front door, but even so she could see ghosts—dozens of them—along the way, in the street, in yards, watching from windows. A ghost boy played catch with an unseen partner. Mrs. Clare, three years in her grave, shuffled to her mailbox in housecoat and slippers. Mary Greer walked beside Veronica, a smile on her face, her head held at a terrible angle. Janine could not see them, and Veronica could sense her concern as she fumbled with her keys. Her mother wasn't home, and that as much as her wet clothing, made her feel cold inside.

"Ronnie? Can I—"

"I'm okay, Janine," she said. "Thank you."

"Are you sure?"

"I'm sure. I'll see you tomorrow." She hoped. She was going to go upstairs, change, call her mother, and if her mother couldn't come home right away, Veronica was going to call a cab and go to her.

Then she turned and wrapped Janine in a big hug.

"That was very brave of you," she said. Over her shoulder,

she could see Mary Greer smiling up at her from the bottom step. Veronica did not turn away.

"It was, wasn't it?" Janine said.

Mary's head slowly began to tilt, and she managed to keep from crying out when it straightened, the vertebrae clicking into place.

"Yes, Janine," Veronica said, not turning away even then. "It was."

```
卌 卌 卌 卌
卌 卌 卌 卌
卌 卌 卌 III
```

I see Mary standing there looking up at me and I can feel my energy coalescing; I can feel myself attaining a gravity I never could feel before. Beholding her as Veronica's little friend from up the street, oblivious, walked right through her, I felt that I could make myself alter the present. I felt so strong I could alter the past and the future as well.

Mary begins to fade from my sight even as Veronica opens the door, stepping around me as she hurries into the kitchen, locking the door behind her.

"You'll protect me, won't you, Brian?" she says, a brief glimmer of relief in her tired eyes. "Just long enough for me to change and get out of here?"

Can she see me?

I try to speak, but I can form no words. I can't even warn her.

So instead, I nod.

In truth, I have no idea if I can "protect" her or not. I am little more than a memory, and the strength of memory often fails the living.

She reaches out, her hand grazing the air where my insubstantial face hangs, and I feel myself grow even stronger.

As she turns, I allow myself to fade from view, conserving what strength remains.

IIII IIII IIII IIII

IIII IIII IIII IIII

IIII IIII IIII IIII

Veronica went upstairs and was out of her wet clothes in moments, changing into jeans and a sweater as swiftly as she could manage. She pulled on her sneakers and took the stairs two at a time. She reached the kitchen phone and began to dial. She planned to be out and away before Bittner could make it there—she had no doubt he was on his way.

The knock on the door startled her so much she screamed and dropped the phone, and it hit with sufficient force to open up the battery compartment.

"Brian!" she yelled, seeing the shadow fall across the pane. "Brian, help me!"

He didn't appear. She heard her name, from a voice that sounded worlds away.

She backed against the kitchen table, pushing it at least a foot along the wall. Dimly, she was aware that if she didn't move it to its original location, her father would be sliced in half. A face crowded into the gap between the curtains, and she shrieked again.

"Ronnie!" Kirk called. He was tapping on the window. "Ronnie, let me in!"

Veronica muttered a word that she was glad her father's

image wasn't around to hear. The dial tone was an insistent buzz from the fallen phone.

She walked over to the door and unlatched it.

"What do *you* want?" she said, standing inside the screen door. But really she was elated; she didn't think she'd ever been happier to see a living person than she was right then. And with a car, no less! If he hadn't had the audacity to look relieved, she probably would have thrown her arms around his neck and planted a big kiss on his cheek. Or his lips.

"Can I come in?" he said. "Please? I want to talk to you."

"What about?"

"You know," he said. "About you hating me and everything."

She made a show of rolling her eyes. "Come on in, then." She turned from him and went to get the bleating phone.

"Thanks," he said, opening the door and letting himself in. "So, can we talk a little?"

"Sure." She pushed the plastic battery cover on the phone until it clicked into place, then she slid the table back to its proper position. "I was just going to call my mother."

"Oh, yeah?"

"Yeah," she said. "Lucky for you I'm in desperate need of a ride. So maybe you can apologize to me on the way as you bring me to her."

"Apologize to you? I think you were the one that mentioned 'hating.' I don't think I mentioned anything about 'hating.'"

Veronica held up her finger to shush him after dialing her mother's number. She waited until her voice mail picked up, then left a message saying that she was going to meet her at work. She replaced the phone on the wall when she was done.

"I'm sorry I said I hated you," she said. "I don't hate you."

Kirk's mouth opened and closed in a comical fashion. Boys, as always, were so easy to catch off guard.

"And . . . and I'm sorry I kept pressing you," he said. "I don't know when to back off sometimes."

"That's okay. It's good, usually."

"I should have . . ."

Veronica shook her head and took her keys from the table.

"No, you were right. I'm in danger. Mr. Bittner is coming for me, I know it."

"You do?"

She nodded. "I do. And I also know how I can make the police listen to us."

"How? Spectral evidence—"

"I know all about spectral evidence; you told me. We'll still show them that. But I also know where Mr. Bittner's first victim is hidden, and the police have no idea that the cases are even connected. He killed a runaway and hid her in the woods off of 95 almost twelve years ago, and no one ever knew."

"You think they'll listen?"

"They'll have to. Mr. Bittner doesn't know it, but she pocketed a few things from his car when he wasn't looking. Coins, a pen, and a credit card receipt. With that, and the more 'spectral evidence' that you can show them, I think the police will have enough to make an arrest."

"They better," Kirk said. "Or . . ."

He trailed off, his eyes scanning hers.

"Or what?" she said softly.

"Or else you'll still be in danger."

She stepped toward him, and his arms went around her, hugging her tightly. She closed her eyes and breathed in. The air around him was scented with cologne.

"How do you know all that?"

"She told me. Mrs. Bittner." She realized that what she smelled wasn't Kirk's cologne, though. It was Brian's.

"*Mrs.* Bittner?"

Veronica nodded. "I went to his house, and—"

"You went to his *house*?" Kirk said.

"Are you going to keep interrupting me?" When, chastened, he assured her he wasn't, Veronica began giving him a shortened version of what she'd experienced, of how the ghosts had surrounded and then entered her.

"I felt their memories when they touched me. That poor woman. His wife, I mean. She killed herself, you know. Hung herself in—"

"In Eva's room," Kirk whispered.

"Yeah," Veronica said, looking puzzled. "How did *you* know that?"

He shook his head. "Wh . . . why did she do it?"

"Severe depression. Kirk, that poor family! I feel bad for *him*, even. Imagine losing a child, your only child, what that must be like."

"On the 29th," Kirk said, thinking of the Fish and his little girl. "Eva. I . . . I took a phone call from the Fish before I came here. He told me. Ronnie, I think he's dead."

"What?"

"I think he was dead when he called me," he said. "He wasn't making sense. He was mostly incoherent and . . . distant. We have to get out of here. He was trying to warn me."

Veronica could see how fearful he was. The smell of cologne in the air seemed to intensify. "What else did he say?"

He grabbed her arm. "I'll get you to your mom," he said. "Then we'll go to the police."

"What else did he say, Kirk?"

"Please," Kirk said as he pulled her toward the door. "Let's just go!"

She looked over his shoulder in time to see a huge shadow looming at the window, and then she was screaming.

Bittner was lucky. He yanked the screen door open, and when he pushed the heavy wooden kitchen door it struck the Lane boy just as he was turning. August lashed out with the hand that held the flashlight, hitting Kirk on the chin and sending him to the floor in a tangled heap. Timing, everything was timing. Wasn't that what this day was all about? His daughter fell back, and August kicked the boy's legs out of the way so he could close the door behind him.

"My daughter," he said, blood dripping from his wound onto the tile. The moment he said it, a man appeared at the table beyond her, and in that instant August hesitated, which allowed his daughter to take a step back.

Why does she cower? he thought. Why doesn't she run to her father's waiting arms?

He reached for her.

Mr. Bittner burst from the doorway and stepped over Kirk, his eyes the red and glassy orbs of a dying animal not fully aware of its fate. His trench coat spread open like great leathern wings, and Veronica saw a wide patch of blood—his?—dampening the tan fabric and the dark suit beneath. There was no sound but that of his swift movement, but it filled the house as Veronica turned and caught sight of her father sitting at the kitchen table. As she ran past and into the living room beyond, she heard Bittner carom off the table, hard enough to send the mail sliding to the floor. He seemed to ricochet in a manner that almost made it seem as though her father's ghost had tripped him.

Thank you, Daddy, she thought.

Veronica ran, her momentary shock at seeing Bittner's form lurching at her gone as she took flight, the image of his black gloves reaching for her etched in her mind. She made it to the stairs at the end of the hall and hauled herself up with the banister, stumbling slightly on the second step.

Where am I going? she thought. There was only one door that locked; the one to the bathroom. She looked up and there was Brian waiting at the top of the stairs.

Her pause was fractional. Her pumping legs took her to and through Brian, and she felt a brief tingle of energy as she passed through his misty form. Below her, Bittner was staggering, hitting walls. The cuckoo clock in the hallway fell and shattered, and she heard him grunt with surprise as he saw the ghost.

She turned, knowing she shouldn't—but where could she go? Her room—the door of which was pressboard thin and without a lock? Out the window? If she jumped she'd probably break both her ankles, and he'd be out the door and on the lawn with his hands around her throat even if he was carrying around a belly full of buckshot. He *had* been shot, hadn't he? Why else would his shirt be soaked through? If only Veronica could last long enough for him to pass out or, better yet, to die.

But what if he died here and didn't leave? she thought. What if he remained a ghost, like her father and Brian, trapped in this world?

Better than me being a ghost, she thought. She shuddered as she made the turn at the top of the stairs, determined to stay alive.

Below her, Brian looked as though he were trying to punch or push Bittner. He'd drifted down two steps and was standing like an offensive lineman across the stairs, but his blows passed through Bittner's clothes and into his body and seemed to have little effect. Bittner swung his hand, which passed through Brian as easily as it would a cobweb. Made bold by the lack of effect that the ghost seemed to have on him, Bittner ascended another stair, passing right through Brian as though he wasn't there at all.

Which, Veronica realized, he wasn't. Brian disappeared.

She watched for a moment longer, just as Bittner screamed and bent at the waist, as though passage through the ghost had given him the worst kind of indigestion possible—either that, or whatever it was that was causing his life to drain out of his side was beginning to catch up with him. He clutched at his stomach, at the dark stain that was spreading across his shirt.

Live, Ronnie, Veronica thought.

Bittner grunted in agony as she willed herself into motion. If she stayed where she was, he could have her in four long strides.

She ran to her room and slammed the door. She look around

328

for a weapon, mentally cursing herself for the extreme girlyness of her bedroom: cushions, pillows, a quilted comforter, and lacy curtains. If she were a boy, maybe she'd have a rifle or at least a machete hidden away in her closet. As it was, about the deadliest thing she had on hand were the cologne-scented cards that had fallen from her magazine and littered her bed.

Her dead cell phone was downstairs, tucked away in a special pouch of her backpack. There was a working phone in her mother's room, but she hadn't had the presence of mind to go for it; she doubted that she would have had enough time to dial before he got to her anyway. Running upstairs was beginning to feel like the height of stupidity to Veronica, but what choice had she had? She'd never have gotten by him to go out through the kitchen door.

There was a low footlocker at the end of her bed. It was filled with deadly weapons like teddy bears, doll clothes, and valentines boys had written her dating back to the third grade. Not knowing what else to do, she dragged it to the door.

She had no intention of trying to use it as a barricade. The trunk itself was heavier than its contents. She could probably lift it over her head and toss it if she was so inclined.

She wasn't. Instead she did a quick mental measurement of the length of the door and set the trunk about six inches away from where she thought was the widest part of its swing. Then she stepped back and tensed herself for a charge.

It almost worked. Bittner hurled the door open, and the sight of Veronica was like waving a red cape in front of a charging bull. He lurched forward, hands grasping at the air in front of him. He wasn't aware of the trunk until he ran into it. His momentum tangled his legs, and he pitched forward onto his face.

Daylight. The open door beckoned Veronica, but Bittner tried to make a grab for her. She leaped over his grasping arm, landing squarely on his back, and then sprang for the hall. She knew she could outrun him. If she could reach the stairs, she'd be home free. The way he looked, he might even bleed out before he escaped the house. Except . . .

Except he kicked at her as she bounded away, and the heel of his shoe caught her just beneath her knee. There was a pop, and she screamed as an explosion of pain shivered throughout her skeleton. Now it was Veronica's turn to hit the floor, and hit it hard.

Maybe it was her father's voice that spoke to her through the swirl of stars. Maybe it was Brian's. Probably it was her own. The voice told her to move, whatever the pain she felt, because if she stayed there, she would surely die. She saw Bittner crawling toward her, dragging himself along like a reptile.

She had a dizzy vision of him, blood trickling from one corner of his mouth like a cartoon vampire, a much lighter hue than the blood soaking his coat and shirt. He was grinning at her, one hand wheeling as the other pushed him up to a sitting position. He steadied his legs as he got to his feet.

Veronica hauled herself to her feet using the railing, the pain in her knee bringing with it a thick feeling of nausea. She managed one step but then fell in a heap at the top of the stairs. She thought she felt his touch, or his breath, on the back of her neck. She turned just as his shoe drove into her side. She felt him crouch and knew he was reaching for her.

She screamed.

"Hush, daughter," he said, his voice soft, almost gentle.

I failed to stop him.

I failed Veronica as I'd failed my Mary. All my efforts were useless, my punches ineffectual no matter how much I tried to focus my hate and anger into them, no matter how much I tried to visualize my vengeance as a hot spike through his heart. The only pain he'd felt was when he'd moved through me, when something in his bowels churned and another piece of his life broke away. But then he was past me and after her again.

She was down, in pain. He was nearly upon her. I could wash over him, let him breathe me in and cluster in the center of his pain, but I knew it wouldn't be enough. Once his hands were around her throat he would fight through the agony and drag her down into death with him.

I could feel the atmosphere around us changing. Sudden death makes the barrier between this world and the next thinner, and their deaths—his and hers—would open small tears.

I heard the boy he'd knocked to the ground groan from the kitchen and thought I might have one more try.

She tried to crawl, but then his knee was in her back and his hands were on her shoulder. He was turning her over.

He rolled her with ease, his strength not ebbing fast enough. She scratched at his face and may have cut his cheek, but he battered her hands aside. He pinned one of her arms beneath his leg. He slapped her and she saw lights, stars, the spirit world. He placed his hand on her throat.

She jabbed him in the belly with her free hand, aiming for the center of the dark red stain soaking his shirt, and he shrieked like a feral cat. She twisted beneath him and made it halfway onto her stomach, but then he palmed her skull and slammed her face-first into the carpet.

He's killing her, I whispered into the boy's ear. *Right now, he is killing her.*

The boy tried to sit up, but his eyeballs seemed loose in their sockets and could not focus. His head lolled to the side and he slumped over. There was a bloody cut from where the door had struck his head.

You have to get up! I screamed. *Don't let him kill again!*

The boy blinked. He tried to stand, but his legs slid out from under him. Consciousness was slipping away from him.

She must be dying, I thought. The veil had been rent open, and ghosts began to manifest. Real ghosts, not the pale images that the Event had left behind. I could feel them take shape in the room.

Hovering, I settled onto Kirk like a second skin.

Veronica tasted tears and blood as Bittner hauled her to him and onto her back. But as he did, she caught a glimpse of what was at the foot of the stairs.

People. A trio of girls. Madeline Bittner, holding the hand of one of them. Mr. Pescatelli joined them, and for a moment Veronica thought he might save her, but then she realized she could see the hallway wall through his transparent body.

They were all reaching upward, their hands pointed at the

monster that was about to kill her, expressions of deep sorrow etched upon their faces. Brian, looking more solid than ever, moved through their ranks toward the stairs.

Not Brian, but Kirk, Veronica realized. But his posture was different, and his eyes . . .

But it was too late. She was on her back, and the animal madness was clear in Bittner's eyes as his fingers probed for her neck.

"Eva!" he yelled, staring into her eyes—staring *through* her eyes—like they were portholes into another world. "Eva, come to me!"

His thumbs were pressing with killing force against Veronica's windpipe. The real world began to fade from view.

She didn't understand what happened next.

Bittner became airborne. He was choking her and then he was flying through the air as though shoved by strong arms.

It was as though gravity had ceased to be for a moment, and then a high wind had come and blown August Bittner away, down toward the waving hands of the ghosts below.

He gasped, a breathless, tortured sound that burned itself into Veronica's conscience. She braced herself for the heavy crash of his body coming back to earth.

But the sound never arrived. August Bittner never landed.

Pain-racked and weeping, gasping for breath, Veronica propped herself up to a position where she could look down the stairs, but of Bittner and the ghosts, there was no trace. She blinked through her tears, certain that her eyes were playing tricks on her—but there was nothing. It was as though the ghosts had caught him and dragged him to another world: a world where he would be the insubstantial one; a world where his fearsome, bloodstained image would disappear in the time it took to pour a cup of tea.

Veronica looked up at Kirk, but it wasn't Kirk. It was Kirk's body and Kirk's face, but the eyes, the consciousness within was not Kirk's. It was Brian's. He smiled at her.

"He's gone," he said, in Kirk's voice.

Bittner was gone. Veronica knew, somehow, that he would not be returning. This was her final thought before she passed out.

I watched the veil tear, and I watched Bittner be borne by many hands into the afterlife. What would existence be like for him there? Would he gain insight, like I believed I had during my time lurking invisibly among the living? Would a living man among the dead be similar to my existence among the living? And would he feel any lonelier than he already did?

I'm surprised at my ability to care. It is as though my hatred burned out like a guttering candle once Bittner's hands were off of Veronica's neck. I have nothing left; no energy at all. I can feel myself shedding molecules like a dog sheds fleas, and this time I do not think they will reassemble in the bathroom, as they had done for so many years. This time, I do not think I will return.

Maybe nothingness will be better than the torture I have endured. Maybe that is the fate of those who end their own lives.

I feel what remains of me ebbing away. But then I see her, waiting for me at the end of the hall.

Mary.

It's time, she says. *Brian, I have been waiting to see you for so long. Really see you.*

She takes my "hand," and I slip out of this boy, Kirk Lane, as easily as consciousness had slipped from him moments before. Mary and I drift along toward where I died. I see that the mirror is glowing, but not from any reflected light. There is a pure white light shining from within the glass.

The veil opens up, and she carries me through.

Ⅲ Ⅲ Ⅲ Ⅲ
Ⅲ Ⅲ Ⅲ Ⅲ
Ⅲ Ⅲ Ⅲ Ⅲ

Kirk awoke without any idea of how he'd gotten to the second floor. But he didn't pause to reflect upon it, because he could see Veronica lying very, very still—red marks livid on her throat.

He called her name. He crawled to her and lifted her gently by the shoulders. *Ronnie*, he called. *Ronnie*. Her head swiveled on her neck, the whites of her eyes showing as they rolled up in their sockets. Her name became an urgent plea in his mouth, and he was having difficulty catching his breath.

But then a fluttering of eyelids. He gave her a gentle shake.

"Brian?" she said. "Brian, is that you?"

"No, Ronnie," he told her. "It's me. It's Kirk. I'm real."

She blinked, and he came into focus. She parted her lips.

"I'm real," Kirk repeated.

She sat up, and he held her, and she held him, fiercely, back.

EPILOGUE

Propped up by one crutch and standing beside her mother, Veronica watched her father lower his paper and smile at her before he faded away for what she knew would be the final time. She could see it in his smile, and she could feel it in her mother's hug and in her breath on her cheek.

Sure enough, 7:13 came and went the following morning without the ghost of Eric Calder. They watched and they waited, but he did not appear. Veronica leaned against her mother, hoping to anchor her with her solidity and warmth. "Are you okay?"

"I am," her mother said, wiping the tears away before they fell into her teacup. "I really am."

Mary Greer was already gone. Veronica and Janine watched for her image every morning as they passed by the former home of August Bittner, serial killer, but she never appeared again. There was no ruffling of curtains, either, upstairs or below. Brian, too, had not appeared since the night of the attack, but Veronica thought she could smell traces of his cologne on the mist when she left the shower.

The ghost world still turned, though. A bleeding specter still howled soundlessly on Case Street. Mrs. Olsen still appeared at her mailbox every day at 3:47 reading a letter from a son who never came home. New ghosts appeared; some faded away and never returned. Eileen Janus would appear randomly, or at least with no discernable pattern, smiling at a classroom that only a few weeks prior had been inhabited by Stephen Pescatelli but was now occupied by a young substitute who would sigh with impatience and glance at her watch until the former teacher disappeared. Mr. Pescatelli, either by a touch of cosmic irony or as proof of one of his various theories, never appeared. And the memory of the phone call he somehow made after his death lingered only as a strange unexplained anomaly in the mind of Kirk Lane.

Kirk took Veronica's hand.

All of the ghosts directly associated with Veronica's life and her ordeal had vanished, but her time with Kirk was not over, and the memories that the touch of his hand brought were the good ones—like sharing a cup of tea with him after a long shift, or kissing him on the couch until her mother came home—while the dark memories they shared grew distant and indistinct. Time heals all wounds, and time will amplify all bonds. Veronica wasn't sure if it was really love, but it was the first time she'd ever thought it might be.

The dark memories of that night were completely lost to Kirk. He recalled nothing from the time he saw Bittner push through the door until he mysteriously awoke upstairs beside Veronica's prostrate body. He asked her if she still worried that Mr. Bittner was at large.

"I don't, really," she said.

"It doesn't worry you that they haven't caught him?" he said.

"His blood was all over Mr. Pescatelli's house, in your house, in his car. He was obviously at death's door, but they can't find him. You aren't worried he'll come back?"

"No. It was all over the news. If he's still among the living, he'll be caught." Veronica smiled. She wasn't sure exactly what had happened to Bittner, but she thought that if there was a veil that could allow ghosts to pass from an afterlife into her world, why couldn't we, in turn, pass through to theirs? But she was tired of theories, and didn't have Kirk's or Mr. Pescatelli's interest in them, preferring instead to live more fully on her side of the veil.

"Besides, we've got another four years before we have to worry again," Veronica said.

Kirk let the subject lie even though it was obvious there was more to the story than Veronica was telling. The news said only that the police were looking for August Bittner in relation to the death of Stephen Pescatelli and for an assault on a sixteen-year-old girl. There was no mention of the ghosts, the grasping hands, the force that had propelled Bittner out into space the moment he sought to end her life, even as there wasn't any mention of Veronica's name. Kirk didn't question further, as he no longer felt the need to solve certain mysteries.

Veronica told the police where they could find the body of Shelly Bonder. When questioned about how she knew, Veronica would say, without further elaboration, that she'd learned of Shelly's location from Mr. Bittner.

Janine only wore her hat and gloves when it was cold out, after exorcising the ghosts from Veronica (who secretly believed that Ghost-B-Gone was nothing more powerful than air freshener).

She started jogging after school, and tried, unsuccessfully, to get Veronica to join her. She spoke nostalgically about going out for the soccer team but worried that her window of opportunity had passed.

There were few attendees at Mr. Pescatelli's funeral other than Veronica and Kirk. The stone above his grave listed names that reminded Veronica that he'd also, like Mr. Bittner, once had a wife and daughter, although Kirk would tell her later that their bodies had never been found in the aftermath of the Event. She thought of Mr. Pescatelli occasionally, and when she did, she had a very clear image of him—an overweight, nervous man, brave in some ways but too frightened to confront ghosts face-to-face. She wondered if it made him happy or sad that his image never appeared in his class, that he never became the subject he studied so intently.

Walking through the rows of the cemetery with Kirk back to his car, Veronica came across a simple marker with the name "Bittner" etched into the stone. Light snow crunching underfoot, she walked behind the stone and saw two names—*Madeline* and *August*. Their birthdates were beneath, as was the date of Madeline's death, while there was just a blank space next to August's.

Madeline's, Veronica noticed, listed February 29, and the year of her death.

"That wasn't a leap year," Kirk said, noticing the date the same time as she did. "It's an odd number."

To the left of the stone, nearest to where Madeline lay, was a slightly smaller stone. *Eva Marie Bittner*, it read. *In the Hands of the Lord.*

• • •

Veronica returned later, and alone, when the sky was as washed out and gray as the stones she walked among.

Smiling, she looked around the empty cemetery, expecting that Eva, Madeline, or her husband's victims would appear and thank her for all she'd done and risked, but none did. The cemetery was free of ghosts.

August Bittner she could barely remember at all. She'd meant it when she told Kirk that she had no fear of his return. Her memory of him became hazy and indistinct, as though seen through a rainy windshield. Even the photo the paper ran of him looked blurred, the lines of his face softened and smeared.

There came a day when Veronica realized that it had been weeks since she'd seen her father's ghost.

The thought came to her in the morning, when she stood with her face pointed at the warm spray jetting from the showerhead. She realized also that she didn't miss his ghost. If anything, its disappearance had freed her to think of the person he actually was, and not just as a sort of metaphysical tape loop. She remembered a man who liked cheeseburgers, cartoons, dark beer, and who needed a small fraction of time to keep for himself. A man who liked to play cards with her, but not board games. A man who would pretend right along with her that her stuffed animals were really real, with feelings that were just as easy to hurt as hers. She remembered a man who liked to hold his daughter's hand when they were in a crowd and also when they were alone. She remembered a man who loved her.

She missed him, but not his image or any of the images that

had faded with the passage of time. She was crying a little when she turned off the faucet, but it was a good feeling. She realized that the only regret she had about any of the ghost experiences was with Brian. Unlike with her father, she had no feeling of closure with him. There was no sense that they had ever said good-bye.

She patted herself dry and wrapped the towel around her body before leaving the shower, and the cool air felt good against her warm, slightly damp skin. She went to the mirror.

Looking up, she saw a familiar face smiling at her in the unfogged glass.

"Hello," she said.